TEXAS WINDS

DANA WAYNE

Cover design by Just Write.Creations

Library of Congress Control Number Data
Wayne, Dana
Texas Winds / Dana Wayne.
1. Contemporary-Romance-Fiction.
2. General-Romance-Fiction.
BISAC: FIC 027020 FICTION / Romance / Contemporary. | FIC 027000 Fiction / General.
Library of Congress Control Number: 2023922685

ISBN: 979-8-9895330-0-8

www.danawayne.com

Chapter One

Storm clouds silhouetted thirty-seven-year-old Jake Holloway in the saddle, unmoving and silent, near the edge of a deep ravine. The cry of an eagle overhead and a jackrabbit scampering in the distance went unnoticed.

A rumble of thunder pierced the gloomy silence, and the horse whinnied softly.

Saddle leather creaked as Jake shifted his muscular six-two frame to assess the approaching storm before returning his gaze to the chasm below, thoughts focused on the past. His chestnut mare, Misty, shook her head and snorted as though complaining about this ritual immersion in self-blame.

How many times had he sat here? How many *I should haves,* and *I'm sorrys* clogged his throat. "Too damn many," he muttered as another roll of thunder interrupted the quiet. "Dammit," he barked at last and tugged on the reins, turning Misty toward the ranch, the yawning abyss of unanswered questions as troubling today as they were four years ago.

They'd argued that morning. In fact, he couldn't remember the last time they hadn't started the day with angry words. But that day began differently.

Jake jerked Misty to a stop and let the past consume him because the pain was better than nothing at all.

Forever etched into his brain, that fateful day remained a vivid memory.

A plate of scrambled eggs and bacon had greeted him when he entered the kitchen. Mary was busy at the stove, wearing her usual attire of black leggings and a long, flowy top. A dark blue bandana secured those long, nut-brown curls he loved into a low ponytail at the back of her neck. Several wayward locks framed an ageless face. Emerald eyes glistened when she offered him a nervous glance. Suddenly, the woman he fell in love with at sixteen stood before him.

Pain and regret vied for dominance as the morning continued to play out in his mind.

Mary had placed a mug of coffee beside his plate and then sat across from him.

"You're not eating?" he'd asked.

She'd shaken her head and took a deep breath. "We need to talk."

Something in her voice made him pause as he scooped a bite of eggs. "Okay." He motioned with his empty fork. "About what?"

She spun the salt shaker on the table, eyes downcast. "I think it's safe to say things haven't been...the same between us for some time."

"You mean because you've slept in the guest room the last three months, and we—"

"I'm tired of fighting," she interrupted softly. "I can't...." She inhaled deeply. "I don't...."

The air around them sizzled with tension as he put down his fork and swiped his mouth with a napkin. "Don't what?"

She inhaled again. "I don't..."

His heart rate jumped, and the instant rush of blood swooshed in his ears. Silent, his chest tightened, and he barely breathed. He didn't need a psychic to tell him disaster loomed like a hidden predator, ready to pounce.

The steady tick of the wall clock highlighted the uneasy silence.

Mary sighed and shook her head sadly. "I can't—I won't pretend anymore, Jake." She straightened her shoulders and faced him. "I want a divorce."

His heart stopped, then raced onward. *What? She can't mean that.*

The swirling in his ears intensified, and his vision blurred as he tried to make sense of the words circling his head like angry bees. *She wants a divorce.*

"There's someone else."

It took a moment for his brain to untangle the words. A shocked heartbeat collided against his chest before anger, white-hot and ferocious, blindsided him. "Who?"

She flinched but didn't look away. "It doesn't matter."

"Like hell!" He rapped his knuckles on the table. "Who is he?"

Back stiff, she didn't break eye contact. "People change, Jake. We aren't the same people anymore. It's time to accept it and move on."

He shoved his chair back so hard it toppled over. "Seems to me you've already done that." He stomped to the sink and gripped the counter.

"You're angry, I—"

"No shit," he barked as he faced her. *And I'm devastated by your betrayal.*

Anger clashed with hurt as he paced in front of the sink. Finally, he righted the chair and clutched the back until his knuckles turned white. Gaze downcast, he slowly shook his head as reality hit home. *She wants a divorce.*

Okay, so things were a little strained lately, but he couldn't see any reason for such drastic action. *Whatever their problems were, they loved each other once; they could again. Right?*

Heartbroken, he faced her. "Why, Mary? Why?"

Eyes averted, she continued to fiddle with the salt shaker. "We're not the same people anymore, Jake." Mossy green eyes glistened with unshed tears when she met his gaze. "We want different things now, have different needs."

He blew out a grief-stricken breath and ran long fingers through dark, unruly hair. He paused a moment, then gripped the chair again. "Is it what I said about wanting a kid? Is that it?" He drank in a deep breath. "I won't push anymore. I promise. I want a child, but I can wait until you're ready."

Her eyes flicked left and right before reconnecting with his. "We both know this ranch is all you've ever wanted, Jake. Or needed. But I need more." She stiffened her back. "I don't love you, Jake."

Stunned silent by the declaration, her words bounced inside his head like pinballs. *I don't love you.*

Chest so tight he could barely breathe, he stared. "You don't mean that, Mary. You can't."

A single tear rolled down her cheek. "I'm truly sorry, Jake. I don't want to hurt you."

"How the hell can seeing someone behind my back not hurt me?"

She hesitated, then squared her shoulders and stood. "I'm going to say goodbye to Honey Bear, and then I'm leaving." She turned for the door and stopped. "Please don't be here...for both our sakes."

Anguish produced a bitter taste in his mouth and forced out words better left unsaid. "Fine. Go." Hands fisted at his side, he stepped back, the urge to shake some sense into her almost too strong to resist.

Mary hesitated, then whispered, "I'm so sorry," before she bolted out the door in tears.

Speechless, Jake watched her leave, hands clenched so tight they throbbed as he struggled to absorb her announcement.

He went to the sink and splashed his face with cold water, ignoring the droplets dripping down his shirt. *How do you fall out of love with someone you've been with since your teens?*

He splashed his face again, but the water did nothing to alleviate the soul-crushing pain eating him alive.

She wants a divorce.

She doesn't love me.

Emotions in turmoil, he tried to pinpoint when things got so far off track, but nothing specific came to mind. More than likely, many petty things morphed into bigger ones, but he was too busy with the ranch to notice.

Maybe it was the vacation he postponed last summer. One of the hottest on record, temperatures passed triple digits daily. He spent every waking hour ensuring the stock survived. He succeeded in saving them, but did he lose Mary in the process?

We just need to talk things through. We can work it out.

With that thought in mind, he stepped off the porch and headed for the barn in time to see her exit astride her favorite mare, Honey Bear. When she passed the edge of the barn, she kicked the horse into a run.

What happened next replayed in his mind like a slow-motion reel. Honey's right front leg buckled when she stepped into a hole near the gate, and she went down, throwing Mary to the ground.

Blood froze in his veins when he saw land on the big iron ore rock resting against the fence. He ran toward her, shouting for his ranch hand to call an ambulance.

She lay motionless on the ground, blood pooling under her head, her right arm lying at an awkward angle. He yanked off his shirt and pressed it against the gaping wound on her head, crying and praying for her to be all right.

The rest of that day and the following weeks became a blur of doctors and specialists who kept Mary alive long enough to give birth to a premature daughter.

He muttered a curse and spurred Misty forward, unable to quash the one memory that haunted him to this day.

Was the child his?

Chapter Two

'*Tell Alexa I'm sorry. I'm just not ready.*'

Alexa Morgan stared at her reflection in the full-length mirror and inhaled deeply, those eight little words forever embedded into her brain. "Why can't I let it go?" she muttered. "It's been four months."

A soft *whoof* from Biscuit, her canine companion of three years, went unnoticed.

"Because he dumped me at the altar, that's why," she seethed. "At the bloody altar. In front of all our friends and family." She sucked air through clenched teeth. "With a fricking text to my mother, no less. The dipstick didn't even have the guts to tell me to my face."

Biscuit pressed his nose against her hand.

She absently caressed his head. "I'm sorry, sweetie. I said I wouldn't talk about it again, but..." Even now, the memory was a painful wound that refused to heal. "He dumped me, Biscuit. Without a second thought." The truth was a hard pill to swallow. "He never loved me at all."

Despite the hurt and mortification of Rodney's callous desertion that day, she had refused to cower in shame. Instead, she had marched into the church with her head held high and informed everyone she'd discovered Rodney was a toxic, self-centered A-hole who didn't deserve her, and in celebration of her good fortune, the party would start at the reception.

Her father and her brother, Bobby, were not so understanding. It took half a dozen people to prevent them from hunting him down like the mangy dog he turned out to be.

Later, the crowd, minus his family and friends who couldn't flee fast enough, cheered when she ceremoniously dumped the beautiful wedding cake in a trash can and turned the pricey reception into a Rodney's-a-creep bash.

Once the party started rolling, she grabbed a bottle of champagne, some mini crab cakes, a side of mac and cheese, and a hunk of chocolate cake for good measure and indulged in a pity party for one.

Over the next two weeks, she returned every gift—except the ones from his side, which she donated to Goodwill. When he dared to ask about them later, she texted where to look.

The honeymoon cruise she paid for and couldn't bear to use became a gift to her brother for not saying, "I told you so," though he had every right. He believed Rodney, a mediocre engineer for a rival company, saw her as a way up the corporate ladder. But if she truly loved him, he would support her.

Only Biscuit knew the bitter truth behind the breakup.

She shook off the unhappy memories. "Suck it up, Buttercup," she lectured herself. "You're thirty-two years old. It's time to put your big girl panties on and decide what you want to do with your life." She paused. "And it's not working for your father's company." She adjusted the chic bun on top of her head. "And I'm tired of being called Alex. It's a guy's name, but Alexa is too formal. I want to use the nickname Andy gave me." She glanced at the dog. "You know him. He's Dad's general foreman." She turned back to the mirror. "From now on, I'm Lexie, not Alex." She meticulously arranged a few ebony curls around her face and nodded. "That's better."

She took a step back and analyzed the image in the mirror. Though she'd lost some weight, and shadows of fatigue left dark smudges under her eyes, the woman staring back was nonetheless attractive. Comfortable jeans faded to a soft blue encased long, slender legs. A royal blue tee-shirt, the front embellished with *Underestimate me, that'll be fun* in glittery silver letters, highlighted an ample bosom, and the narrow silver belt accentuated a slim waist. Snappy silver and black slingback sandals completed the look.

Intelligent blue eyes scrutinized the finished product. "What do you think, Biscuit?" She turned around and inspected her jean-clad butt over her shoulder. "Nothing says 'structural engineer,' does it?" She adjusted the horn-rimmed glasses on her face and frowned. "More like a bored schoolteacher."

Biscuit tilted his head left and right, then shook his head and sat by the front door.

She sighed, picked up her phone, added a reminder to call Bobby from the road to let him know she got a late start, and stuffed it in her bag. Out of habit, she wedged a pencil in her hair as an unexpected rumble of thunder got her attention. "No, no, nooooo." She retrieved her phone, pulled up the weather app, and scowled at the forecast. "Fudgesicle and ice picks. Showers off and on all afternoon, and maybe some tomorrow." She returned the phone to her bag and took a breath. "Great. By Wednesday, it's sunshine and blue skies." Bolstered by that touch of good news, she glanced back at the woman in the mirror. "You can do this, Lexie. Two weeks of peace and quiet to find yourself is doable." She grabbed her bag and the dog's leash, then headed out the door.

The impromptu vacation was her mother's idea. Concerned that Lexie worked too hard—she did, and she wasn't taking care of herself—she wasn't, Rose Morgan suggested a vacation. Once the seed was planted, Lexie couldn't wait for it to happen. For the first time in months, she had something positive to look forward to, something that had nothing to do with her father's company, HRM Construction and Engineering, or *Rodney the Creep.* Granted, she'd have to mix a little business in next week, but other than that, her assistant could handle anything that came in, and Lexie was free to do as she pleased.

Resolve in place, she ignored the light, misty rain and quickly hugged Biscuit after he jumped into the back seat. "I don't know about you, but I can't wait to see Dallas in the rearview mirror." She settled behind the wheel, exhaled loudly, and twisted the ignition with new vigor. "Dad understood when Bobby left the company to follow his dream. Hopefully, he'll do the same for me." She backed out of the drive. "I just have to figure out what my dream is."

Determined to find the answer, she put the car in gear and headed north. "Can you believe we're actually doing this?" She glanced at the dog. "At a quaint cabin in the woods, no less. Bobby said the place is called Twin Lakes. It's private, with only four cabins. One on each side of the lake." She twirled one long ringlet of hair around her finger. "There's a fishing pier, too. Gosh. I haven't been fishing in years. I remember camping at Lake Texoma once, and Dad tried to teach me to fly fish. One of my favorite memories." A momentary cloud fell across her good mood. "Then the company started growing, and those opportunities fell by the wayside." She released the curl and wrapped both hands on the steering wheel. "Their website says they provide fishing tackle, so who knows? Maybe I'll see if I remember what he taught me. Oh, and there's deer and other animals around, too." She shook her finger at Biscuit. "But you can't chase them." She upped the speed on the wipers as the shower strengthened. "I hope this rain goes away soon." She squared her shoulders, fixed on remaining positive. "But, hey, a bad start means a great finish, right?"

Biscuit's reply was a soft grunt before he stretched out on the back seat.

"Fine. Take a nap, but you'll miss all the beautiful scenery." A few minutes later, she entered the ramp for the interstate and barely stifled a surprised curse when a guy in a red Corvette cut in front from the far lane to exit. "Idiot," she grumbled. "I won't miss this mess at all."

Her bright outlook dimmed when the misty shower turned into a deluge two hours later.

She read the road sign up ahead. "Comanche Springs, fifteen miles. Finally." Anticipation made her antsy. "Twin Lakes is somewhere near here. I was supposed to call Bobby for directions, but I'd rather hit town first and grab something to eat." She glanced in the rearview mirror, then back to the front. "Dang, this rain is getting on my last nerve. The forecast I saw when we stopped for gas said clearing skies by now."

The hypnotic slash of the windshield wipers prompted her to crank up the radio. But not even her favorite music lessened the sudden uncertainty enveloping her.

She fingered the heart-shaped charm dangling from the chain around her neck. A gift from her brother when she turned sixteen, it never failed to soothe her.

An unexpected clap of thunder followed by a flash of lightning off to the left startled her. "Dammit!"

Biscuit's gentle 'woof' sounded like disapproval.

"Good grief. You're worse than Mom. I'll put money in the jar when we stop." Growing up around construction sites, she picked up quite a selection of colorful expletives. It wasn't until *Rodney the Creep* came along that she succumbed to the urge to use them. All of them. More than once.

Enter *The Swear Jar*. Her mother, bless her meddling little heart, gave her one soon after *the event,* as she called it, hoping to improve her vocabulary.

By the time Lexie finished everything, she had progressed to a gallon-sized jar. Lately, though, the contributions declined, and the newest container was a half-gallon plastic jug inscribed with *Swear Jar* in red nail polish.

"What's wrong with me, Biscuit?" She sighed and chewed her lower lip.

A sharp bark had her glancing back. "I know, I know. It wasn't me; it was him. But was it? I mean, the same thing happened with Gary. Well, not exactly the same. I was still in college then, and Gary at least ended things before we got that far." She swallowed hard. "Maybe Mr. Right doesn't exist." The notion brought an ache to her throat. "Maybe I'm not meant to be a mom, either. Maybe I'm meant to be alone."

Misery threatened to edge past her defenses, and her heart twisted as she recalled the pivotal conversation with Rodney the day before the wedding. She had excitedly told him she was late, as in *late*, and the possibility of pregnancy existed.

His reaction hit her like a gut punch. "How could you be so careless? You've ruined everything."

The resentment in his voice still wrenched her heart, and she shook her head. "I can still see Mom's face when she handed me the phone. And poor Dad. He was speechless." Rodney's text had been brief and cold. *Tell Alexa I'm sorry and good luck. I'm just not ready.*

"Good fricking luck?"

The words scraped over her broken heart like a razor blade. He cared nothing about her or the child. Their child.

Ultimately, the pregnancy was a false alarm. Probably due to the stress of planning a wedding, striving to meet her father's expectations, and endless hours on projects around the state. But the end result didn't change—no happily-ever-after for her.

"Enough." She made a slicing motion with her hand. "I refuse to let anything spoil our vacation."

Biscuit nosed her cheek again.

She sighed and leaned into his doggie kiss. "You always make me feel better." Reinvigorated, she gripped the wheel. "But you could have warned me he was a jerk. Dogs are supposed to sense these things."

He shook his head as though to say, 'It's not my fault.'

"Okay, fine. But still, you could have at least hinted he was an ass."

She ignored his sharp '*whoof*' and looked ahead, the pain an open wound that refused to heal. "I'll never be a mom", she whispered, gripping the wheel tighter. "Enough. It is what it is. I need to focus on this vacation and accept that I'm destined to be an old maid working for my father in a job I don't like and get on with half a life." She took a deep, calming breath. "But reality truly sucks."

Biscuit shook his head.

"I'm trying to be a realist here." She shifted in her seat. "Fairy tale endings are for other people. Not me. I'm done."

The dog whined and looked around her out the side window.

She followed his gaze and squinted. "Oh no. Hogs. A whole slew of them." Focusing on the road, she slowed her speed. "I read somewhere that over a million feral hogs live in Texas." She quickly rechecked their location. "Marci told me a bunch destroyed her parents' entire backyard last year. Even tore down the fence." Another nervous glance at the unpredictable hogs made her heart rate jump. "Dammit. They're changing direction." She tapped the brake and snapped, "Down. Now."

Immediately, Biscuit stretched out on the back seat.

Suddenly, rain poured from the clouds despite clearing skies up ahead, and a loud popping noise sounded a split second before the Ford Edge swerved hard to the right.

Between the rain and the aftermath of a blowout doing fifty-five miles an hour on a rain-slick road, she didn't see the hogs head straight for her until it was too late. She hit one, maybe two, with the left fender. Or perhaps they hit her; she wasn't sure. The impact came as she hit a large puddle on the highway, and the vehicle hydroplaned. Out of control, she held on to the wheel as the car spun around and skidded off the other side of the road, landing with a sudden teeth-jarring stop in a muddy ditch, facing the opposite direction.

The airbags deployed, filling her eyes, nose, and mouth with choking powder. Glasses askew, she coughed and pushed against the material, groping for the button to lower the window. Unable to see, she eventually got the front windows down, and fresh air wafted in along with sprinkles of rain. Momentarily stunned, she sucked in the moisture-laden air, righted her glasses, and took a moment to regroup.

As her foggy mind cleared, she assessed the situation. The car rested at an awkward angle in the ditch. The blowout happened to the right front tire. She had no idea what damage the hogs did to the left side, but she was going nowhere any time soon. And she was still some distance from her destination.

Annoyed, she shook her head slightly, and a wave of dizziness washed over her, followed by the first inkling of a headache. She touched a knot on her left temple and stared at the crimson liquid coating her fingers. She pulled down the sun visor and looked in the small mirror. Blood dripped from a cut on her forehead, down her cheek, and onto her new blouse. "Pop tarts and buzzards," she grumbled, grabbed a takeout napkin from the console, and pressed against the cut. "Ouch." She shifted in the seat, testing for aches, knowing most wouldn't show up until tomorrow. The only bright spot was the sudden shower ended almost as fast as it started, and clear skies showed in the distance.

Biscuit's whimper drew her back to the moment wind sent her heart rate through the roof. "Please don't let him be hurt." She struggled with the airbags and seat belt, then leaned over the console toward the back, thankful her luggage and supplies hadn't been thrown forward.

The dog lay on the floorboard, wedged in behind the passenger seat. Unable to reach him from this angle, she tried to soothe him with her voice. "Hang on, sweetie. I'm coming."

Knowing the hogs were unpredictable and dangerous, she looked around before getting out and saw they were nearly out of sight across the road.

Fighting another wave of dizziness, she fumbled with the door. The vehicle's right side pitched downward in the ditch, which made opening the driver's side door more difficult. "Crap on a cracker," she snarled as she wrestled with it and stepped out. A surprised yelp escaped when the heel of her snazzy new sandal slid off a jagged rock, and her left ankle folded, followed by unbearable pain up to her knee. Unprepared, she tumbled out, landing hard on the rock as her forehead banged against the bottom of the door. Only a last-minute reflex kept it from closing on her head. "Oomph."

Stunned, it took a moment for her mind to clear before she struggled to stand, using the door for support. Upright at last but unable to put weight on her injured foot, she leaned on the vehicle and saw a hog lying on the other side of the road. Quickly averting her gaze, she felt something near her eye and swiped at it, dismayed to find more blood on her fingers. "Great. Must be where I hit the door." Jaw tight, she moved, only to discover walking was impossible. "Son of a bucket."

She closed her eyes, did a mental ten-count, then eased down on the muddy ground and crawled to the passenger side door, gritting her teeth against the pain as she dragged her foot along. "Only for you, Biscuit," she muttered, "would I ruin my favorite jeans. And my new shoes."

After several attempts, she stood on one foot and wrenched the door open. "Oh, baby, are you all right?"

He whined and tried to wiggle toward her.

"No. Stay. Stay."

Thankfully, the angle made the car door stay open, and using it for balance, she hopped and slid to the front, jerked open the door, and nudged the seat forward.

Biscuit whined again.

"Wait, baby. Stay. I'm coming." She grabbed her phone from the cup holder, shoved it in her back pocket, then pulled her pistol from the glove box and secured it in the specially made pouch of her purse.

A few agonizing moments later, her companion was free and sat in the back seat. He whined again and moved to get out. "No. Stay put. No point in both of us being muddy and wet."

A quick exam showed no visible injuries, though he yelped when she touched his front left paw. "You'll be okay, baby. I'll get you to a vet as soon as possible."

Ankle and hip throbbed in unison, and a growing headache added to the misery mix.

She took a breath and looked around. The front bumper dug into the far side of the muddy embankment, and the blown-out tire rested in muck halfway up the rim. Dingy water in the ditch swirled around her feet and leached up her mud-coated pant legs. Her disgusted gaze took in the filthy jeans and soaked and blood-coated tee shirt. "Crap," she muttered. "Brand new shoes." She swiped a hand across her cheek, leaving a streak of bloody mud in its wake. "Great way to start my first vacation in years."

She adjusted her grip on the door and blew wet hair away from her mouth. "Alrighty then."

Muttering under her breath, she reached past the dog and plucked the half-full *Swear Jar* from the floorboard. An irritated swipe at the wet hair clinging to her cheek left more muddy streaks behind. "Time for the big guns." She placed the jug on the seat near Biscuit and pulled two soggy one-dollar bills and three quarters from her pocket. She took a breath and ceremoniously dropped the quarters through a slot cut into the lid, mumbling after each one. "Damn. Damn. Dammit." She took a deep breath and crammed the wet bills through the hole. "And son-of-a-bitch."

"Don't reckon that's gonna help much."

An f-bomb exploded before she could stop it.

CHAPTER THREE

S tartled by the man's deep voice, Lexie swore and spun around, tossing the jar over her shoulder as intense pain shot up her leg. Off-balance, she grabbed the door to keep from falling on her rear as the jug landed with a mushy thump at the stranger's feet.

The brim of a dark Stetson cast his face in shadow, but there was no disguising his frame. Tall, at least six-two or three, shoulders a mile wide, with long, muscular legs encased in worn jeans. Muddy work boots covered his feet, and well-used leather gloves stuck out of his front pocket. Rain dripping from the brim of his hat left wet trails on his pale blue chambray shirt, and the rolled-up sleeves revealed tanned, muscular forearms.

He hesitated, then picked up the jar, one corner of his mouth curling up as he read the inscription. "I'm guessing that last word is expensive," he said as he passed her the container before stepping back.

His husky, just-woke-up voice raced through her like fine wine, leaving her momentarily speechless. "It is," she snapped and took the jug. "Five bucks." She glanced past him and noted a grime-coated, black Ford F250 crew cab parked behind him on the shoulder of the road. *Holy crap. I never heard a thing.* She eyed her bag, mentally calculating how long it would take to reach the pistol inside if needed. "You shouldn't sneak up on people. I have a gun. And I know how to use it."

He made no effort to approach, just stood there, hands on his hips. "Are you hurt?"

She gripped the door tighter when her throbbing ankle threatened to fold again. "No. I'm good."

"You have blood on your face. And mud."

His intense gaze traveled up and down her body, causing an involuntary shiver.

"Were you ejected?"

"No. I slipped when I got out."

He tipped his head toward the back seat. "What about the dog?"

She glanced at Biscuit, who showed no concern over the stranger's sudden appearance, and noted a little blood on the side of his mouth. How did she miss that before? "Biscuit!" Dismissing the man, she leaned against the car and ran her hands over the dog again, checking more thoroughly for anything broken. "I'm so sorry, baby. I'm so sorry."

The dog stoically endured her frantic exam with only a slight whimper when she touched his front paw before moving to his mouth. "Come on, baby, open up." She slowly pried his jaw open and saw blood on his tongue.

"Looks like he bit it. Probably on impact."

It took tremendous effort not to react to the unexpected voice behind her left shoulder. "Yeah. Probably. I'll have him checked out when I get to town."

He looked at the luggage piled in the back of the SUV. "Where you headed?"

She glanced up and discovered walnut-colored eyes watching

Biscuit, his square jaw visibly tense. His face was rugged and somber, bronzed by wind and sun and covered with dark stubble. No laugh lines around full lips, and unspoken pain was alive in dark, fathomless eyes. In a heartbeat, his expression changed, switching to closed-off and distant as he took two steps back, hands stuffed in his front pockets.

"I'm on vacation." She saw no need to elaborate.

"Comanche Springs has a good vet, but he's at my ranch right now." He pointed to the arched entry on the opposite side of the road: *Indian Creek Ranch*. "I'm Jake Holloway."

She hesitated. "Alexa Morgan." She pointed toward the dog. "And that's Biscuit."

A surprised expression briefly crossed his face, and then he paused as though debating with himself. "I'd try and pull you out, Miss Morgan, but it's likely to make bad matters worse if there is damage we can't see."

She shook her head. "I appreciate the offer, Mr. Holloway, but it's gonna need a tow." The pain in her ankle ratcheted up a notch, and her hip throbbed. Unwilling to admit this to a stranger, she gripped the door tighter and stuck to the facts. "Blowout on the right front before I hit the hogs, who did a number on the left side. I doubt the wheel will even roll. I'll just call Triple-A."

"Take too long." He pulled a cell phone from his back pocket and punched in a number. "Hey Paul, it's Jake. Fine thanks. A lady hit some hogs out on Forty-Two by the main gate... No, she's fine. Had a blowout before she hit 'em...Yeah, there's one on the side of the road... Okay. I'd pull it with the truck, but I'm not sure about other damage." He looked around her to the front seat. "Yeah, airbags deployed...That's what I thought. How soon can you get it...thanks, man, 'preciate it. She'll be at the house."

Be at the house? Uh-uh, nope. No way.

He put his phone away and eyed Biscuit. "Does he bite?"

"Not unless I tell him to."

"My daughter is in the truck, and I need to get her home. Tell him not to bite." He extended his hands toward Biscuit, then stopped and glared when she didn't immediately comply.

For reasons she couldn't explain, she said, "It's okay, baby. It's okay."

Jake nodded and stretched his hands toward the dog so he could sniff. "Hey, big fella. I'm gonna take you to my truck. Okay? Just take it easy and let me help you."

Biscuit whined once and looked at Lexie.

She let go of the door long enough to rub his nose. "It's okay, baby."

Holloway gently scooped up the dog and turned toward the pickup. "My mother and sister are at the house. My sister's a nurse practitioner and can look at your injuries while Brett checks out the dog."

Before she could voice any objections, a high-pitched cry – a child's cry of fear, came from the truck.

"Daa-dee!"

———◆———

Katie's cry put Jake in motion. He edged past the woman as the wail increased in volume.

The dog looked at him and whimpered.

"She's okay, boy. Just woke up and didn't see me." Jake opened the front door, and Katie's howls dwindled to soft sniffles.

By the time he got the dog in the front seat, the whimpers had stopped altogether. Wide, hazel eyes blinked twice, and her heart-shaped mouth formed a small 'o'.

"Doggie," she cooed and reached toward Biscuit.

"No!" The reprimand sounded harsher than he intended, and her face crumpled again. Before the tears started, he softened his tone. "He's hurt, Katie."

She hiccupped softly and snuffled. "Doggie got boo-boo?"

"Yeah. He has a boo-boo, so don't touch him, okay?"

"Okay, Daddy."

He clenched his jaw. The words always hit him like acid, and he reminded himself for the thousandth time she wasn't to blame for the situation. "I'll be right back. I have to shut the door so the doggie won't jump out, but I'll be right back, okay?"

"Okay."

He pulled out his phone and speed-dialed his sister, Donna. "Hey. Are you still at the house...Good...No, no, nothing's wrong. A lady had a run-in with some hogs out by the gate... Will you please just stop and listen?" He pinched the bridge of his nose and exhaled loudly. "I'm not sure of her injuries. Hard to tell because she's covered in mud, but she does have a couple of cuts on her face. I thought maybe you could take a look at her. Paul's gonna tow her car to the shop. And I think she's Bobby's sister... I know that—look, she can wait at the house until Paul gets the car and go from there, okay...Fine." He ended the call, took a calming breath, and turned to look for the woman, expecting her to be right behind him

Instead, he cursed under his breath when he saw her leaning on the SUV, a massive bag slung on one shoulder as she placed a call. He strode toward her and stopped several feet away.

"District Attorney Morgan, please. His sister, Alexa, calling." She held his gaze and waited for the call to go through. "Hey, big brother. I know. I got a late start. And, well, I had a little accident...I'm fine, really. We both are...I had a blowout and a run-in with stupid hogs at the same time, and my car is pretty much toast." She shoved hair from her face, smearing more mud on her cheek, and heaved a disgruntled breath. "Just listen a minute. Jake Holloway was nearby and—oh, okay."

Slightly rounded sky-blue eyes met his. More striking than beautiful, with a smooth, olive complexion devoid of makeup and eyes the color of a summer sky, she exuded both strength and vulnerability that drew him like a moth to a flame. *Dammit. I don't need this.*

"He suggested I wait at his house until my car is dealt with." She paused, and those baby blues never wavered. "I see...But I'm going to need a rental...Are you sure? I don't want to be a bother...Thanks, Bobby." She extended the phone toward him. "He wants to talk to you."

"Hey." He scanned her body again. "Aside from a mud bath and some nicks on her forehead, no serious injuries. Donna is at the house and will check her out...No problem. I got this." He ended the call and passed the phone back to her.

She dropped it into the voluminous bag on her shoulder.

"So, you're Bobby's little sister? The one he wanted the cabin for?"

"Yeah. I'll be staying at a place called Twin Lakes. He said you'd drop me off there. He'll come by after work and bring something for me to drive until I see about my car."

Jake didn't mention Twin Lakes was on his land, and he'd built the cabins as rentals two years ago to offset the unpredictable income from ranching. Given his intense attraction to her, he couldn't decide if having her nearby for two weeks was good or bad. "We need to go. I have to get Katie home."

She visibly tensed before taking a cautious step forward, then stopped and grabbed the door, face contorted in pain.

"You said you weren't hurt," he snapped and stepped forward.

She snorted. "A sprained ankle and a sore hip are nothing. I've had worse playing flag football with Bobby and his friends."

"Can you walk, or do I need to carry you?"

She huffed. "I don't think I can put weight on it." She tried another step but faltered, and he grabbed her arm.

"Okay. Give me the bag." He draped the handle over his shoulder and hesitated. The thought of her frame against him momentarily derailed his train of thought. He gave himself a mental kick and cleared his throat. "I'm going to put my arm around your waist to help you walk, okay?"

Her jaw clenched and released. "Yeah." Her straightforward gaze lasered in on him. "Just so you know, Mr. Holloway, I may limp doing it, but I can still kick your ass if necessary."

The remark surprised him, and he thought he may have even smiled. "Understood."

A heartbeat passed before she shyly slipped her arm around his waist. The moment she leaned against him, he shot into sensory overload. Dormant nerve endings rapidly stirred to life. Everywhere they touched tingled. His pulse quickened, and a ripple of excitement raced through him. Each rapid beat of his heart became a drumbeat in his ears. Her light floral scent and the smell of warm, rain-soaked skin teased him. He couldn't move. Couldn't breathe.

A shiver wracked her body, and her startled gaze bore into him before she flushed and gripped his waist. "Let's go," she whispered.

Does she feel the connection, too? For a moment, his body refused to move. *Been too long. That's all. Too damn long.*

Slim and toned, she wasn't someone who sat behind a desk all day despite looking like a librarian with those horn-rimmed glasses and a pencil sticking out of her hair. He struggled not to notice how her damp clothes clung to her body like second skin. She was the perfect height, too, maybe five-seven, with long legs and nicely rounded hips that meshed perfectly against him. The bun atop her head was lopsided, and damp curls tickled his cheek as they started toward the Ford.

Disgusted with himself, he took a small step forward, then another. Once they reached his truck, he held her steady with one arm and opened the rear door.

Cheeks a lovely shade of red, she glanced at him, then down at her mud-caked clothes and sandals.

"This is a work truck, Miss Morgan. A little mud won't hurt it."

The soaked V-neck tee stretched across full breasts when she straightened, their puckered tips hard to ignore. He swallowed hard and fought to keep his eyes on her face. When he realized he'd have to lift her into the truck, he had to clear his throat to speak. "Turn around and put your back toward the seat. I'll hoist you up."

He read the argument in her eyes. "Unless you can manage on one foot."

Jaw tight, she gave a quick shake of her head. "I can't."

"When I lift you, put your right foot on the running board. You should be able to balance yourself and slide onto the seat. But hang on to me till you're steady." He didn't wait for her to agree before he gripped her waist.

Her hands trembled as she rested them on his biceps. "I'm ready."

Their eyes met and held as he slowly lifted. His over-heated body reacted instantly, and he barely stifled a groan.

Her grip on his arms tightened, and her lips parted. Then she closed her eyes and searched for the running board with her un-injured foot. Once balanced, she opened her eyes but averted her gaze as she maneuvered onto the seat. She grunted in pain when her injured ankle bumped the threshold as she hoisted herself into the truck.

"Are you all right?"

Lips tight, she took a quick breath and glanced at Katie, who watched with wide, worried eyes. "Just peachy," she muttered through clenched teeth and leaned back in the seat.

"I'll put your stuff in the back. Then we'll head for the ranch." He pointed toward the gate. "About half a mile down that road."

"Thank you."

She kept her eyes closed, and he couldn't help but wonder if the pain put such a bright flush on her cheeks and made the pulse at the base of her throat jump—or something else entirely. He shook his head to banish that line of thought and stepped back.

"There's just a suitcase, my laptop, a few groceries, and a bag of dog food." She finally opened her eyes and faced him. "And I'm sorry to be so much trouble."

"No problem." He briskly walked away without another word.

It was going to be a long two weeks.

Lexie eyed the man as he stomped off – there was no other word for his determined stride and tried to make sense of the intense reaction he elicited.

Awareness had jumped to hyperdrive the moment they touched. Heat from his massive frame warmed her in more ways than one as they walked to the truck.

Breath had lodged in her throat when she faced him, the hardened peaks of her breasts almost touching his chest as desire flooded her veins like molten lava.

Their eyes met and held. *Did he feel it, too?*

Slow seconds ticked away. Did she breathe? She couldn't remember. She had closed her eyes to prevent him from seeing the effect he had on her as he slowly lifted her into the truck.

It was like nothing she'd ever experienced before. It was scary, intriguing, and exciting at the same time. She opened her eyes. *No. No. No. I am not going there.*

She leaned forward to check on Biscuit, who lay curled up in the front seat, eyes closed, breathing steady. Then she turned to the child, who eyed her with open curiosity.

"Hi there. My name is Lexie. What's yours?"

One foot bobbed up and down a couple of times. "Katie."

"Such a pretty name for a pretty little girl."

"You fall down?"

Lexie chuckled at the child's quick assumption. "I sure did. Good thing your daddy was around to help me."

Katie eyed the blood on her forehead and frowned. "You have a boo-boo."

She nodded. "A tiny one, but it doesn't hurt." She waved toward the dog in the front seat. "His name is Biscuit."

"He got boo-boo?"

"Yeah, but he's gonna be fine, though. Both of us will be."

She glanced at Biscuit, then back to Lexie. "I wike doggies."

"Me, too."

Her foot stopped, then bounced a couple of times before she spoke again, her voice barely above a whisper. "Can I pet him?"

"Well, let's wait until the doctor says it's okay. Then you may pet him all you like." She winked at the child. "He loves being petted by pretty girls."

Katie's smile slowly developed, and her face lit up when it did. "Tank you, Wexie."

And just like that, the child stole her heart. "You're welcome, Katie."

The driver's side door swung open, and Jake climbed behind the wheel. "I'll bring your stuff to the cabin after you and the dog get checked out."

Katie sank back into her seat and gave Lexie a side-eyed grin.

"I'm sorry to be so much trouble," Lexie repeated. "I'm sure you have more important things to do."

"No problem," he grumbled and set the truck in motion.

Her physical reaction to him was one thing; the fact she found herself at ease in his care and unruffled by his gruff nature was something else entirely. Maybe it was because Bobby liked and trusted him. Her instincts were usually pretty reliable. Well, except for Rodney-the-creep. But that was different. Today, her gut simply said, 'handsome man with a kid.' That's it. No Spidey-sense of caution, no creepy crawlies down her back.

But one question did give her pause. *Is he married?*

She noticed Katie glanced at Jake, then ducked her head, one foot bouncing up and down. She didn't appear frightened, nervous maybe, but not scared. Before she could give it any more thought, they rounded an extensive stand of pecan trees, and a sprawling ranch lay before them.

A large two-story house, reminiscent of French Colonial/Neoclassical design, sat between two ancient live oak trees, its stark white paint and black shutters gleaming against a clearing sky. A small balcony on the second level highlighted impressive French doors with narrow floor-to-ceiling windows on each side. Baskets of ferns and bright red begonias accented a deep wrap-around porch that circled the home.

Intricately etched glass covered a massive oak front door, and New Orleans-style gas lamps hung on either side.

A swing suspended from the ceiling on the right held colorful pillows. A few rocking chairs and small tables added a welcoming feel to the space.

Corrals were visible to the right, and a large red barn and several outbuildings disappeared behind the house.

"Wow. This place is beautiful."

"Thanks."

He pulled into the gravel-covered circle drive and stopped at the front entrance, where a woman waited on the porch. Vaguely familiar, she was tall and slender, wearing jeans and a pullover top. Dark chestnut hair brushed the tops of her shoulders. Where Jake was solemn and distant, her expression was open and friendly.

She looks familiar. Where have I seen her before? I hope she's his sister and not his wife. Lexie quickly dismissed the idea as folly and told herself she wasn't interested, even as her body called her a liar.

The woman came down the steps and waited for Jake to stop. "How'd it go today?"

"Fine." He turned to face Lexie. "Sit tight. I'll give you a hand." He slid off the seat and opened the back door, talking over his shoulder to the woman. "That's Bobby's sister, Alexa Morgan. When we get inside, can you look at her ankle, too?"

While Jake worked to get the child out of the car seat, the woman came around as Lexie opened her door.

"Hi. I'm Donna Holloway. Mr. Congeniality's younger and more cordial sister." She glanced to where Jake was unhooking Katie from the car seat. "Hey, sweetie. Did you have fun today?"

"Uh-huh." Katie pointed to Biscuit. "Doggie."

Jake removed her from the car seat's restraints and spoke to Donna. "Mother inside?"

"Yeah. She'll be out in a sec." She quickly scanned Lexie's face. "Any other cuts?"

"No."

"Other injuries?"

"Twisted my ankle, then landed on a rock the size of a Volkswagen when I fell." She rolled her shoulders. "I'm sure the seat belt left bruises, too."

An older woman walked out the front door, drying her hands on the apron around her waist. Smiling, she reached for the child's hand as Jake set her on the porch.

"Wexie's doggie got boo-boo," said Katie as she took the woman's outstretched hand.

"He does?" She looked at Jake.

"Donna can fill you in while I get her inside."

"Okay," said the woman, who turned to Katie. "I have fresh cookies and milk in the kitchen." She nodded to Lexie, then turned, and they went inside.

Jake walked around the truck as Lexie slid off the seat.

Biscuit started to rise, and Jake barked, "Stay."

Much to her chagrin, the dog sat down at once and waited.

While she processed her dog's acceptance of someone else's command, he scooped her up and headed for the steps.

"What are you doing? Put me down."

"You can't walk on that ankle." The ghost of a smile softened his stern features. "Besides, your feet are caked in mud."

"Take her to Mimi's bathroom," instructed Donna as she rounded the front of the truck, then dashed ahead to hold the front door open. "I'll grab some towels and meet you there."

Despite having her in his arms, Jake used a boot jack beside the door to tug off each boot, then walked inside in his stocking feet.

Bombarded by a flurry of sensations, Lexie clutched his shirt in one hand and tried not to think about the ripple of muscle underneath.

Chapter Four

Lexie remained silent as Jake carried her through the foyer, down a short hallway, and into a tidy bedroom. Before she could voice the questions in her mind, he entered a small ensuite bathroom.

"This used to be my grandmother's quarters." Jake placed her on the closed commode lid. "Now it's a guest room."

Lexie noted a compact walk-in shower opposite the toilet equipped with grab bars and a removable seat. Pale yellow paint and pictures of daffodils brightened the walls. A frosted glass window covered with a yellow and white striped café curtain allowed muted light, and a colorful yellow non-skid mat sat in front of the shower.

Her perusal ended when he took a step back. Irked to be in his debt—again, she met his gaze. "I know I'm saying this a lot, but thank you. Again."

His nod was brisk. "I'll take the dog—what's his name again?"

"Biscuit."

"I'll take Biscuit to the barn and have Brett check him over, though I didn't note anything to cause alarm."

The small room was even smaller with him in it, and she looked everywhere but at the man who loomed over her, sending her pulse rate up several notches. "Um, okay."

Donna squeezed in behind Jake with towels over one arm and what appeared to be a red shirt over the other. She placed the shirt on the vanity and draped the towels over the shower door before turning to Jake. "Go. She needs to get out of those wet clothes."

He turned, then stopped at the door. "I'll leave your bag on the bed after I get Biscuit looked at." He tapped the trim around the door and spoke to his sister. "She's staying in the small cabin at Twin Lakes. I'll take her there later."

"Good," said Donna. "You'll be close by."

He left without responding, and Donna got down to business. "I know your ankle is probably hurting like crazy right now."

"It is for a fact."

"I need to check it out, so bear with me. I'm betting it's a bad sprain versus anything broken, but the exam will hurt. Afterward, I'll help you onto the shower seat. You should be able to manage things from there."

"I can –"

"You don't want to spend the rest of the day covered in muck." Donna squatted on the floor, removed the right sandal, and gently lifted Lexie's left foot, stopping when she cringed. "Sorry. I know it hurts."

"It's okay." Lexie kept her teeth clenched to avoid making a sound as Donna worked the sandal off her injured foot and carefully examined it.

A few tense moments later, she stood and crossed her arms. "I don't think it's broken. We can do an x-ray tomorrow if you want, but I think it's just a bad sprain. It could be a grade two, but I'm thinking a one is more likely."

"What's the difference?"

"Grade two means you may have a partial tear in the ligaments, whereas a grade one means you just stretched them when you fell. Either way, we treat it pretty much the same, though grade two takes longer to heal."

Lexie couldn't keep the exasperation from her voice. "Some vacation this is turning out to be. How long before I can walk on it?"

She shrugged. "Depends—grade one, probably a week. A grade two could be anywhere from four to six weeks. In either case, stay off it totally for two or three days. We can try a boot when some of the swelling goes down. You'll need to wear it while walking until it's healed." She dropped the shirt over the handle on the shower door. "Let's get you in the shower."

Lexie looked down at her muddy clothing, then the beckoning shower. "I'm filthy."

If Donna heard the remark, she ignored it. "Leave your clothes on the shower floor. I'll put them in the laundry later."

Embarrassment sent heat racing to Lexie's cheeks. "I'm so sorry about all of this."

Donna reached for her hand. "Don't be. It's not like you planned for this to happen."

"I know, but y'all are doing so much...."

"You'd do the same in our shoes. Besides, your brother is married to my best friend, so you're kinda like family."

"Tina's your best friend?" She stood on one leg as Donna helped her into the shower and moved the shower seat closer to the controls. "You were maid of honor at their wedding."

"I'm surprised you remember. That was like six years ago."

"That green dress was stunning on you."

Donna stopped and looked up. "Thank you."

Lexie shrugged. "You're welcome." She lowered herself onto the seat. "How long have you known Tina?"

"Since we were in grade school." Donna handed her the detachable shower wand and a wash rag. "You should be able to reach the controls from there." She took a step back. "Soap and shampoo are in that cubby hole. Take your time. I'll check on you in a bit."

Twenty minutes later, ankle and head throbbing in unison, Lexie leaned against the vanity and eyed the dark bruise on her hip and the one building across her chest. "Just flipping great," she complained, then sat on the commode seat and toweled her hair dry as best she could.

The shirt Donna left was a soft cotton jersey sporting the name and number of an NFL quarterback. She slipped it on, then stood beside the commode to examine her reflection in the mirror. Face burning, Lexie tugged on the hem, which caught her mid-thigh. "No way in hell am I wearing this without pants," she muttered. "It swallows me and still doesn't reach my knees. Hope my stuffs in the bedroom."

Ignoring the dizziness, she hobbled and hopped to the bed, using the wall, dresser, and nightstand for support. By the time she reached the bed and the open suitcase lying near the foot, she couldn't decide which was worse—the dizziness that made her stomach roll or the headache pounding against her temples. Eyes closed, she eased down on the bed and took several deep breaths, irritated she had nothing to take for the pain.

She fumbled around in the case for panties, quickly pulled them on, and dug out a pair of grey sweatpants. A bra wasn't worth the effort.

A light knock sounded on the door. Expecting Donna, she placed the pants in her lap. "Come in."

The door opened, and Donna walked in with Jake right behind her. "Judging by the look on your face," admonished Donna, "you overdid it. You should have waited for me to help." Hands on her hips, she stopped beside the bed. "Would you like to lie down here or in the den?"

"I don't—"

Ignoring her, Donna turned to Jake. "Help her to your chair in the den. It's more comfortable, and we can elevate her foot."

"No," stammered Lexie. "I don't...."

Jake moved to her side and slowly reached for her right arm. "No point arguing, Miss Morgan. She's bossy as hell and never takes no for an answer. Come on. I'll help you up."

Acutely aware of the jersey's length, Lexie clutched the sweats in front and slowly stood. The moment she was upright, her balance wavered, and Jake quickly drew her against him. One arm automatically encircled her waist, anchoring her to his side; the other paused in front, and she instinctively grabbed it with one hand.

Air whooshed from her lungs. Her heart pounded out an erratic rhythm as the impact of his nearness overwhelmed her.

"You okay?"

A huskiness she hadn't noticed before filtered through his voice. The warmth of his body penetrated the thin fabric of her shirt and prickled her flesh. She cleared her throat, pretending not to be affected. "Yeah. Who knew standing on one leg was so difficult?"

As if to emphasize the point, her body wobbled again, and his hold tightened. The sensory effect of such a gentle grip shocked her. Desperate, she tried to manage a casual conversation. "Um...Biscuit. How is he?"

"Fine," he muttered, his voice throaty and coarse. "Nothing serious. A little nick on his tongue, left paw has a slight sprain. He's in the den with Katie."

He slowly guided her toward the door, and she glanced up. "Thank you for taking care of him. And me."

Eyes the color of deep, dark chocolate drilled into hers. Breath once again caught in her throat, and rational thought vanished. Her breasts tingled against the soft fabric of her shirt as unexpected—and unwanted desire rushed to the surface.

Suddenly, his jaw tensed, and his eyes turned glacial and guarded.

In one forward motion, she was in his arms. She closed her eyes and tried to ignore the sensation of his bare arm against the back of her thighs. With her cheek pressed to his chest, she heard the strong thump of his heartbeat and seized the wrinkled pants like a lifeline.

Long strides took them back down the hall, where he turned left and entered a comfortable den filled with masculine, overstuffed leather furniture arranged around a stunning stone fireplace. He stopped at the closest chair and gently eased her into it.

"I have work to finish," he snapped at Donna. "You gonna be here a while?"

She punched his shoulder. "Go. I got this."

Biscuit limped over, tail wagging furiously, and licked Lexie's outstretched hand. "Hey, baby." She ran her hands over his ears. "Are you alright?"

Biscuit's exuberance caused him to bump her ankle, and she

couldn't stifle a surprised yelp of pain. Lexie pointed to Katie, who stood near the fireplace. "Go, boy. Go play with Katie."

Immediately, the dog trotted over and sat beside the child.

She inhaled. "Can you give me a hand getting these sweats on?"

"I'm so sorry. I should have thought to ask before Jake brought you in here."

Once suitably covered, Lexie leaned back in the chair, gritting her teeth against the pain pulsing through her body. "Thanks."

"No problem. I'm sorry. I didn't think about how you were dressed until I saw your face turn red." She snorted. "But I bet *he'll* think about it every time he wears it from now on."

Heat flooded her face as she recalled his breath teasing her cheek and his bare arms against her thighs as he carried her here. *Holy mother of pearl. What is happening to me?*

Donna waved one hand in front of her face. "I'm sorry. I have this habit of saying what I'm thinking before I think of what I'm saying." She shook her head, then pointed toward the chair's right arm. "The controls to recline are there. Let me grab a pillow off the couch, then tilt back until you're comfortable. I'll hold your foot." She eased the pillow under her injured ankle when the footrest extended.

Mrs. Holloway entered with an ice bag under her arm, a medicine bottle, and a glass of water in her hands.

"Here's the ibuprofen you asked for, dear," she said to Donna, "and the ice pack." She placed the items on the end table beside the chair and spoke to Lexie. "Can I get you anything, dear? Coffee, maybe, or iced tea?"

Lexie would kill for a cup of coffee but hated further infringing on their hospitality. "I can't impose anymore, Mrs. Holloway.

You've all done so much already."

"It's nothing anyone else wouldn't do for someone in your situation. Besides, you're Bobby's sister, and he's practically family. And please, my friends call me Aggie."

Gentle brown eyes glowed with an inner peace so profound it suddenly made Lexie yearn to know her secret. "Thank you...Miss Aggie." She rolled her lower lip inward, succumbing to temptation. "Honestly, I could use a cup of coffee."

"Just made a fresh pot. How do you take it?"

"Just black, please."

"I'll be right back."

Agnes headed for the kitchen while Katie knelt near the fireplace, her head close to Biscuit's ear. Her lips moved, and her head bobbled as she appeared to lecture the dog, complete with a finger pointed at his nose. The sight warmed Lexie's heart.

Biscuit emitted a soft 'woof' as though in agreement with whatever she said, then lay down on the hearth.

Katie patted his head, then walked to the edge of the couch on Lexie's right. Wide hazel eyes studied her without comment.

Lexie took a deep breath and looked at Katie. "It's so nice of you to talk to Biscuit."

The child ducked her head and then looked up. "Bis-tit sor-re he hurt your foot," she offered solemnly. "He won't do it again."

"I know, sweetie. He didn't do it on purpose. He's a good dog."

Soft chestnut curls bobbed up and down as she bobbed her head and inched closer. "Aunt Dee fix your boo-boo?"

"She sure did."

Soon, the child stood near the footrest, and she eyed the dark bruises with concern. "I sor-re you got hurt."

Touched by her empathy, Lexie wiggled the big toe of her sore foot. "I'll be good as new in no time. See?"

Donna passed two pills and water to Lexie. "Ibuprofen for pain and inflammation. Two every four to six hours."

Lexie swallowed the medicine and prayed the stuff kicked in sooner rather than later.

Silent, Katie inched up the arm of the chair.

Something in her doe-like eyes pulled at Lexie's heartstrings. And then it hit her. *Lonely. The child is lonely.* Lexie understood that feeling more than she would ever admit, even to herself, and ignored the pain. "Thank you for keeping Biscuit company, Katie. He gets kinda scared around people he doesn't know."

She glanced at the dog who lounged in front of the fireplace. "He does?"

"Uh-huh. But having a friend to talk to helps a lot."

Enthusiasm seeped into hooded eyes. "I be his f'end."

"Oh, would you? I know he'd like that."

She looked down, then back up, and Lexie's breath caught at the budding hope hovering in the depths of the child's eyes.

"I can be your f'end?"

Lexie swallowed hard. "Absolutely."

A tentative smile graced the child's face as Katie leaned forward. "Can you weed?"

Puzzled, Lexie replied, "Uh-huh."

"Katie—"

"It's okay, Donna." Lexie studied the child. "Why do you ask?"

Katie worked her way to the end table, tiny fingers trailing along the arm of the chair. "Can you weed me a sto-ree?"

Surprised, Lexie hesitated. "Of course. Do you have a book you like?"

"Uh-huh," said Katie. "I get it." She sprinted off down the hall.

"I'll be damned."

Donna's soft expletive caused Lexie to frown. "What's wrong?"

Donna shook her head. "She's said more to you in the last five minutes than she has to me in weeks."

As Lexie digested her statement, Donna changed the subject. "Don't get up without assistance," she instructed. "And I don't think you should go to the cabin tonight."

"Why not?"

She pointed to her foot. "No weight on that for at least two, maybe three days. We'll have to see how it goes. And trust me on this, tomorrow you're gonna be sore all over."

Lexie opened her mouth, but Donna didn't give her a chance to reply.

"The cabin isn't far from here, about a mile or so, and we'll get you moved over later. Jake said they have some crutches in the barn you can use until you can put weight on your foot. And I talked with Bobby while you showered. He and Tina will be by when they get off work." She glanced at her watch. "It's four-thirty now, so I'm guessing maybe an hour. He knows you're staying here tonight and said to call him if you need anything from town."

During Donna's speech, Aggie returned with a steaming mug of coffee and a saucer of peanut butter cookies, still warm from the oven. The aroma made Lexie's mouth water.

"She's right, dear," said Aggie. "You won't be able to get around for a day or two." She nodded as though the decision was final. "The guest room is ready, and I insist you stay here at least tonight. We'll move you to the cabin tomorrow or the next day."

"Miss Aggie, I –"

"Katie asked her to read a story," said Donna, both brows raised as she cast her mother a meaningful glimpse.

Aggie's eyes widened, and her mouth dropped open. She placed the coffee and cookies on the table and glanced between them. "She did?"

"She's gone after a book."

"I don't understand," said Lexie. "What's the big deal?"

Katie bounced down the hall, stopping when she saw her grandmother and aunt.

Aggie grinned and took Donna's arm. "Come along, dear. You can help me finish getting their supper ready."

The two women left the room without another word, peeking behind them as they headed for the kitchen.

Lexie pointed to the book Katie held. "Is that what you want me to read?"

She glanced toward the departing women, then slowly dipped her head.

Lexie's head and foot throbbed with each beat of her heart, but she pasted on a pleasant expression and motioned the girl forward.

Katie took one tentative step, then another, stopping when she reached the chair and handed the book to Lexie.

Upon seeing the title, she clutched the book to her chest. "*Where is The Pokey Little Puppy* is my favorite book ever. My brother read it to me when I was little." A quick inspection showed it appeared new, its binding crinkling when she opened it.

"I wike doggies."

"So do I."

Katie glanced toward Biscuit. "Can Bis-tit wisten, too?"

"Sure." Lexie snapped her fingers, and Biscuit limped over. "Sit." Both dog and child sat beside the chair.

Biscuit licked Katie on the cheek, and she giggled. "I wike Bis-tit."

"He likes you, too." Lexie took a fortifying sip of coffee and offered the snacks to Katie. "Cookies aren't good for doggies, so we can't share with him, okay?"

"Okay."

Katie sat cross-legged on the floor, nibbling on her treat, one arm around Biscuit as Lexie began to read.

Chapter Five

Distracted, Jake rubbed the silky nose of the mare Dr. Brett Austin examined while alternating visions of Miss Morgan clouded his mind. From frazzled and muddy beside her car to animated and smiling as she talked with Katie in the back seat to fresh from the shower wearing his favorite Chiefs jersey.

But the most disquieting of all—the effortless recall of light peach-scented shampoo on damp hair and how his skin still tingled from the touch of his arm on her bare leg.

Try as he might, he couldn't banish the images from his mind. Something about her drew him as no woman had in years. It charmed, angered, and confused him all at the same time.

I don't need this. I don't want it.

But he couldn't get her out of his mind.

"This one should foal in October."

The vet's disembodied voice floated near the edge of Jake's consciousness, though the actual words didn't penetrate. "Hmm."

"The other two can be bred next week."

"Uh-huh."

"The purple one has blue feathers."

"'kay."

"And polka dots."

"Whatever y—," Jake stopped and stared at his friend. "What did you say?"

The vet laughed and slapped him on the shoulder. "You haven't heard a word I said."

Jake stepped back, ignoring the unfamiliar rush of heat to his face. "Lot on my mind today."

"Anything to do with the lady who owns the dog I checked over earlier?"

"No," Jake snapped as he turned the horse loose in the corral and hung the halter on a nail.

Brett's laugh was deep and hearty. "Right. I can't wait to meet her." He fell in step with Jake as they walked toward his truck. "But will have to wait for another time. I have three more farm calls today, and Beverly has plans for us this evening."

"I thought your new partner was supposed to help lessen the load."

"Sean gets walk-ins today." Brett gave him a side-eyed look. "You talked to him yet?"

He ignored the question. "Why come back here? I thought he liked San Antonio."

"Clinic changed hands. I don't think it was a smooth transition."

They stopped at his truck, and he opened the door. "Besides, small-town life is better. I'll email you my report since your mind was preoccupied and didn't hear a word I said."

"I heard you," snapped Jake.

"Of course, you did."

Annoyed, Jake watched him leave, then went to the kitchen door and removed his boots before walking inside. Donna and his mother sat at the breakfast bar, cups in hand.

"Do you ever smile anymore?"

His sister's question made him pause as he poured himself coffee. "What?"

"Smile. You know..." She mimicked pulling up the corners of her mouth. "Make a happy face."

He ignored the question. "How is she?"

Donna gave a disgusted sigh. "She's fine. I don't think it's broken, just a bad sprain. She needs to stay off it for two or three days."

He joined them at the bar, grabbed a cookie off the plate, and devoured it in one bite. "Can one of you stay with Katie while I take her to the cabin?" He took a cautious sip of coffee and waited.

"She's staying here tonight."

Despite the steel in his mother's voice, he argued. "What? No. She can't stay here."

"Why not?"

A reasonable reply escaped him. "Because."

Agnes made a dismissive gesture with her hands. "Anyway, I've already told her she's staying. At least for a night or two."

"She'll be sore the next few days," Donna said. "Plus, she can't walk and needs someone to help her."

"I've got a ranch to run. I don't have time to babysit." Coffee sloshed from his cup as he plunked it on the bar.

"You haven't even tried to find another nanny," said Donna sharply.

It was difficult to argue with the truth, so he didn't bother.

"I know you keep hoping Mrs. Ackerman will come back, dear," said Aggie softly, "But her parents are both in poor health and need her there."

He knew that, of course, but hated the hassle of looking again. Finding Mrs. Ackerman, an older widow with grown children and grandchildren, had taken weeks. Since then, there were three others, none lasting more than a month—mainly because they were more interested in him or his two ranch hands than Katie.

Knowing she needed some other interaction, he enrolled her in daycare three weeks ago, but it still left him in a bind for the afternoons when he had work to do. Disgruntled, he wiped the sloshed coffee up with a napkin. "That's why I have y'all around to help."

Agnes gave his hand a motherly pat. "Which is why I hired someone for you. She'll be by Wednesday or Thursday afternoon to get acquainted with things, and y'all can discuss her schedule."

She hired someone. Without him even meeting her? "What?"

"You heard me. You wouldn't do it, so I did. And yes, I checked her references. Her name is Elizabeth Adams, but she goes by Beth. She's 43, divorced, has one daughter and a granddaughter about Katie's age." She continued before he could interrupt. "She will pick her up from daycare and stay until you are home. She agreed to do light housework if needed and to fix your supper."

He stared at his mother in silence, unable to formulate a suitable rebuttal.

"And, she can be available on short notice, like if you decide to join the real world and date again."

The words buzzed around his head like angry bees. His own mother put him in the crosshairs of another husband-hunting divorcée.

"I see the wheels turning, Jake." Donna rubbed a hand on his arm. "Mom and I interviewed her together. And checked her out.

She'll be fine."

He swung around to face his sister. "And neither of you thought to include me in the interview process?"

She sputtered. "Like you'd be there." She swilled the last of her coffee. "She moved here from Dallas a couple of months ago. Owned a small daycare center there. Had to sell it after the divorce. She's polite, soft-spoken, sense of humor." She poked him in the shoulder. "Which she will sorely need around you."

He tilted his head back and stared at the ceiling. His life was a runaway freight train, and he was powerless to stop the wild ride. "I can't go through this again." He focused on his mother. "You know what happened before."

Agnes patted his hand again. "It's the Holloway charm, sweetheart. They can't help themselves. But I think you'll be safe with Elizabeth. Food is in the oven when y'all are ready to eat."

He needed to regain control of something—anything and switched to his houseguest. "Lexie can't stay here," he muttered, refusing to acknowledge he fought another losing battle.

"Bobby should be here anytime." Donna rose and placed her mug in the sink. "I understand he's bringing a vehicle for her to drive. It's her left foot, so she can probably manage it, but not for a couple of days at least." She grinned as she came around and poked his shoulder with one finger. "Besides, you could use some female company besides us."

"I don't want company," he growled. "Especially not another meddling female."

"Oh, no, sweetheart," Agnes cooed. "She isn't meddling." She rose and kissed his cheek. "We are." She turned toward the back door and stopped. "I left the crutches Cody brought by at the end of the bar."

He ground his teeth in frustration. "She's not staying."

If either woman heard his refusal, they ignored him.

"I need to get home before your father sends out a search party." Agnes picked up her purse. "I'll pick Katie up tomorrow from daycare."

Donna walked toward him and stopped. "Katie asked Lexie to read her a story."

The news shocked him. She seldom asked him, or anyone else, to read. "What?"

She shrugged. "For whatever reason, your house guest reached a part of Katie none of us have thus far. If I were you, I'd keep her around a while."

Speechless, he watched them walk out.

Katie asked a stranger to read her a story.

The thought bothered him more than he expected.

He learned parenting from a loving mother but a distant father. Consequently, he wasn't a touchy-feely guy and was always out of his comfort zone with Katie. He tried his best to do right by her, even though her unknown sire haunted him.

And while he worked hard not to, he sometimes got frustrated trying to get the child to respond. She wasn't non-verbal; she talked but was terribly shy and easily intimidated, making it difficult for him to get what he considered proper responses from her.

In a burst of clarity, it saddened him to realize he couldn't remember the last time he heard her laugh or even smile.

He had hoped being around other kids in the daycare center would bring her out of her shell. The owner, Mrs. Tompkins, told him today she remained hopeful despite little progress thus far.

Is it me? Has the past so hardened me I've lost the ability to show love?

Disgusted, he pushed the stool back and stomped to the end of the bar, grabbing the crutches as he marched toward the den.

He rounded the corner and froze.

He couldn't hear the words, but their body language spoke volumes. He'd never seen this animated side of Katie. She leaned on the arm of Lexie's chair, her face beaming with delight as Lexie brushed a chestnut curl behind Katie's ear and placed a kiss on her forehead. The gesture was so feminine, so motherly, it took his breath away.

Suddenly, he realized what was missing from Katie's life.

And his.

Katie's charming giggle made Lexie momentarily forget the pain pulsing through her body.

"Bis-tit needs a boot wike wittle puppy." Katie patted the dog's head and rose to lean on the arm of the chair.

Lexie handed her the book. "He has an old tennis shoe of mine he likes to chew on."

"Wike Pokey Puppy?"

"Just like him." She ran her fingers through the soft ringlets around the child's face and tucked them behind her ear. "Why don't you put the book back, so you'll know where it is next time."

"Tank you, Wexie."

Impulsively, she kissed the child's forehead. "You're very welcome."

"I be back."

When Katie skipped away, Lexie leaned back and closed her eyes. Each beat of her heart thumped against her skull like a hammer, and she couldn't stifle a groan as she gently massaged her temples.

"Is Katie bothering you?"

Jake's coarse voice startled her, and she jumped, jerking her foot, which immediately doubled her pain level. "Dammit!"

"Sorry. Didn't mean to startle you." He leaned the crutches against the end table. "How much does that word cost?"

"A quarter," she snipped and met his unreadable gaze.

He fished a coin from his pocket and silently placed it on the table.

The unexpected action took her by surprise. "Um...thanks." *Okay, so maybe he's not such a jerk after all.*

He gave a light shrug of dismissal. "Can I get you anything? Maybe something for the headache?"

She leaned back and tried to reconcile her mixed feelings about the man. Jerk—not a jerk—insensitive—sensitive. "I took something half an hour ago. It should kick in soon."

His stiff posture made her think he was angry or perhaps sad. She didn't know him well enough to decide which, and his face revealed nothing.

"I'd suggest you lie down a bit, but Bobby should be here soon."

The mention of her brother caused her face to crease in dread. He would no doubt arrive in big-brother-protector mode, and she wasn't in the mood.

The pain was one thing; the imposition on strangers added another level of distress. "I must apologize again for being such a bother." She closed her eyes and resisted the urge to rub her aching temples again.

"It's no bother."

She snorted. "Bull."

Katie sprang back into the room but skidded to a stop when she spotted Jake.

His expression softened as he looked at his daughter, and Lexie did a double-take. The transformation was incredible. And sexy. She closed her eyes briefly to corral her wayward thoughts.

"Did you thank Miss Morgan for reading to you?"

Katie gave a solemn nod.

He cleared his throat. "Okay. Good."

His gaze skipped around the room, and he appeared lost for words.

Lexie stepped in and spoke to Katie. "That book was my favorite when I was your age."

The child pulled at the hem of her shirt. "I wike doggies."

Jake cleared his throat. "Miss Morgan—"

"Lexie. My friends call me Lexie." She didn't specify only one person called her the name she'd officially adopted just this morning. To everyone else, including her over-protective brother, she was Alex.

Jake rubbed one hand on his thigh, which she interpreted as a nervous sign.

"...um...Lexie. Try to rest before your company arrives." He held out his hand toward the child. "Come on, Katie. Time to eat."

Katie hesitated, then walked to Jake and took his outstretched hand.

"Mother left supper warming in the oven. I'll bring you a plate when you're ready."

"Thanks. Maybe later." Her empty stomach growled in protest, and warmth flooded her cheeks. "Mr. Holloway—"

"Jake."

"...Jake. Thank you."

As if on cue, the sound of wheels on gravel drifted in from outside.

Jake released Katie's hand and headed for the front door without a word, leaving them staring at his retreating back.

The pounding in Lexie's head made her grit her teeth a moment before turning to the girl. "Thank you for sharing your book with me today. I really enjoyed it."

Katie returned to her spot by the chair. "You weh'come."

"I think you might know my brother. His name is Bobby, and his wife is Tina."

Katie nodded.

Lexie lowered her voice and grinned. "Just between us, he might be large, but he's really just a big ole teddy bear."

Katie blinked, then giggled. "He is?"

She placed her arm around the child and leaned in. "Yep."

Jake walked in with Bobby and Tina close behind.

Her brother stopped beside the chair; his handsome face filled with concern. "You look like h—" His gaze darted between Lexie and the child cradled against her. "Alex, are you sure you're okay?"

Katie flinched at his booming voice, and Lexie hugged her tighter. "It's been an eventful day, for sure."

Biscuit limped over to welcome the newcomers, and each took a moment to say hello before Bobby lowered his voice and spoke to Katie.

"Hey, there, Lil Bit."

Katie produced a tentative smile and snuggled closer to Lexie.

Tina stepped forward and handed Katie a book with a dog on the cover. "I found this the other day and thought you might enjoy it."

She took it without comment.

"What do you say, Katie?" asked Jake.

"Tank you, Aunt Tina," she mumbled.

"You're very welcome. I'd be happy to read it to you some time."

Katie held the book close to her chest. "Wexie can weed it to me."

The newcomers didn't react to Katie's dismissal of the offer; instead, they directed their attention to Lexie.

"Come on, Katie," Jake said. "Let Miss Lexie visit with her family."

Katie hesitated, then spoke to Lexie. "You weed to me tomorrow?"

"Of course."

Her timid gaze darted to the newcomers before handing Lexie the book. She took Jake's hand, and they headed for the kitchen, Biscuit trailing behind.

"I think you have a new member of your fan club," said Bobby with a grin.

Lexie shrugged. "She seems lonely to me."

Her brother squatted down and touched her arm before critically scanning her face. "That's a nasty knot on your head, Alex. Are you sure you don't need to go to the hospital or anything?"

"I'm fine," she insisted. "Some bumps and bruises and a sprained ankle. I'll be sore for a few days, but nothing serious." She sighed. "My car, though, is another story."

"Yeah." Bobby gently rubbed her hand. "I spoke to Paul earlier and gave him the insurance information. He thinks they will total it."

"I figured as much. Dang hogs."

"Well, look on the bright side," said Tina as she stood behind her husband. "You weren't seriously hurt, and now get a new ride."

"Why did Jake call you Lexie?"

Bobby's question surprised her. She avoided his direct gaze since he was the one who tagged her Alex soon after she was born. "It's something Andy—you know, Dad's general foreman, started a few years ago." She paused. "It's not as if I don't like your nickname; it's just ...."

"I think it suits you better than Alex," said Tina.

"She's right." Bobby tapped her nose in a show of affection. "But you could have told me, all of us, in fact, you didn't like being called Alex."

"I didn't want to hurt your feelings."

"So, Lexie," said Bobby, dragging out the new name, "Let's talk about you."

Time passed quickly as brother and sister discussed the accident, the cabin, and her plans for the next two weeks. It spoke volumes about Bobby's respect for Jake when he expressed no concerns about her staying the night at his house and moving to the cabin tomorrow.

"Tina stocked the cabin for you, so you don't have to go shopping anytime soon."

"I did ask your mother what foods you liked," said Tina, "And made sure there was plenty of coffee and a couple of steaks. Oh, and two bottles of your favorite wine," she added with a wink.

"Thanks for checking on me and arranging for the cabin, the food. Just everything."

Bobby patted her hand. "You're exhausted, so we'll go now." He stood, fished a set of keys from his pocket, and placed them on the table. "We left Tina's Escape outside for you to use. It's easier to get in and out of."

"Oh, no, I can't take Tina's car."

He kissed her forehead. "Of course, you can. She'll drive the Bronco, and I'll have an excuse to ride the Harley to work."

She looked between the two of them. "All I have done today is say I'm sorry for being such a bother."

"It's no bother, and you know it," said Tina.

"Thank you."

"You're welcome," said Tina. "Now, can I bring you anything else from town, Alex—I mean Lexie?"

"I think you have all the basics covered. Thank you." She nodded toward her injured foot. "Hopefully, I can go to town by the weekend."

"Well, if you can't, just call me, and I'll pick up anything you need."

"Thank you. Again." She sighed. "I have to be off my foot for a few days, but I hope to go to the cabin tomorrow." She pointed to the crutches resting beside the end table. "I can use those to get around."

"I'll say goodbye to Jake, and we'll go." Her brother paused and swallowed hard. "I'm so glad you're okay, kiddo." He took a breath. "And I called Mom and Dad earlier, but they hadn't landed from New York yet. I left a message for one of them to call me."

"Thanks. I appreciate your help."

Once he was out of sight, Tina smirked. "Now, tell me how you managed to get smiles from Jake and Katie both."

Chapter Six

Jake lifted Katie to the barstool and scooted it forward.

"Doggie eat, too, Daddy?"

The question from the habitually quiet child took him by surprise. "Yeah. I'll fix his supper, too."

She leaned around where she could watch. "I wike Bis-tit."

He grabbed the bag of dog food he'd brought in earlier and scooped some into a bowl by the back door. The dog waited for him to finish and step aside before eating with gusto. He stared at the mutt for a heartbeat, suddenly realizing he had no qualms about him being in the house. Maybe because Katie reacted so strongly to him, or perhaps his owner—he shut down that line of thought and went to the sink to wash his hands. Next, he fixed Katie's plate, added a glass of milk, and placed it in front of her.

"Tank you."

He absently wondered if her sudden spurt of manners came from the daycare and made a mental note to thank Mrs. Tompkins. Then, anticipating a drawn-out meal, he carefully tempered any impatience in his voice. "You're welcome. Now eat."

She picked up her fork, stabbed a sliced carrot, and poked it in her mouth. While she chewed, she picked up a green bean with her fingers and stuffed it in, too, feet bouncing against the breakfast bar.

Her relaxed behavior and eagerness to eat caught him by surprise. She tended to dawdle to the point he ground his teeth in frustration. Before he finished the thought, she shocked him again by speaking without a prod.

"Wexie hun-gee, too." She stuffed two beans in her mouth.

He sat beside her, coffee cup in his hand. "She has company right now."

"Unca Bobby is a teddy bear," she mumbled around a mouth full of food.

"A what?"

As if suddenly realizing she spoke, the child stilled and ducked her head.

"Katie?" Jake asked softly. "Why is he a teddy bear?"

At first, he didn't think she would answer, but slowly, she cut her eyes toward him, uncertainty clouding her face. "Wexie said he's a big teddy bear."

Jake grinned at the image of Bobby, a six-three, two-hundred-seventy-pound former linebacker, as a teddy bear. "You know what? I think she's right."

The hesitant smile transformed Katie's face. Suddenly, more than anything, he wished to keep it there.

"I wike Wexie." She swallowed and looked at him with soulful, expectant eyes. "You wike Wexie?"

You have no idea. "Yeah, I do."

Katie swatted her hair away from her face and resumed eating.

On impulse, Jake got up, went to the junk drawer near the sink, and pulled out a rubber band. Katie sat still while he carefully secured the shoulder-length tresses behind her neck. "How's that?"

"Tank you, Daddy."

Jake's heart stumbled as he asked himself once again how he could be so conflicted about his feelings. She was a kid, crying out loud. A good one. And she needed him.

The image of her response to Lexie tore at his conscience.

He cared for her, bathed and dressed her daily, provided for her, and read to her when she let him. Hell, he even tried to do something with her hair.

But was he a good father? Or more like his own? A man who thought hard work and providing for his family showed love enough? A man who kept everyone at arm's length, even his children.

A gulp of coffee lodged in his throat when he realized this was the first time he referred to himself as Katie's father.

As though sensing his scrutiny, Katie glanced his way, rosy cheeks full of food, and her tiny lips pursed as she chewed. Gone was the uncertain expression she typically wore. In its place was one of contentment, even happiness.

His heart gave another little jerk.

She resumed kicking her feet against the bar and chewed.

It's been four years, Holloway, he chided himself. *Let it go.*

But he couldn't.

Mary's unknown lover was out there somewhere. *Did he know or wonder about Katie? What if he decided to push for answers?*

"See, Daddy?"

Katie's voice broke through the turmoil in his head.

"I make a happy pate." She reached for a paper napkin and wiped her mouth.

Jake assumed the *happy plate* phrase came from daycare and made a mental note to remember it. "Yes, you did."

The angelic face looking up at him, so full of trust and—something else gave him pause. *Will I ever be able to give her what she needs? Do I even have it to give?*

He shook off the disquieting thoughts, reached for the plate, and hesitated. "I think a happy plate deserves chocolate ice cream, don't you?"

She sat up straighter, face beaming. "Yes!"

⊗

Lexie shifted in the chair and winced. Movement of any kind brought a new ache to life. The two pills she took earlier may as well have been candy for all the good they did. Eyes closed, she tried to will the throbbing away. When that didn't work, she sighed and turned to the end table, searching for the bottle of ibuprofen, only to stop when her phone rang.

She glanced at the caller-ID and groaned. Craig Bennett. The supervisor for the Marshall site was a royal pain. He'd asked her out several times, not the least put off by her continued refusal. Although good at his job, he was the most irritating man she'd ever met. The type who thought a woman should be flattered by his interest. His egotistical behavior grated on her nerves.

She briefly considered letting his call go to voicemail, but he would likely contact her father and say she wasn't answering his calls—the jerk.

"Morgan."

"You plan on showing up today or not?" he snipped. "Unlike

you, I got someone waiting to go out with me."

She visualized his haughty stance, chest out, dark, beady eyes scanning her head to toe, mouth turned up in a lewd smirk.

"I said I would come by before Friday." She heard him inhale, no doubt prepping for his usual array of cutting remarks or innuendos and spoke first. "But my plans have changed."

"That a fact?"

She pinched the bridge of her nose. "Something happened today, and I'll be out for a few days."

"Anyone I know?"

His snicker chafed against already frayed nerves. "I'll be by sometime Monday afternoon. We'll do the final walk-through then." She pressed her head against the back of the chair and rubbed a spot between her eyes with one finger.

"Think you can tear yourself away long enough to send me the specs on the West Texas project?"

She made no effort to temper the disdain in her voice. "Ask your secretary. She signed for them at eleven-thirty today."

There was a slight pause before he scoffed, "Have fun with your *plans*." His emphasis on the last word made it sound vulgar as he ended the call.

The encounter, coupled with the headache, left her drained and, to her dismay, on the verge of tears. Eyes clinched She dropped the phone in her lap and took a deep breath, the pain in her head so severe her stomach threatened to purge its skimpy contents of coffee and cookies.

She'd dealt with his type before, but Craig took things to a whole new level. Thankfully, this particular contract ended next week. Unfortunately, her father put him on the job in West Texas. Even though contact would be minimal, none was preferable.

She sighed and considered reporting him to HR. While irritating and obnoxious, his behavior wasn't precisely harassment.

Maybe I'll just put a bug in the director's ear, just in case.

She bit her lip when her stomach gave an unhappy roll. *Oh, no. Please. Not that.*

A noise drew her gaze toward the hallway to the kitchen.

Jake strode in carrying a food tray, impassive face giving nothing away.

Katie skipped in behind him, and Lexie forced a genial expression.

"Guess what, Wexie? I made a happy pate, and Daddy gived me choc-it ice ceam."

She failed to hide the slight wince when she spoke. "Wow, that's great."

Jake placed the tray on the coffee table and faced her. "How bad is it?"

Chagrined at his easy assessment of her condition, she grimaced. "A five on the Richter Scale."

"Which means closer to an eight." He moved to the end table and picked up the medicine bottle. "Donna said you could have more if needed."

"I do."

He shook the pills in her hand and passed her the glass from the tray. "I hope sweet tea is okay."

"It's fine." She swallowed the pills and sat back. "Thank you."

"Are you still sick, Wexie?" Katie's soft voice radiated concern.

"A little bit, sweetie, but I'll be okay soon."

She gently patted her arm. "Me and Daddy make you all better."

She prayed the artificial grin didn't look like a scowl. "That's so sweet of you, Katie. Thank you."

Jake cleared his throat. "As soon as you eat something, I'll help you to bed." He tilted his head toward the coffee table. "Mother made Katie's favorite—meatloaf and veggies. I wasn't sure what you'd eat since Donna also said nausea might be an issue."

The mention of food made her stomach growl in anticipation, even as her headache warned she might regret it. "Maybe the food will help. I haven't eaten much since breakfast."

"Let's get you situated."

A few minutes later, the tray rested across her lap, and she sampled the meat. Her stomach didn't protest, so she took another cautious bite, followed by a sip of tea.

Katie and Biscuit stood beside her chair and watched.

"I'm going to give Katie her bath," Jake said stiffly. "I'll be back in a few minutes." He took the child's hand and left the room.

Halfway through the meal, the headache hadn't improved, and her stomach was iffy at best, so she pushed the plate away.

Jake returned and placed the tray on the coffee table. "You okay?"

"Not sure."

He nodded and extended his hand. "I'll help you stand, then take you to bed." His shocked expression froze.

For a split second, she forgot to breathe.

"I mean, I'll help you to bed."

Eyes wide, she avoided his gaze. "Okay," she stammered, gripping his outstretched hand, and wobbled on her right leg as reality crashed in.

Supper was seconds away from ending up on the floor.

Chapter Seven

Jake watched the color drain from Lexie's face when she stood. *Aw, hell.*

He caught Katie's wide-eyed expression as he scooped Lexie in his arms. "Stay here with Biscuit, okay?" He hurried toward the bathroom without waiting to see if she obeyed.

"Oh, God," Lexie murmured, fingers pressed to her lips. "I'm gonna be sick."

"Hang on. Almost there."

Once inside, he raised the commode lid with his foot and lowered her feet to the floor. He barely got her in position before she bent double and hurled.

The retching didn't bother him; he'd dealt with worse things on the ranch. But he had little experience dealing with sick people. The few times Katie fell ill, his mother or sister was there to help.

Out of his comfort zone, he tried to keep the hair away from her face with one hand and support her shaking body against his with the other. Between heaves, she trembled like a new foal standing for the first time, and sympathy washed over him. "It's gonna pass," he said softly. "You'll be okay."

When the worst appeared over, he gently shifted her to the sink, and she gripped the counter with both hands, arms shaking so much he doubted she'd hold herself up for long.

He filled a small glass with water and held it while she sipped and rinsed her mouth.

She avoided his face in the mirror and stammered a weak "Thank you" before crumpling against him.

He carried her to the bed, gave a silent word of thanks to his mother for turning back the covers, and gently laid her down. He grabbed a couple of pillows from the settee by the window and tenderly elevated her injured foot before pulling the covers to her waist.

The only movement was the erratic rise and fall of her chest as she breathed.

He rubbed his chin and glanced around the room, then returned to the bathroom and wet a rag with cool water. She didn't protest when he sat on the edge of the bed and gently wiped her face before folding the rag over her forehead. "Bobby was right. We should have had you checked out at the hospital. I'm calling Donna."

"...no."

"You could be—"

Silent tears leaked from her tightly clenched eyes, and he froze. *What the hell did I do wrong?*

"...don't."

"Don't what? If the pain is so bad it makes you cry, then something is seriously wrong."

Her lips quivered, and a soft sob escaped.

Now he felt like an ass. On top of being hurt and sick, he'd made her cry. Humbled, he rubbed the back of his neck. "Look, I'm sorry if I upset you, Lexie, but this can't be normal." *Like I got a clue what constitutes normal female behavior in this situation.*

She sniffled and took an uneven breath. "...too much."

Too much? What's too much?

He stared at the weeping woman until his befuddled brain finally connected the dots.

Talk about your bad days. She totaled her car, can't walk, is in so much pain she upchucked her dinner and is at the mercy of a stranger with zero comfort skills. And then there was the phone call. Whoever was on the other end upset her, too.

He took the rag from her forehead and gently wiped the tears. "As bad days go," he said softly, "yours is a doozy."

She sniffed and hiccupped twice. "I...hate crying."

"If anyone has a right to, it's you."

She whimpered and clenched her eyes. "...don't...be nice."

He sat back and stared. *Don't be nice? What the hell?* "I'm just trying to help."

Granted, he probably sucked at it, but he *was* trying. He shook his head. It was an exercise in futility to figure out how a woman's mind worked. And he had no time for lost causes. "Fine," he grumbled, "I won't be nice."

She made a muffled noise. Whether a snort of laughter or another crying jag about to start was unclear, so he switched gears. "I'm calling Donna to make sure there's not something else happening we need to worry about."

She took a deep breath and opened her eyes. Red-rimmed and puffy, their crystal blue depths touched a piece of his soul he thought long dead and buried.

His stomach churned and a band tightened around his chest. *I gotta get out of here.*

Before she said anything else, he walked out to place the call.

Baffled, Lexie watched him leave, then pulled the rag over her eyes. Something upset him just now, but she was too dismal to dwell on it. He was a confusing enigma with so many contrasts.

She shifted on the bed and flinched. She was miserable; everything, even the hair on her arms, hurt.

But that was nothing compared to the humiliation of Jake—a total stranger—supporting her while she hurled.

And to top it off, she'd cried—cried, dammit, in front of the man! In her whole adult life, only Biscuit ever saw her cry, even after the Rodney debacle. But his compassion was her undoing. Unexpected and sincere, it touched a part of her no one had before. Her defenses crumbled when he gently wiped her face with that stupid rag.

In her world, self-control was vital. Show weakness, and someone used it against you. But in the brief time she'd known Jake, she'd been practically helpless. Good lord, he even held her steady as she puked! On top of everything else, she blubbered like a baby in front of him.

She sighed. *Things could only go up from here, right?*

But did she *want* things to go up?

Her heart gave an emphatic 'yes,' but could she trust such a fickle organ again? After all, it believed Rodney loved her, and look how that turned out.

Dejected, she rubbed her temples. *Scarlett had the right idea; I'll deal with it tomorrow.*

A soft whine made her peel the cloth from her eyes to peek over the side of the bed.

Biscuit's nose rested near her hand, and Katie stood beside him, hair still damp from her bath, one arm lying across the dog's neck.

Concern clouded her face. "I sor-ree you sick."

"Thank you, but I'll be better tomorrow."

"Katie," Jake's gruff voice made the child jump. "Don't bother Miss Lexie right now."

It wasn't hard to form a scowl as she glared at him. "She's not bothering me."

He stopped beside the bed with a glass of something clear and a sleeve of crackers in his other hand. "Donna thinks you may have a slight concussion." He frowned and held up the glass. "Evidently, I'm the only person on the planet who didn't know you give ginger ale and crackers to someone with an upset stomach."

Despite her headache, his annoyed expression generated kindness. "That's a staple in mom's kitchen."

His tone softened when he spoke to Katie. "Can you hold these for me?" He handed her the crackers and pulled a pill bottle from his shirt pocket. "This, too."

She took one in each hand and held them against her chest.

He placed the glass on the bedside table. "I need to help her sit," he said kindly. "So, I need you and Biscuit to move back a little, okay?"

Silent, she pulled the dog aside.

Once she was sitting up, Jake sat on the side of the bed and handed her the soda. "Just a sip or two to start," he muttered. "Then we'll try the crackers."

A few tense minutes later, stomach cooperating with the light snack, Jake handed her two pills. She leaned back and closed her eyes. "The list I'm indebted to you for is getting longer."

"You've had a long day. Try to rest." Jake stood and took Katie's hand. "Donna will come by tomorrow to check on you. Night light by the bathroom door comes on in the dark." He paused and cleared his throat. "Donna insists I check on you during the night."

Her eyes flew open, and she made no effort to hide her surprise. "That's not necessary."

"She insisted." He paused. "I'll try not to wake you but if you do and see me, don't be frightened." Plainly uncomfortable with Donna's order, he cleared his throat again. "I'm not some kind of pervert." He took a step back. "I'm harmless."

Maybe it was the compassion and sympathy he'd shown her to this point or the fact her brother trusted him, but whatever the reason, she wasn't at all concerned and wanted to repay his kindness with understanding. "I know, Jake."

His shoulders visibly relaxed, and he nodded toward Biscuit. "Do you want him in here?"

One look at Katie's face made the decision easy. "Would it be okay with you if he kept Katie company tonight?"

Surprise flashed in dark eyes before he nodded. "It's fine." He snapped his fingers, and Biscuit came to his side as he turned off the light and left.

The quiet semi-darkness brought blessed relief. Tension ebbed away, and she surrendered to sleep, soothed by the memory of warm, gentle hands and midnight eyes.

Chapter Eight

Jake swallowed the frustrated 'dammit' before it escaped his lips and cleaned the splashed coffee off the counter. Thanks to his houseguest, he was clumsy and unsettled this morning after a restless night. True to his word, he checked on Lexie several times. Heat burned his cheeks as he recalled standing beside the bed like a damn pervert watching her sleep. The lines of pain and frustration were gone in slumber, and those ebony locks contrasted sharply with the white pillowcase and accentuated the paleness in her cheeks. An unexpected surge of protectiveness surprised him. Off-balance, he turned and walked out.

On his last visit, however, she was restless. Her body twitched and jerked as her head rolled side-to-side. Her breath shuddered, and she moaned softly, hands moving as though to ward off or maybe reach for something. He knelt beside the bed and gently caressed her cheek with one finger while folding his big hand around her smaller one. "Shhh," he whispered repeatedly. "It's over. You're safe. Everything will be fine."

Suddenly, she whimpered, lifted her head off the pillow, and jolted awake. She had blinked rapidly, eyes darting around the room, her breath barely more than fearful gasps before frightened eyes locked on his.

Surprised, he froze, then stammered, "You had a bad dream. But it's over. You're safe."

Silent, she continued to stare, then slowly relaxed as comprehension dawned.

He waited a moment, then moved to stand

She gripped the hand covering hers. "...will you...."

Silent, he resumed his position, her hand tightly clasping his. She took a slow, shaky breath, blue eyes shimmering in the muted light. "...thank you."

It was some time before her eyes drifted shut and her body relaxed in peaceful sleep.

He had probably stayed longer than necessary. He told himself he couldn't leave until he was sure the distressing dream wouldn't return. But the truth was, he didn't want to go and refused to consider why.

Back in his room, sleep eluded him for hours. When it finally came, it brought unwanted images he couldn't escape. Even wide awake, they invaded his thoughts: Lexie's tenderness with Katie, her helpless tears last night, holding her in his arms, pressing against his body, and soothing away her troubling dream. Each image resurrected sensations he thought long gone.

Protectiveness.

Longing.

Desire.

He scrubbed one hand over his face. *No. Not now. Focus on something else.*

He sipped his coffee while he made breakfast, adding extra bacon and eggs for his visitor.

Katie happily munched on cereal, sneakered feet bouncing

against the bar, Biscuit at her feet. She hadn't complained when he woke her earlier and even grinned as he brushed her hair and added a barrette to one side. Just twenty-four hours ago, her actions were almost robotic. Today, she acted, well, like a happy kid, or at least how he thought one would. While the change was subtle, he noticed the difference.

It can't just be Lexie. It has to be something else. The dog, maybe. Lexie couldn't possibly have such a strong influence this fast.

He gave a disgusted snort when he realized she'd had the same effect on him.

Enough. Focus.

He concentrated on not burning the eggs and mentally lined out his to-do list in a futile effort to get his mind off Lexie. *Need to fix a downed fence on the west property line. I can pick up the new part for the baler after I drop Katie off at daycare. But then Lexie will be alone in the house. What if she got up and fell? Maybe I should wake her first? How will she react to last night?*

The fact he couldn't stop thinking or worrying about her irritated him, and he ground his teeth in frustration.

"Where's Wexie, Daddy?"

He placed eggs and bacon on his plate, added a canned biscuit, and placed it on the bar. "Still asleep, I guess."

"I wike Wexie."

A grunt sufficed for a reply as he returned to refill his cup.

Just then, Lexie stumbled into the kitchen on crutches, feet bare, still wearing his jersey and grey sweatpants, ebony locks brushing her shoulders. Her movements were slow and deliberate, and her mouth formed a tight line across her face. A bruise he hadn't noticed before peeked under the neck of her shirt. The bump on her forehead wasn't as big, but a dark bruise remained. The nicks on her face were scabbed over, red, and slightly swollen. A brief, indefinable emotion flashed in her ocean-blue eyes before it disappeared.

Uncertain, he stepped toward her and stopped. "Good morning." He motioned to his spot at the bar. "Um, sit down. Please. Can I get you some coffee?" He ignored the sudden rush of pleasure as the memory of holding her hand until she fell asleep played out in his mind.

She cleared her throat. Cheeks flushed a bright pink as she met his gaze. "...thank you, Jake." She took a quick breath. "For...everything."

Those words, softly spoken, played hell with his concentration. Joy warmed him from within as they regarded each other. "You're welcome." He stepped back. "Have a seat, and I'll get your coffee."

She shuffled forward and stopped. "I don't suppose you know where my glasses are, do you?"

"I think you left them on the end table last night when you got sick. I'll get them."

"No, please. Eat your breakfast first."

"See, Wexie," said Katie as she pointed to the plate. "Daddy make you beck'fast, too."

She jerked her gaze to his face. "I can't take your breakfast."

"I made enough for both of us." He placed a mug of coffee by the food. "In case you got up after I left."

She lingered, then sat down. "Thank you. Again."

He didn't miss the tight grimace as she leaned the crutches against the counter. "Need anything for your coffee?"

She wrapped her hands around the cup, inhaling the hearty

brew. "Just black, thanks." She took a cautious sip. "Ahh, nectar of the gods."

"Did you sleep okay?" The moment the question left his mouth, he wanted to drag it back because of the sudden rush of memories it evoked.

Her flushed expression said she shared at least some of his thoughts.

She cut her eyes toward him, then quickly looked away. "Yes. I did."

"Um, how do you feel this morning?"

"Didn't know I'd be this sore."

"What about the ankle?"

She was slow to answer. "Better than yesterday."

"But…"

"Still hurts."

He filled another plate with scrambled eggs, bacon, and a biscuit, then sat on the other side of Katie. "The biscuit came from a can, but it's not bad. Eat before it gets cold."

She cleared her throat. "I, um, I think I'll be able to get around all right with those." She indicated the crutches. "So, if I could impose on you once more to get me to the cabin, I'll get out of your hair."

He refused to acknowledge how much the thought of her leaving bothered him. "Donna will be here soon. We'll go with what she says."

"I've imposed long enough."

"Are you weaving, Wexie?"

Jake caught the light tremble in Katie's voice, and sadness erased the happy expression she'd worn earlier.

"Just to the cabin by the lake," said Lexie. "I'll still be close."

"But I want you to stay here." She looked down at the dog. "And Bis-tit, too."

Lexie opened, then closed her mouth and glanced at Jake.

"We'll wait till Donna gets here to decide. In the meantime, little girl, finish your breakfast. I need to get you to daycare."

"I wanna stay wif Wexie."

He caught the surprise in Lexie's face before she quickly recovered. "Maybe another time, Katie."

"Are you still sick?"

"A little, yes. But I'll be better once I finish this delicious breakfast your dad made."

"Daddy make you better?"

Her cheeks flushed bright red, and she avoided eye contact and spoke to Katie. "Yes. He did."

"He's a good Daddy."

The knot in his stomach rose to his throat, and Jake swallowed hard before he spoke. "Lexie will be here when you get home, Katie," he said firmly. "Now finish so we can go."

"You wait for me?"

Lexie paused, then reached over and tweaked Katie's nose.

"Of course. I'll be here when you get home."

Katie resumed eating and thumping the bar with her feet.

Lexie waited before trying a cautious bite of eggs.

"Everything all right?" Jake asked. "Stomach's not upset?"

"Mmm," she mumbled around a mouthful. "It's fine. Didn't realize how hungry I was."

"Well, crackers and ginger ale don't count as food."

"If you make a happy pate," gushed Katie, "Daddy give you ice ceam."

"Really? I'll remember that."

Out of practice with casual conversation, Jake cleared his throat. "Bobby tells me you're an engineer."

She nibbled a slice of bacon. "I've always enjoyed making things. Dad makes things, so I became an engineer."

Something in her voice made him wonder if the job choice was hers or her father's. "Don't see many female engineers."

A frown came and left quickly, then she gave a half-shrug, making him wonder again if she liked the job or did it for her father.

"It can be a challenge at times, but I manage."

The image of her threatening to kick his ass yesterday made him grin. "I'm willing to bet you do more than just manage."

Their gazes met over the top of Katie's head, and he forgot to breathe.

The immediate connection was almost tangible. When her eyes widened, and her mouth formed a silent 'o', he knew she felt it, too.

Whatever *it* was.

Her chest rose and fell on a short inhale. She licked her lips and stammered, "Thank you," before redirecting her attention to breakfast.

It took him a moment to recover his balance. "I'll be in and out this morning and gone most of the afternoon, so just make yourself at home."

"Okay."

"Don't hesitate to call if you want me. I mean, if you need anything."

She didn't look at him. "I'm managing with the crutches, so I'll be fine."

Unable to leave it at that, he spoke up. "Despite our short acquaintance, Miss Morgan, it's obvious you are not only a beautiful woman but a strong, intelligent, and self-reliant one, too." He toasted her with his cup. "And can do anything you put your mind to."

His remark brought their gazes together again. This time, though, her smile was one of gratitude. "Thank you for saying that."

"You're welcome." He nodded toward her cup. "More coffee?"

"Yes, please."

A change in the atmosphere surrounded him as he refilled her cup. He couldn't put a finger on it, but he felt more relaxed than he had in ages. The comfortable silence bordered on intimacy, and Jake allowed himself a rare moment of indulgence before reality stepped in. *This is temporary. She's leaving soon.*

"Finish your breakfast, Katie." He set Lexie's cup by her plate. "I'll get your glasses."

He returned, handed her the eyewear, and tapped Katie on the head. "You done, kiddo?"

"I done." She pushed the empty cereal bowl aside and wiped her mouth with a napkin.

He added the bowl and juice glass to the growing pile in the sink, then wiped her face and hands with a wet rag. "I have a couple of errands to run after I drop Katie off. I'll be back in about an hour. Donna should be here any time." He tossed the rag toward the sink and helped the child down. "Need anything before we go?"

"I'm good."

Reluctant to leave, he took Katie's hand. "Um, I'll be back soon."

She grinned at the child. "Have fun today, Katie."

"Bye, Wexie. See you 'waiter."

Biscuit rose to follow, and Jake snapped his fingers. "Stay." The dog returned to his spot by Katie's chair, and Jake chanced another look at his houseguest. Out of nowhere came a longing so intense it shocked him.

Longing for a complete family.

For answers.

For her.

Chapter Nine

Lexie stared at the closed door and tried to make sense of his unsettling effect on her. No one, not even her former fiancé, caused such fluttering and swirling emotions. Especially last night when she woke from a troubled dream to find him holding her hand.

Heat bathed her cheeks when she recalled practically begging him not to go. He hadn't said anything, just held her hand. She had no idea how long he knelt there, and it didn't matter. What did matter was she needed him—and he stayed.

The last thing she remembered before drifting back into a dreamless sleep was the warmth of his hand and the comfort of his presence.

Which, when she stopped to think about it, was like seven kinds of crazy. But strangers or not, their connection went beyond the length of acquaintance. The short breakfast interlude felt right somehow, and she wondered if he sensed it, too.

Her analytical mind needed answers, and the part of her struggling to find meaning in her life pushed for resolution.

With the clarity of hindsight and time to think, she realized she never truly loved Rodney. At least not the deep, abiding love her parents shared. It shamed her to think maybe she saw him as her last chance for the home and family she longed for, which was totally unfair to both of them.

That ah-hah moment didn't make his desertion any less hurtful, but it did help put things in perspective.

Which brought her back to Jake.

When he insisted she could do anything she set her mind to with such conviction, Lexie knew she *could* do anything. The million-dollar question was: what?

"Fine. I can do anything," she muttered. "So, what's it gonna be? What will make me happy?"

Biscuit looked up when she spoke.

"And since when do you obey anyone but me?"

His tail swished across the floor.

Lexie returned to her breakfast and carefully ate every bite, her mind continually drifting back to Jake. The air of detachment around him contrasted sharply with the compassionate man who cared for her last night.

And what about this apparent connection between the three of them? There was something there, but what? In another burst of insight, she wondered if father and daughter were lonely and simply reacting to her forced presence.

When her mind considered the possibility of filling the void in their life, she immediately quashed it. *No. I'll be gone in two weeks, and they'll be back where they started. Or worse. I can't do that to them.*

But the idea refused to go away. Maybe the sad truth was she was just as lost and lonely and grabbing at straws.

Lexie straightened and forced herself to take stock of the aches and pains instead. Every muscle in her body had protested when she rolled out of bed earlier, making the crutches more of a challenge. But she slowly got the hang of walking with them. Even though she had slept in her clothes, they were fine for today. After a moment's hesitation, she struggled into a bra as she sat on the side of the bed, wincing in pain before the aroma of coffee pulled her to the kitchen.

The excruciating headache had lessened to moderate pain, and her stomach appeared happy with breakfast. Her ankle continued to throb, but it was bearable with limited movement.

She sighed and looked at her plate, then the dishes in the sink. The island ran parallel to it, with no chairs on the sink side and maybe five feet of space. "That's doable." She pushed her stuff across the bar and slid to Katie's chair, then Jake's, ignoring the pain in her foot and dragging the crutches along. Using one of them and the bar for support, she maneuvered a stool between the sink and the island, put her dishes on it, then shifted them to the counter. "Got it," she said with satisfaction.

Proud of doing something constructive, she ignored the discomfort and balanced on the crutches at the sink, making short work of the dishes, stacking them neatly in the drain on the right.

The window over the sink provided a panoramic view of the ranch. Giant oak and pecan trees shaded the expansive backyard, and a tire swing hung from one gnarled branch. A flagstone patio, complete with an outdoor kitchen and pergola, came off the end of the porch. Further on, fences outlined pastures dotted with horses and cows.

She leaned forward to get a better look and decided the closest pasture appeared to contain Longhorn cattle, though she was too far away to be sure.

Two other fields contained large ponds, the water shimmering in the morning sun, and puffy white clouds stood out against a bright blue sky. "Wow," she whispered. "Just...wow."

After one last look, she rested on the stool and examined the tidy kitchen. Open and L-shaped, it sported a separate dining area off to the right of the breakfast bar, where three large windows let in natural light and provided another impressive view of verdant pastures and a massive red barn. An open door past the refrigerator led to the laundry room.

Biscuit nudged her leg, and she scratched his head. "I don't know about you, but I think I could live in a place like this," she murmured, then shook her head. "Stop it."

Biscuit nuzzled her leg again, and she resumed scratching. "Maybe I need some space, though, to think clearly," she muttered. "But Katie would be so disappointed if I left."

Biscuit exhaled a snort, and she stopped petting. "It has nothing to do with Jake. It's Katie I'm concerned about."

His ears perked up, and he looked toward the windows. A dark blue pickup came down the drive and disappeared around the corner of the house.

"Probably Donna."

A few minutes later, she came through the back door. "Well, nice to see you up and moving around. Any issues this morning?"

"A little wonky with the crutches, but I'm learning."

"How's the pain?"

"Consistent."

She moved in front of Lexie. "Let me take a look." After a careful exam, she stood and placed her hands on her hips. "It's still swollen, so keep it elevated as much as possible today."

She didn't give Lexie a chance to say anything as she continued. "I'm going to wrap it this morning. I'll do a walking boot when the swelling is down. In the meantime, remember RICE. Rest. Ice. Compression. Elevation." She looked at Lexie's bare feet. "Are you okay, or would you like some socks or something?"

"I should have dug out a sock and maybe a sneaker for my good foot this morning."

"Mind if I look after I get you settled in the den?"

"No, of course not. My bag is on the settee."

Twenty minutes later, foot wrapped, elevated, and ice pack secured, Donna set a tray on the end table and prepared to leave. "There's ibuprofen on the tray and some water. Be careful moving around. You're not used to the crutches, and we don't want you to fall. Jake is usually in and out all day, and Mother will bring Katie by when she gets out of daycare."

"Does she come every day?"

"Pretty much. She either cooks or brings something from the house. If she didn't, they would live on cereal and sandwiches. Speaking of which, have you had breakfast?"

"Yes. Jake fixed something."

Dark brows edged upward. "He did? Please tell me it wasn't cereal."

She laughed. "No. Bacon and eggs. And a biscuit."

"I'm impressed."

Lexie let the comment slide as curiosity got the better of her, "Um, I was wondering...."

"About what?"

"Um, Katie's mother...." Immediately, she regretted the question and waved a hand in front of her face. "Never mind. It's none of my business."

Donna eyed her for a moment before she answered. "She died when Katie was born."

"Oh no."

"There was a riding accident." She shook her head sadly and paused as though gathering her thoughts. "She suffered a severe head injury and was unconscious for weeks. The day Katie was born, something went wrong, and they did a C-section." She took a breath and continued. "Mary didn't survive."

"I am so sorry," said Lexie.

Probing dark eyes searched her face. "My brother is a strong man, but he's been through hell. He doesn't let many people in." She gathered up her bag of supplies. "I'll bring a boot tomorrow to try if the swelling is down. You'll be able to walk, but you might need the crutches until you get used to it."

Lexie accepted the change in topic. "How long will I have to wear it?"

"Probably just a week or so. We'll see how it goes."

"Surely I owe you something for this house call, at least?"

"Like I said yesterday, you're practically family." She turned toward the kitchen. "If you need anything, Jake knows how to reach me."

Alone, Lexie allowed her mind to wander. *His wife died giving birth, and he's raising Katie alone.*

The memory of him being there when she woke from the bad dream resurfaced.

It was the crash all over again. But this time, she was trapped inside, and water reached her waist. She could hear Biscuit's terrified wail but couldn't get to him. Monstrous hogs pawed at the doors and windows, and their savage growls terrified her.

When she jolted awake, frightened and disoriented, Jake was there, holding her hand. His gentle, soothing voice comforted her and turned the troubled vision into one that later disturbed her on an entirely different level.

She placed her hand over her racing heart. *What is happening to me?*

Unsettled by her train of thought, she leaned back and mentally constructed a to-do list for today. It took less than five minutes to realize she could do nothing today. Her head and ankle throbbed in unison, and every muscle in her body protested movement of any kind. Unaccustomed to lying around, restlessness warred with the discomfort of her injuries.

She looked around the tidy den and saw little to occupy her time since she rarely watched television. "I can read that book I brought with me. Or maybe do some sketching." She drummed her fingers on the arm of the chair. "Except my stuff is in my bag in the bedroom." She looked down at her ankle, tried to wiggle it lightly, and gasped when pain raced up her leg. "Okay, bad idea." Resigned to vegetating, at least for the moment, she lay back in the chair, Biscuit beside her on the floor.

Sighing deeply, she closed her eyes, visualizing the peaceful scene from the kitchen window, and let it lull her into a light slumber. Soon, the images morphed into a dream of her walking beside Jake, his strong fingers laced with hers. They stop and face each other. She smiles up at him, awaiting the kiss her body suddenly craves.

Chapter Ten

Jake walked into the kitchen, surprised to find the dishes washed and stacked in the drain. He knew his mother had not come by because his dad had a doctor's appointment today. Donna told him she'd stopped by briefly but said nothing about the dishes.

Which left Lexie.

A frown creased his brow as he stalked toward the den. She was supposed to be taking it easy, not washing his dishes. He rounded the corner, then stopped as he saw her reclined back in his chair, sound asleep, lips curled up in a sexy smile. His body, apparently on high alert around her, responded quickly as his mind conjured up things that might produce such a smile.

His mouth suddenly became bone dry. He closed his eyes, then stared at the ceiling, trying to break the connection to his brain. *What's happening to me?*

Biscuit's soft yelp drew his attention.

"Quiet, boy," he whispered through parched lips. "Don't wake her."

He took one last look, then forced himself to turn away, only to turn back when she moaned softly, fingers of one hand rising slightly toward him.

Blood pounded through his veins as his fingers tingled and curled inward with the insane need to touch her extended hand.

Suddenly, her legs shifted, and a soft cry escaped as her face contorted in pain.

"Lexie?" He stepped toward her. "Are you all right?"

She blinked rapidly and bit down on her lower lip. "Jake? What are you doing here?"

Her bewildered expression was charming. "I live here."

Eyes tightly clenched, she shook her head. "I know that." She faced him. "I thought you had errands and stuff."

He fought to appear relaxed when he was anything but. "Just came by to check on you." He paused. "You're supposed to take it easy today."

"As you can see," she snipped, "I am."

"After you cleaned up the kitchen."

"Washing dishes was the least I could do." She huffed out a breath. "Besides, I'm not good at doing nothing."

"Isn't that what folks on vacation do?"

Her mouth twisted in an annoyed smirk. "I wouldn't know. Haven't had one in years."

"Seriously?"

"'fraid so."

"Ever heard the expression about all work and no play?" Memories of all the delayed and canceled trips he'd been responsible for mocked him as he waited for her reply.

"Yeah, well..." She rubbed one hand on her thigh. "No fun going alone."

Her comment stunned him. How could she not have someone special? And why was he pleased about it? "Well, you're on vacation now, so take it easy." He tilted his head to one side. "What had you planned to do while you were here?"

"I don't know, read, sketch. Go fishing."

"You like to fish?"

Azure eyes sparkled with humor. "Does that surprise you?"

"Well, yeah."

"Dad took Bobby and me fishing a lot when we were kids. Until work took over, then the trips were few and far between. But those are still some of my favorite memories." She leaned back and chuckled. "I remember this one time I caught a big ole grinnell."

"What's a grinnell?"

She snorted. "It has several different names, bowfin, mud pike, dogfish. You can find them in a lot of backwater creeks and streams. Basically, it's a trash fish because it's bony and difficult to cook. It's a heck of a fighter, though, and fun to catch. I hooked a big one, but he came off the hook close to the bank. I was maybe eight then and not about to lose the biggest fish I ever caught, so I waded out to get him."

He chuckled as the story unfolded, easily imagining the scene she described.

"I yelled for Dad to come help. He and Bobby came running around the bend." She was laughing now and stopped to get her breath. "They thought a gator was after me. When they saw me standing knee-deep in muck, trying to splash him up on the bank with my hands, they sat down and laughed until they cried."

"Did you get him?"

"Of course."

"What did you do with it if he wasn't fit to eat?"

Happiness bubbled in her voice. "I insisted we bring it home and cook it for supper. Mom wouldn't touch it, so Dad supposedly cleaned and cooked it for me." She slowly shook her head. "Looking back, I think it was probably that big catfish he caught. Whatever it was, I thought it was the best-tasting fish ever."

"So, you and your dad are pretty close?" He couldn't say why her answer mattered, but it did.

Brows furrowed in thought, she nipped her bottom lip. "He's like two people—a father and a boss, and both are different." She paused. "Growing up, he took time for the fun stuff. But as we got older and the business grew, it meant less family time. But we made the most of it when it happened. So, yeah, we're close." She shifted in the chair, and a spasm of pain made her wince.

"Donna's gonna kill me if you've hurt yourself." He looked around and pointed to the medicine on the end table. "Do you need this?"

She rolled her lips inward and briefly closed her eyes. "Please. I should have already taken some."

He shook out two pills and handed her the glass of water. "There's no ice in it. Do you want some?"

She shook her head and took the medicine. "Plain is fine."

He passed her the television remote. "Where's this book you were going to read? Or the sketch stuff?"

She sank back in the chair as her cheeks flushed a pretty shade of pink. "Um, if you don't mind, there's a canvas bag on a chair in the bedroom. All my sketch stuff is in there."

"Okay."

He returned a few minutes later and passed her the bag. "What do you sketch?"

One shoulder lifted in a light shrug as she pulled out a well-used sketch pad and pencil, then placed the bag on the floor. "Whatever catches my eye." She ran a hand over the book, her expression thoughtful. "Drawing and coloring are relaxing and therapeutic."

She nodded toward the tote on the floor, lips curled up in that sexy smile he looked forward to seeing.

"I have coloring books in there, too, if you're ever in need."

While coloring itself held no interest for him, he'd do it in a heartbeat if it meant spending time with her. Despite his long to-do list, he enjoyed her company and wasn't ready to leave. "Need anything else before I go?"

"I'm good." She tapped the pad. "Thanks for bringing this."

"Got your cell phone handy?"

She pointed to it on the end table, and he handed it to her. "Add my number." As soon as the words left his mouth, he regretted the authoritative tone and added, "Please."

She appeared to bite back a grin before she did what he asked.

"I have a lot of maintenance stuff on tap beginning on the far west property line, so I'll be gone most of the day. Cell service out there is iffy, but call anyway if you need me, uh, anything."

"I'll be fine. And I'll behave." She crossed her heart and grinned.

He smirked. "Well, if you can behave for more than a few minutes, I might take you fishing one evening when you're better."

Her eyes widened. "I'll hold you to that."

Thoughts of alone time with her sent warmth flooding through him. *Not good. Not good.*

An indefinable emotion flashed in her sky-blue eyes so fast he almost missed it. His heart stumbled in response when her intense gaze dropped to his lips.

He took a sketchy breath, noting bright spots of color on both her cheeks. "By the way, I cleaned your shoes last night and left them on the porch to dry."

"Thank you."

He dipped his chin and strode toward the kitchen.

Biscuit whined and followed.

Jake stopped, and the dog barked once and looked at Lexie, tail wagging furiously.

"What? You want to go with Jake?"

Biscuit woofed, and his tail swished faster.

Jake rubbed his chin. "I'm okay with him going. If you don't mind, that is."

Biscuit yapped again, bouncing up and down on his front paws as though he knew he was the topic of conversation.

"Fine. Go with Jake. You've been cooped up too long anyway."

The dog darted to Jake's side, tail wagging so fast his butt shook.

"He's a city dog," she said softly. "So, keep an eye on him, please."

"I will." He turned, and Biscuit raced ahead of him to the back door.

Thoughts racing, Lexie watched in fascination as Biscuit disappeared around the corner. He'd never shown any inclination to befriend anyone, especially a man, before. Yet, in the last twenty-four hours, he'd included father and daughter in his inner circle. And now happily followed Jake to who knows where.

Maybe he picked up on the vibes she sent out. Vibes that shouted, 'I like this man'. "No," she mumbled. "It's nothing like that."

But her heart kept asking, 'Are you sure?'

Flustered, she caressed the well-used pad filled with scribbles, flowers, animals, and people. Art intrigued her from an early age. She once toyed with becoming an artist or maybe illustrating children's books until her father persuaded her to pursue an engineering degree. It seemed like a good idea then but had recently lost its appeal. *Was it too late for a career change? What do I want? What about Jake?*

Being so attracted to someone she just met was mind-boggling, but she couldn't deny the unsettled feelings she experienced around him.

And then there was Katie. The child needed someone. Was she that someone?

"No," she grumbled. "Do not go there." She opened the pad, tapped the pencil on the edge, and stared at the blank page, Jake's face filling her mind.

Distracted by her restless train of thought, she slammed the pad closed and leaned back in the chair, letting her mind wander, not surprised when it settled on Jake. Everything about him intrigued her, from his rugged good looks to his sexy ghost-like smile that vanished in a flash—even his day-old scruff and brusque manner.

But what surprised and charmed her the most was his genuine tenderness and thoughtfulness and the almost shy way he extended those things to Katie.

An unexpected warmth surged through her. An intriguing figure of a man, big and powerful, yet vulnerable, too. Something about him called to her soul, and she was powerless to stop it.

Alarm bells sounded in her head.

She'd do well to heed them—but she wouldn't.

She couldn't.

Chapter Eleven

True to her word, Lexie spent the day in her chair, getting up only to use the bathroom or grab a drink from the kitchen. While she dozed some, she was so uncomfortable she didn't get much rest.

Though not as bad as last night, her head still throbbed with each beat of her heart. The soreness encasing her body when she got up this morning hadn't lessened as the day wore on, and her ankle hurt with any movement.

She couldn't reach the pills on the end table without stretching, which was simply more effort than she wanted to expend. A long, hot bath would do wonders, but her room only had a shower.

She opened her eyes and glanced at the grandfather clock in the corner—four o'clock. Aggie should be by with Katie soon. Guilt washed over her when she considered going to her room before then. She was lousy company right now but couldn't disappoint Katie.

Resigned, she tried to relax when she heard the back door open and Katie's excited voice.

"Wexie? Where are you?"

The child came running into the den, a page in her hand. "I coh-red this for you," she said brightly, extending the page toward her. "It's Bis-tit."

She took it and smiled at the four-year-old's attempt to color. "Oh my, Katie," she gushed. "I love it."

She looked around the room. "Where's Bis-tit?"

"He needed to get out of the house, so your dad took him to work today. He'll be back later."

The disappointment on her face was acute.

"But, as soon as your dad gets home, you and Biscuit can play."

"Okay. You weed me a stor-ree now?"

Expecting the request, she gave an inward groan. "Sure. Which book?"

Aggie entered, tying an apron around her waist. "Don't bother Miss Lexie, Katie. She needs to rest."

"It's okay, Miss Aggie."

"Can I get you anything?"

"I'm fine, thank you." She looked at Katie. "Why don't you get the book you want me to read?"

One book turned into three. Then it was show-and-tell time with her favorite stuffed animal, a fluffy brown bear, and her favorite pj's, the blue ones with a puppy on the shirt. Lexie did her best to smile and encourage Katie's interaction, but the headache and general discomfort made concentration difficult.

Aggie finally rescued her a little after five. "I know it's a mite early for you, Lexie," she said, "but supper is ready, and I can fix a plate if you like."

Lexie shook her head. "I hate to ask this, but..."

"But what, dear?"

"I wondered if there was a tub where I could soak some of this soreness out." Belatedly realizing the request may be too much, she hurriedly added, "The shower in my room is fine, I just—"

"Of course, dear. Jake should have thought of that." She rubbed her hands on her apron. "There's a tub in the other guest room down the hall, but the one in the master is better. It's a jacuzzi tub."

"Master? Uh, as in Jake's room?"

"Yes, but he won't be home for a couple of hours yet." She grabbed the crutches. "Come along. I'll help you get settled."

Katie wanted to help, too, and by the time Lexie pulled out a change of clothes for her to hold and walked to the master, she felt like she'd run a marathon. Aggie placed towels and body wash within reach, and once assured she could navigate alone, they left and closed the door.

She sat on the edge and carefully lowered herself into the bubbling water, adjusted the jets, and let the soothing heat leach the soreness from her body.

The headache continued, but she ignored it, leaned back, and closed her eyes.

An hour later, a soft knock on the door drew her from a relaxed doze.

"Lexie, dear," called Aggie through the door. "Are you all right?"

"I'm so sorry, Aggie. I fell asleep. I'll be right out."

Her soft laugh filtered in. "Take your time, dear. Katie is fed and bathed, and your supper is on the stove when you're ready. Jake should be home soon, too."

"Okay. Thank you." Embarrassed at taking so long, she hurriedly emptied and cleaned the tub, dried off, then dressed in capris and a tee shirt, all while sitting on the side of the tub.

Her body was more relaxed, and even the headache lessened in severity. The ankle throbbed, but, hopefully, wrapping it when she sat down would help. She cast one more longing look at the spacious tub. "I have got to get one of these for my apartment," she murmured, then grabbed the crutches and attempted to stand when the door swung open, and Jake walked in.

Jake was two steps into the room when he heard Lexie's squeal of surprise, followed by a sharp "Dammit" as she fumbled with the crutches.

He rushed forward and grabbed her against him as the crutches hit the floor. The bun on top of her head tickled his nose, and the subtle smell of his soap on her skin short-circuited his brain.

"You cussed," he managed at last.

She poked a finger in his chest. "You scared me."

"Sorry. Didn't expect to find anyone in *my* bathroom." He made no move to release her.

"Aggie said I could use it," she mumbled against his chest. "To soak the soreness out."

He adjusted his hold, securing her against his chest, his hands resting on the small of her back. Hands clutching his upper arms, she didn't protest. "Did it help?"

She nodded without glancing up.

"I should have thought to suggest it this morning."

"That's what Aggie said."

He heard the smile in her voice. "Yeah, well, it's not every day I have a damsel in distress in my house." He kept his voice light, enjoying their gentle sparring. "Is the swear jar in your room?"

She huffed out a breath. "Yeah, well, you startled me, so you owe the quarter." She pulled back enough to glare at him, but a sudden yawn ruined the gesture. "Oh, my goodness." She struggled to get a hand in front of her mouth. "I guess I'm more relaxed than I thought." She stepped back, only to crumple when her bad ankle folded. "Fudgesicle!"

"Dammit, Lexie," he mumbled and scooped her in his arms. "You stepped back on your hurt foot."

"Thank you, Captain Obvious," she snipped. "What are you doing?"

He didn't answer. He couldn't. Once again, having her in his arms sent him into sensory overload.

His chest hurt with the effort it took to get air in his lungs. Everywhere they touched, nerve endings tingled and stirred. Long dormant desire exploded to life as he hurried down the hall to her room.

She made a slight noise, and her hand fisted in his shirt.

He made the mistake of looking down—and stopped in his tracks. Every need, every desire that besieged him was reflected in the eyes locked with his.

She sucked in a shaky breath. Her mouth moved, but no words came out.

"How come Wexie can't walk?"

The innocent question from Katie broke the spell, and Jake shook his head. "She hurt her sore foot again." He started down the hall, only to meet his mother near Lexie's room.

"What happened?"

"She stepped down on her bad foot and nearly fell."

"Oh no." Aggie stepped aside and let them pass. "I just turned down her bed."

Jake was grateful for the presence of his mother and Katie, for it prevented him from making an utter fool of himself.

He entered the small bedroom and, once again, laid her gently down. "Where's the wrap for your foot?"

"Still in the bathroom." She swallowed hard. Her jaw clenched and released. "I was going to put it back on in the den."

"I'll get it," said Aggie and rushed back down the hall.

Jake stood beside the bed, emotions all over the place.

"Is Wexie okay, Daddy?"

Katie stood just behind him, Biscuit at her side. "Yeah, she'll be good as new soon."

"Here's the wrap," said Aggie as she hurried back into the room.

He took it and moved near the end of the bed. "I'm going to sit down and put your foot in my lap, okay? I need to wrap it."

She took a deep breath and nodded.

He sat and tenderly lifted her foot and lay it across his thighs. "Mother, can you get the ice pack, please? And the ibuprofen off the end table by her chair."

"Of course. Come along, Katie," she said. "Daddy needs to help Lexie, and we're in the way."

"Damn, Lexie," he said as he made the first wrap. "That's some bruise. And it's still swollen. We need to keep it elevated tonight and ice it."

"Once again, I must apologize for being such a bother."

"You're not a bother."

She snorted. "Yes. I am." She waited until he looked up. "Thank you."

"Here's the ice pack and medicine," said Aggie. "And I brought some water."

"Thank you. Give her two of the pills, please."

"I took some earlier, but I think I need more." Once she downed the medication, she returned the water glass to Aggie. "Thank you."

His mother stepped back and placed the medicine bottle on the table. "I'll bring you a tray shortly, dear. What would you like to drink?"

"I hate putting you all out so much."

"Don't give it another thought," said Aggie. "I'll be back with your dinner in a jiff."

"Thank you, Miss Aggie," she said softly. "For everything."

"You're welcome, dear." She walked out, Katie in tow.

Lexie watched Jake as he wrapped her foot. "How did you know how to do that?"

"Football. High school and college." He glanced up as he expertly wound the bandage. "Lot of sprains." When he finished wrapping, Jake put two pillows under her foot, added the ice pack, and pulled the covers over her like last night. Then he bent down and uncovered the injured foot. "In case we need to change out the ice pack later." He stood with his hands on his hips. "Crap. I didn't think about eating. Do you want to try and sit up now?"

She hesitated, then nodded.

Jake got her propped up against the headboard, her face inches from his. When he caught her watching his lips, self-control nearly vanished.

"Jake?"

That one whispered word from her hit him like a jackhammer.

Thankfully, his mother's timely appearance kept him from making a huge mistake, like kissing her senseless, and he quickly stepped back.

"Here you go, dear," said Aggie as she placed the bed tray before Lexie.

"Thank you. Again." She smiled at the older woman.

"My pleasure." She looked at Jake. "I'm going now. Katie is in the den with Biscuit. I called Donna to see if we needed to do anything special, and she said no. She'll come by in the morning to check but said to call her if needed."

She left, and Jake looked at the woman who dominated his thoughts since their first meeting. Had it really only happened yesterday? "Can I do anything else for you?"

"No. I'm good. Thanks."

"I'll come back later for the tray."

"Okay."

He nodded and walked out.

It was going to be another long night.

Chapter Twelve

The hot bath yesterday did wonders for Lexie, and she woke up feeling much better. She stretched and nestled into the comfy bed as last night's events replayed in her mind.

When Jake returned for the supper tray, he pulled a chair next to the bed, and they chatted like old friends. He told her how much Biscuit seemed to enjoy himself in the field and asked if he might take him out again today, and she agreed. Then he surprised her by insisting she use the tub anytime she wanted while she was here.

Katie came in soon after to say goodnight with a book in her hands. When she agreed to read the story, Katie surprised them all by climbing into bed beside her. When she glanced at Jake, his expression softened, and his eyes glistened as he mouthed a silent 'thank you.'

She had to swallow hard before she could read.

When the story was over, Katie was fast asleep.

Something she couldn't put a name to swept over her as she stared at the sleeping child. Tears stung the backs of her eyes, and she blinked rapidly to keep them in check. Her heart skipped and stuttered with happiness like when she first thought she might be pregnant. She breathed in the delicate baby smell and tenderly kissed the child's forehead. When she glanced up, she saw the same look on Jake's face before he cleared his throat and stood.

Neither spoke as he leaned over Lexie to pick the child up. His face turned as red as hers felt, and he avoided looking directly at her when his arm brushed over her chest. His mumbled "good night" followed him out the door.

It was some time before sleep claimed her, and when it did, she dreamed impossible dreams filled with father and daughter.

"Enough already." She shook her head, bringing her thoughts to the present, grateful the headache was minimal today. "What is wrong with me?" She glanced at her watch: six-forty-five. On a typical day, she would have finished a five-mile run, showered, had a light breakfast, and be on her second or third cup of coffee. "That's it. I need coffee. I wonder if Jake has it ready?"

Too many conflicting emotions begged for attention. Just the thought of seeing him this morning made her pulse jump, whether in anticipation or dread, she couldn't say. "Rrrggg. You're a hot mess, woman." She slapped both hands on the bed. "A hot mess."

Resigned, she tossed the covers back, set the warmish ice bag aside, and slowly swung her legs over the side of the bed. While she was still sore, it wasn't nearly as bad as yesterday, and her ankle didn't throb as much when she hobbled to the bedside table to retrieve the crutches.

Face washed, hair gathered in a ponytail, and one sneaker on, she pasted on a smile and headed for the kitchen.

❈

Jake sighed and sipped his coffee, trying to get his chaotic mind to focus. Thanks to another restless night, he'd overslept, rushed to get Katie dressed, nearly burned the bacon, and had yet to brush her hair or tie her shoelaces.

Thank goodness the child wasn't a fussy eater and seemed content with the extra-crispy bacon.

She took a bite of jelly-coated toast and pushed unruly curls from her face. "Is Wexie's foot still hurt, Daddy?"

"I'm sure it's better this morning."

She looked at the stove. "Did you fix her beck-fast?"

I barely got yours done. "Not yet, but I will."

She nodded and pushed at her hair again.

Jake sighed. "I've gotta find your hairbrush. Don't get down until I get back."

"Okay."

He dug out the brush and a hair clip, returned to the kitchen, and found Lexie pulling a coffee mug from the cabinet.

He cleared his throat. "Good morning."

She jumped and slowly turned to face him. "Good morning."

He put the hair stuff on the bar. "Go ahead and sit. I'll bring your coffee."

"I'm not helpless."

Even her peevish comment couldn't dampen his suddenly high spirits. "No, you're not. But you can't carry hot coffee with those." He nodded toward the crutches.

Lips pursed, she grunted and headed for the barstool beside Katie.

Biscuit jumped from his spot on the floor and greeted her, tail wagging. "Hey, baby." She bent down and rubbed his ears, and he licked her face. "I hear you had a great time yesterday." When his wagging increased, she chuckled. "Yeah, I know. You want to go out again today." After another pat or two on his head, she sat down.

"Does your foot still hurt, Wexie?" asked Katie.

"Yeah, a little bit."

Katie turned to Jake. "You make beck-fast now, Daddy?"

"Oh, no, please," said Lexie. "Just coffee is fine."

He hesitated. It wouldn't hurt if Katie were a little later getting to daycare, would it? It's not like she had to punch a clock or anything. "I haven't eaten yet, either," he said as he placed the coffee in front of her. "Bacon and eggs all right with you?"

"Please don't go to any trouble on my account."

"It's no trouble."

She cocked her head to one side. "Yes. It is. But thank you."

Katie brushed the hair from her face again. *Dammit. Her hair. I can't stay focused this morning.*

Bacon in one hand, a skillet in the other, he glanced at Lexie. "Would you mind doing something with her hair? I'm a little behind this morning."

Eyes wide, she nodded. "Sure."

Katie handed her the brush and clip. "You make it wike yours?"

"Well, I'll need a scrunchy." She looked at Jake.

"I have no idea what a scrunchy is," he said as he put the bacon on to cook. "But I can probably find a rubber band."

She shook her head. "It breaks the hair. I'll use mine, then redo it later."

He couldn't see how a rubber band could break hair but didn't argue the point as she pulled this red do-dad from her hair and placed it on the counter. His mouth filled with saliva when that glorious ebony mane fell around her shoulders. His thoughts scattered like dust in the wind as he stood there staring at his house-guest like a mule at a new gate.

Get a grip, cowboy, and don't burn the bacon.

Lexie tried to focus on the child, not the father, as she picked up the brush and turned her chair. "Okay, kiddo, let's get you prettied up." A long-forgotten memory made Lexie smile as she gently ran the brush through silky curls. "My mom used to brush my hair like this every day," she said softly. "I loved it." She probably took longer than necessary to finish the task but wanted to prolong the moment. "There you go, sweetie," she said at last. "A perfect ponytail."

Katie's musical laugh as she swung her head side-to-side made Lexie's day.

"Wook, Daddy. I have a tail wike a pony!"

"I can see that." He flipped the bacon, then looked at Lexie. "Thank you."

The moment their gazes met, her stomach fluttered, and tingles raced along her spine. *Holy mother of pearl.*

"My pleasure." What was it about him that turned her insides to mush and left her speechless?

She tucked her hair behind her ears and grabbed her coffee for something to do.

"Can I bu-sh your hair, Wexie?"

Katie's question caught her off-guard, and she started to refuse, but one look at her face and Lexie caved. "Jake?" When he turned around, she smiled. "Can I sit her on the counter for a minute?"

The expression on his face went from shocked to tender in a heartbeat. "Yeah."

She sat Katie on the bar, noticed the untied laces, fixed those, then picked up her cup and turned around as the child skimmed her hair with the brush.

"You have p-itty hair, Wexie."

"Thank you, sweetie." More at ease than she'd ever been, Lexie sipped her coffee as Katie brushed. She exhaled slowly and let the happiness surrounding her seep into every pore. Having her mom brush her hair was always special, but this surpassed it. She didn't waste time trying to define her complex feelings; she simply enjoyed them.

When Jake announced breakfast was ready, she sat Katie back in her chair.

"Is Wexie's hair pi-tty, Daddy?"

He stopped in the process of setting down her plate. "Yeah. Very pretty."

Another shared look, and the connection grew.

"Thank you." She swallowed hard. He was so damned sexy that her heart did a happy dance, and she looked away to regain control.

He appeared to suffer a similar affliction as he stumbled while sitting on the other side of Katie.

She pushed the eggs around on her plate. "Um, do you have much to do today?"

His fork stopped before his mouth, and both brows shot up. "Yeah. Always a lot to do on a ranch." He paused. "After I take Katie to school, I have more repairs to do, then stock to feed." He waved his fork in the air. "That kind of stuff."

"So, do you do this every day?"

Again, that confused look on his face, as though he couldn't believe she'd be interested. But she really was. Whether it was because it concerned him or because it was interesting wasn't something she wanted to examine now.

"Ranching is a 24/7 job." He swallowed a bite of eggs, his voice warming to the topic. "This is calving season, so I check for new ones daily. And then one of my Longhorns, Dolly, is due to calve any day now, too."

"Do you name all your cattle?" She smiled when he looked up. "Or just some?"

He wiped his mouth on a paper towel and grinned. "Just the special ones."

The comfortable atmosphere returned as the conversation grew.

"After I drop Katie off, I need to go by the feed store." He cleaned Katie's face and hands with a wet rag. "I'll stop by for Biscuit when I get back."

Hearing his name, the dog jumped up and looked at Jake.

He pointed to the floor. "Not yet, big guy."

Biscuit whined and sat back down.

"I'll be gone again most of the morning," he said as he helped Katie down. "But call me if you need anything."

"I will."

"And Donna will be by at some point with that boot thing she mentioned yesterday."

"Whew. The list of things I owe you for keeps growing."

When he smiled, the bottom dropped out of her stomach.

His eyes darkened. "Maybe we can find a way for you to pay me back."

Before her jumbled mind could summon a snappy retort, he was gone.

Chapter Thirteen

Jake left Katie at daycare and drove to the feed store, his mind fixating on his parting comment to Lexie. *Maybe we can find a way for you to pay me back.*

He shook his head in disgust. The surprised look on her face sent an embarrassed flush to his. What the hell possessed him to try and flirt in the first place? He sucked at it.

"Been too damn long," he grumbled as he parked and walked inside. He swallowed a groan when he saw he'd have to deal with Janet.

Just damn perfect.

In a moment of insanity three months ago, he'd agreed to her request to have dinner together—a decision he regretted almost immediately. They had different expectations for the evening, and things didn't end well. She'd avoided him ever since.

But not today.

"What can I do for you, Jake?"

The sexy purr in her voice surprised him and contrasted sharply with the iciness she'd shown him since their first and only night out.

"Need some feed and supplies delivered." He passed her the list. "Today or tomorrow, if possible."

Her fingers skimmed his as she took the list. "Haven't seen much of you lately." She leaned on the counter, exposing her generous cleavage. "I missed you."

He ignored the invitation in her voice. "Any idea on time? I want to make sure someone is there to help unload."

Undeterred by his lack of enthusiasm, she continued. "I could make the delivery myself if you like." Her voice dropped, and her finger edged toward his hand on the counter. "At the end of the day, so we could...talk."

"Hey, Jake."

Brett Austin's voice saved him from having to address her blatant invitation. "Hey, Brett." The men shook hands. "How's it going?"

Brett turned his back to Janet and rolled his eyes. "Good. How's Biscuit today?"

"Great. Taking him out with me again when I get back." He grinned. "She thinks he's a city dog, but I'm convinced otherwise."

"I can't wait to meet her. How long is she staying?"

Brett's comment, no doubt made for Janet's benefit, bothered Jake. Partly because he didn't like other people knowing his business, and secondly, he didn't know what she would do with the information. Too late to worry about it now.

"Couple of weeks."

"Good. Bev and I will drop by sometime this weekend."

"Sounds good."

Brett tipped his hat to Janet and left.

"A woman is staying at your house?" A shadow of resentment swept across her face, and anger clung to the edge of her words. "Who is she?"

"Let me know about the delivery time."

He felt her icy stare like a knife in his back as he walked out the door.

———◆———

After Jake and Katie left, Lexie did the dishes and returned to her chair in the den. The prospect of sitting there all day put her teeth on edge. Donna wouldn't be by with the boot until after lunch, so she had time to kill.

"My dirty clothes are still in the shower," she said to the wall. "I could do my laundry." She looked at Biscuit, who still pouted about being left behind by Jake, and ignored her. "Good grief. He's coming back for you."

Huffing an annoyed breath, she put the ice pack on the table, lowered the footrest, and eased off the chair.

A few tense minutes later, she held on to the shower door and used one crutch to pull her clothes within reach. Rolling everything into a ball, she quickly discovered it would be difficult to carry them and walk. "Not a problem." She twisted the ball tighter and secured it by tying the pant legs together. Then, she looped the bundle over her wrist and wrapped her fingers around the crutch. She glanced at the dog watching by the door. "See. Easy-peasy."

When she reached the laundry room, her arms hurt, and sweat dotted her brow. "I can do anything," she muttered, leaning on the machine. "I can."

Once the washer started, she turned and found Jake scowling at her, both hands planted on his hips, Biscuit at his feet. "What are you doing?"

She raised her chin and glared. "Knitting a sweater."

One corner of his mouth inched upward. "Besides being a smart ass."

"I can't do nothing all day again."

He stepped toward her. "Donna will pitch a hissy fit if you don't do what she says. Trust me. I know."

Before she could react, he put the crutches on the washer and swung her into his arms.

Seemingly of its own volition, her arm slipped around his neck. "What are you doing?"

"Knitting a sweater."

"Don't be using my stuff on me."

His smirk sent her stomach on a roller coaster ride. She gave his chest a playful swat, rested her hand over his heart, and tried to ignore the tingles racing up her arm.

"I like it better than mine."

"You seem to have made a habit of carrying me around." The minute the flirtatious statement left her mouth, she ducked her head in embarrassment.

"You complaining?"

"...No."

He paused, and she glanced up.

"Good."

Her gaze dropped to his lips, just inches away, and her heart skipped a beat. *Hot pockets and popsicles.*

He swallowed once and continued walking.

When he lowered her to the recliner, his face inches away, she forced herself to look at the buttons on his shirt instead of those enticing lips. "I'll go crazy with nothing to do."

"I repeat, isn't that what folks do on vacation?"

His warm breath touched her cheek, and she could barely breathe. She delayed moving her arm from around his neck a beat too long. "Maybe."

He gently placed a pillow under her foot and secured the ice pack. "Even though your ankle is not as swollen, you need to keep it elevated until Donna says otherwise."

"Fine," she grumbled. "She'll be by after lunch today. Maybe I'll get a reprieve then."

He placed his hands on his hips. "Well, you still have your sketch stuff. And you mentioned a book you wanted to read."

She thought of the steamy romance novel in her suitcase. No way would she ask him to bring that. "I'm good with my sketch stuff for now."

"Don't move around too much."

She made a cross over her heart. "I promise I won't get up any more than necessary."

One dark brow lifted as his lips turned up in a teasing smirk. "Don't think I didn't catch the word 'necessary.'"

That smoldering look did amazing things to her insides. Unable to come up with a snappy retort, she shrugged.

He appeared reluctant to leave as he glanced around. "Thank you for doing Katie's hair. She loved the ponytail." He rubbed both hands on his thighs. "She couldn't wait to show it off."

"I'm glad. She's such an adorable child. I can't imagine how difficult it is to be a single parent."

A shadow crossed his face, then quickly disappeared. "And thank you for doing the dishes. Again."

"Just trying to keep my pay-back list manageable."

A heartbeat passed before something intense flared in his scrutiny. "Maybe we can negotiate."

Immediately, the air around them sizzled as desire sparked between them like an electrical charge. She froze and sucked in a breath, wondering again how it was possible to feel this way about a virtual stranger. And would this attraction bring happiness or heartache?

He took a long, deep breath, his eyes never leaving hers. "You and I...we have things to discuss. Later."

"Yes," she whispered, unable to say more.

He turned for the kitchen, stopped, and walked back to her. Shaking his head, he closed his eyes. "This is crazy," he muttered.

Then he bent down and kissed her like he was starving, and she was a seven-course meal.

Chapter Fourteen

Jake couldn't get that damned kiss off his mind. He hadn't planned on doing anything more than picking up the stupid dog and leaving. But the site of her in the laundry room, lop-sided bun on top of her head, and those sexy-librarian glasses perched on her nose were too much. And picking her up—again, wasn't the smartest thing to do, either. Maybe he should send her to the cabin now while he still maintained a scrap of restraint.

The woman had him tied in knots, unable to focus. How could it feel like he'd known her forever instead of a few days?

And the way she was with Katie blew him away. Just having her in the house brightened his day.

Then why send her away?

The hammer grazed his thumb a second time, and he stopped, crossing his arms on the fence post. He had two choices, and both presented negative results. At the house, she was a temptation hard to resist. But her absence would make it a dark and lonely place. Again.

"I'm damned if I do and damned if I don't," he muttered.

His gaze drifted to Biscuit, who zipped around, sniffing the ground and chasing butterflies. Despite his unsettled thoughts, he smiled—something he'd done more of this week.

Regardless of what Lexie said, Biscuit was a country dog. And a well-trained one, too. Just like yesterday, if he strayed too far and Jake called, he immediately obeyed.

"Maybe I should get a dog," he muttered. "Lot less trouble than a woman." He returned to work and hammered another staple into the post with renewed vigor, his mind a chaotic cluster of past and present memories fighting for dominance.

The anguish of Mary's betrayal and the child he knew nothing about until the accident put him in a dark place for a long time. Self-preservation dictated his heart remain inaccessible. Never again would he allow someone close enough to hurt him that way.

And then, out of a gloomy Texas sky came a ray of sunshine with electric-blue eyes.

From the moment he saw her, muddy and bedraggled, leaning on her car, she'd captivated his thoughts. The logical portion of his brain argued involvement was a mistake since she would leave in two weeks. But the rational side was no match for the part of him suddenly in need of company.

The realization hit like a thunderbolt, and he caught the tip of his thumb when he hammered another fastener into the post. "Dammit!" He stepped back, inspected his thumb, and swiped his forearm across his brow as the sad truth sank in.

He was tired of silent, solitary meals, with no one to share the day's activities with or even another person's company. And he was damned sick and tired of cold sheets and lonely nights.

Though actual dates were few and far between, he still went out. At least he had, until his last couple of ventures into that realm distorted his outlook. Seeing how things had changed since he last made the circuit was discouraging.

Comanche Springs was a small town, and single women were limited. He quickly discovered most weren't interested in getting to know *him* as a person. They either wanted a good time or an instant commitment. And none wanted a ready-made family.

He sighed deeply and squinted at the sky; his brow creased in thought. "I guess Janet was the last one," he mumbled, then raised the hammer only to stop mid-swing. "What an unmitigated disaster."

He was shocked when she asked him to dinner the first time and politely declined by saying he had no sitter for Katie. When she asked a third time, he felt obligated to accept but insisted on meeting her at the restaurant.

As disaster dates go, it was monumental.

Halfway through the appetizer, she started listing expectations for their relationship—in detail. At first, her brazen attitude shocked him, then ticked him off, and he was impatient for the ordeal to end. Later, when she returned from the ladies' room, he told her Katie was ill, and he had to get home, then paid the check and left.

Two days later, she showed up at the house uninvited, breezing through the door before he could stop her.

Angry heat flushed his body at the memory of her not-so-subtle invitation as she brandished a bottle of wine at him, even with Katie right behind him.

Livid at her presumptuousness, he curtly informed her a relationship was out of the question.

Instead of being put off, she took a step toward him, her perfume overpowering and unpleasant, as she used her body to entice him.

Stunned by her boldness and apparent lack of concern for Katie's presence, he took her by the arm and guided her out. With a terse 'goodnight,' he closed the door firmly behind her, ignoring the harsh words she shouted as she left.

Disgusted with hidden agendas and false people, he stopped going out.

Which may explain his intense reaction to Lexie. "That's it," he lamented to Biscuit, who now lounged at his feet. "It's been too long, and I'm just reacting to a sexy, attractive woman."

The dog cocked his head as though listening, and Jake grunted. "That's all it is."

Repair work completed, he tossed the tools into the back of the truck and guzzled a bottle of water. Sighing deeply, he plopped down on the tailgate and poured water into a cup for the dog.

Biscuit's tail swished back and forth as he eagerly lapped it up.

"Why can't I get her off my mind?" Jake swatted a horsefly circling his head and looked skyward as though the answer lay among the drifting clouds.

When the water was gone, the mutt rested his head on Jake's thigh, and he gently rubbed the smooth fur, giving his thoughts free rein.

From their first meeting, she fascinated him. Without question, she was a beautiful woman, but the attraction went beyond her looks. She was a breath of fresh air and a balm to his weary soul, and he flat enjoyed her company.

And the way she spoke of her father, a man who worked hard but still managed to make time for family, provoked thought. Should he—could he become a better family man?

His jaw tightened as a childhood memory surfaced. His father wasn't mean or cruel, but Jack Holloway was old school. Family time didn't exist in his world. A man didn't show emotions and kept his children at arm's length. He worked hard to protect and provide for his family and didn't rest until the work was done.

He sat up straight. *Am I doing the same thing to Katie?*

The thought left a bitter taste in his mouth. He stopped petting and rested his arm on the dog's back. "I've known the woman for what? Three days and she has me questioning everything in my life." He crumpled the plastic water bottle and tossed it in the truck bed. "And spilling my guts to a damned dog."

Biscuit glanced up and sniffed.

"Fine, you're special but still a dog." He inhaled a whiff of sage and watched a hawk slowly circling overhead. "What *is* it about her? An innate kindness or goodness, maybe?" The hawk's lazy orbit continued. "And Katie...she's a different kid around her."

A flurry of questions swirled through his troubled mind. *Is my distance the reason Katie attached so quickly to Lexie?* Though his mother and Donna interacted with the child, the level of response was different with his houseguest.

What does it all mean?

He froze as another wave of guilt consumed him. *Oh, God. Does Katie feel unloved?*

Before he could explore those troubling issues, his cell rang. Surprised, he quickly checked caller-ID, disappointed to see it wasn't Lexie. "Hey, Cody. What's up?"

His ranch hand didn't waste time. "Dolly's...bites...her leg."

The signal faded in and out, but he got the message. Dolly, his prized Longhorn cow, evidently suffered a snake bite of some kind. Likely a rattlesnake as he'd seen two over the last week. Snake bites weren't usually fatal for cattle due to their immense size, but infection was a real possibility, especially if the injury happened hours ago.

Dolly was due to calve any day now, and infection at this point could prove disastrous.

"How bad?" Jake slid off the tailgate and motioned Biscuit to follow.

"...two spots...leg...swollen...her...corral by the barn...called vet."

"On my way." He opened the door, and the dog jumped in.

Laundry finished, Lexie put fresh sheets on the bed, which was a chore by itself, repacked her suitcase, and placed it, her laptop, and her purse by the back door, assuming she'd move to the cabin later today. The pain in her ankle lessened to a bone-deep ache, unless bumped it. Or moved it. The crutches made getting around doable, so there was no excuse to stay longer. Other than the fact she wanted to, of course, which made no sense at all.

Besides, Jake was probably ready for her to leave.

"If that's the case, why did he kiss me this morning?" When her troubled mind couldn't find a suitable reply, she shook her head. "You're a hot mess, woman," she told herself again as she sat back in the recliner and dug out the sketch pad. "One hot mess."

An hour later, she added another wadded-up effort to the pile in her lap. Out of habit, she looked around for Biscuit to gripe to, belatedly realizing he was off with Jake.

Lucky dog. At least he's doing something—with Jake.

She ground her teeth in frustration and pushed her head against the chair's cushy back. "I am so bored! How do people do this all day?" With a disgusted grunt, she put away the sketch materials, stuffed the crumpled pages in her pocket, and stood.

After tossing the sheets in the trash, she walked onto the porch to retrieve the shoes Jake cleaned last night. Noise from the corral drew her to the edge of the porch, where she watched two men guide a limping Longhorn into a small metal enclosure inside a larger corral connected to the barn. Once inside, one man took hay from the truck bed and placed it in front of the massive bovine while the other dug a cell phone from his pocket.

Curiosity urged Lexie forward, and she carefully stepped down to the flagstone patio and made her way to the corral.

Two men, the picture of working cowboys in dusty jeans, plaid western shirts, and beige, sweat-coated Stetsons, strolled forward and met her at the wooden fence.

"Morning, ma'am," said the one who made the phone call.

"Good morning." She peered over the chest-high fence. "Wow. She's gorgeous. And those horns have got to be at least a six-foot span."

"Six and a half feet, ma'am," he said with pride.

She smiled and turned to him. "I'm Lexie Morgan."

He touched the brim of his hat. "Cody Martin, ma'am." He indicated the man beside him. "This here is Derek Miller."

Derek flashed a charming smile and pointed to the cow. "And that's Dolly."

"Nice to meet you both." She turned back to the Longhorn. "Her coloring is so unusual." She side-eyed the men and grinned.

"It looks like someone flicked rust-colored paint on a white cow, then added a rusty stripe on her back for good measure." She glanced at Cody. "Why is she limping?"

"Snakebite. Probably a rattler. We have some around here."

"Oh no." She jerked her gaze back to Dolly. "Will she be okay?"

"Most likely."

The animal stood with the injured leg barely touching the ground as she nosed the hay.

"Cattle are big, and the amount of venom secreted is usually small, so the main concern is infection. Unless she happened to get bit on the face or neck."

"What happens then?"

"Well," offered Derek as he leaned on the fence, "a bite causes swelling. How much depends on a lot of things. But if she got bit around the nose or mouth, she might suffocate before we could help her."

A red pickup truck with a veterinary service emblem on the side came barreling down the road and stopped near them. Two tall, athletic men wearing bright white shirts with red logos over one pocket and neatly starched jeans stepped out. The passenger grabbed a bag off the seat and openly studied her as he approached, then flashed a good-natured smile, revealing a dimple in his left cheek.

The driver spoke first. "You must be Biscuit's mom." He extended his right hand. "Brett Austin." His grip was firm but gentle. "Been looking forward to meeting you."

"Lexie Morgan. Thanks for checking him over. And please send me a bill for your trouble."

"My pleasure. And no charge. I didn't do anything but look at him." He turned to the man beside him. "This is my new associate, Sean Taylor."

Sean extended his hand. "Nice to meet you, ma'am."

"Same here, Dr. Taylor."

She didn't miss the spark of interest in his hazel eyes as they shook hands.

"Just Sean, please."

Brett glanced at Dolly, then Cody. "Didn't know it was her."

"Yep. Two bites on the leg."

He turned to Sean. "Let's see what we got."

Lexie watched as the men worked together to secure Dolly against the back fence, then carefully examined her leg. She couldn't make out Brett's words as he worked, but his tone was easy, and the animal barely acknowledged him.

When Jake's truck approached from the west, she sighed and waited for the lecture sure to come.

He stepped out with Biscuit on his heels and strode toward her. "Working on another sweater, I see."

"Trying my hand at mittens this time."

"You must not want to go fishing after all."

"For your information," she grumbled. "I have been sitting in that blasted chair for the last hour."

One dark brow shot up. "Wow. A whole hour?"

A sudden blush bathed her face in heat. "I can't sit all day and do nothing."

He didn't comment as he climbed over the rails and headed toward Dolly.

Biscuit scooted under and followed.

She admired Jake's strong gate as he walked away. The man was all muscle, sinew, and raw sex appeal, wrapped in faded jeans and a chambray shirt. The effect he had on her was both exciting and scary. His blatant sensuality was one thing, but his softer side, especially around Katie, did crazy things to her. Sometimes, it seemed he didn't know what to do, but he tried anyway, which endeared him even more.

And Katie. Since meeting her, the dream of being a mother returned with a vengeance.

Was this—whatever connection with Jake genuine, or did this sudden longing cloud her judgment? He affected her on so many levels she couldn't be objective, especially with him nearby.

But the thought of leaving, even going to the cabin, was painful. *What am I going to do?*

Jake made a hand signal to Biscuit as they neared Dolly, and he promptly sat down as Jake squatted beside Brett.

It was difficult not to compare Jake to the vets crouched beside him. He was taller by three or four inches, but they all had muscular bodies that spoke of hard work. She guessed their ages to be mid-thirties.

Brett's thick, tawny hair tapered neatly at the collar, and dark eyes framed a handsome, square face, accented by touches of humor around the mouth and eyes. He wore a wedding ring, but Sean did not.

As she observed Sean, the term 'devilishly handsome' came to mind. Smooth, olive skin stretched over high cheekbones, and his firm mouth curled as if always on the brink of laughter. Medium-brown hair full of sandy-red highlights fluttered in the afternoon breeze.

Sean's good looks and easy smile reminded her vaguely of her ex, and it surprised her to realize the reminder wasn't painful.

Just then, another car came down the driveway and steered toward her.

Once the older Taurus stopped, Aggie stepped out and looked at Lexie, her face flushed. "Oh, good, you're still here and walking." Her voice was harried and rushed as she glanced into the pen. "And Jake's here, too." She turned and opened the back door of her car. "I wasn't sure what I'd find when I got here."

Curious, Lexie hobbled forward as Aggie moved to the back passenger door.

"The daycare had some kind of water pipe break." She opened the door and helped Katie out. "They will be closed until at least Monday of next week, maybe Tuesday. They couldn't reach Jake, and since I'm down as emergency contact, they called me." She adjusted her stylish jacket and opened the driver's side door. "Sorry to rush off, but today is my bridge club, and I need to scoot." She blew a kiss to Katie and got behind the wheel. "See you later."

Before Lexie could respond, Aggie turned around and drove off.

Chapter Fifteen

J ake wasn't surprised to see Sean assisting Brett and extended his hand. "Heard you were back."

"Prodigal son and all that," he said as they shook. "Was gonna give you a call when I got settled."

"Sounds good. But you're buying," Jake said as he crouched beside Brett. "How is she?"

"Got hit twice. One lightly punctured the skin. The other is deeper. That's where the damage is concentrated." He continued cleaning the wounds as he spoke. "Judging by her condition, it happened several hours ago."

"I saw a couple of rattlers last week," offered Jake.

"No way to be certain," said Brett. "But that's a good possibility. At this point, the best we can do is antibiotics and something for the pain, swelling, and inflammation. She's too close to calving for steroids."

While snake bites in cattle were rare, they happened, so Jake knew the routine.

Several long moments later, Brett stood and looked at Sean. "Go ahead with the shots." He addressed Jake. "As long as it doesn't get infected, she should be fine."

Jake listened to Brett's instructions, then turned to the two cowhands who waited nearby. "Put her in a stall with fresh hay and water."

"On it, boss," said Derek as he turned for the barn.

"Anything else, Brett?" Jake heard a car coming down the drive but didn't check it until Brett finished. When he glanced around, he saw his mother drop Katie off and leave again. "Let me see what's going on. I'll be right back."

He walked to where Lexie stood, Katie at her side. "What's happened?"

"Some kind of pipe break at the daycare," said Lexie. "They will be closed until probably Tuesday of next week. And today is Aggie's bridge day."

It took a moment for the statement to process. "Closed?"

"Yeah, until they get whatever broke fixed."

He glanced at Katie, who stood partially hidden behind Lexie. His first thought was she looked scared. Of what? His reaction? He made sure to keep his voice light. "Well, you get to stay home for a few days."

The child nodded but didn't speak.

"Did Miss Amy like your ponytail?"

"Uh-huh. Her said it was pitty."

"And she was right." He looked to where the vets still worked on Dolly. Thankfully, medication for the swelling and antibiotics should address the problem. But the rest of his plans for the day were shot because now he'd have to stay home with Katie.

Lexie spoke up as he considered options.

"I'd be happy to watch her if you have more work to do. I mean, if you're okay with that."

Surprised, he looked at her. "Are you sure? What about your

ankle?"

"Well, as you can see, I'm getting around fine on crutches. And Donna will be by with the boot after lunch."

Her languid smile made his pulse jump.

"And it's the least I can do."

"I can stay wif Wexie?"

The upbeat spark in Katie's voice got his attention.

"Looks like it." He faced Lexie. "Are you sure? I don't want you to hurt yourself."

"I'll be fine." She grinned at Katie. "We both will."

A quick check of his watch showed it was almost noon. "Did you eat lunch at school, Katie?"

"Uh-huh."

He turned his gaze to Lexie. "What about you?"

"I'm good."

His stomach chose that moment to emit an audible growl.

Lexie reacted immediately. "I saw sandwich makings in the fridge. How about I fix you one before you return to work?"

"You don't have to do that."

"Hey, Jake," called Brett.

"Coming." He turned to Lexie. "Don't worry about me. I'll get something later." He gave Katie what he hoped was an encouraging smile. "Mind what Miss Lexie says." Then he returned to the corral to see what else was about to screw up his day.

With Katie happily coloring a dog picture torn from one of her books, Lexie discovered half a pound cake under a glass dome and checked off dessert. She retrieved the sandwich makings she'd found earlier and placed them on the bar along with a plate and utensils.

Once Katie knew what she was doing, she wanted to help, so Lexie let her place turkey and cheese on the bread. When she put the cake on a saucer, Katie said he liked peaches on top. A pantry search produced a can, which she opened and let Katie spoon some into a bowl she placed beside the cake. "That's so his cake won't get soggy," she told Katie and placed the remainder in a plastic bowl in the fridge.

Finally, she added sliced tomatoes, onions, and lettuce on the side for the sandwich, just in case.

Lexie stood at the refrigerator filling a glass of ice with tea when Jake entered the back door, Biscuit on his heels. "Hey. Just in time." She put the pitcher back in the fridge and closed the door with her hip, carefully balanced on one crutch.

His shocked expression gave her pause, but it was too late to worry now.

"Wook, Daddy! Wexie made you a sam'ich," gushed Katie. "I helped, too."

He glanced at the plate on the bar, then back to Lexie. "You didn't have to do that."

Uncomfortable, she shrugged and indicated the glass in her hand. "It's a little late to ask, but is tea okay, or would you rather have water?"

"Tea is fine, thanks." He took the glass and placed it on the bar, then ensured Biscuit had food and water before he washed his hands at the sink.

Lexie hobbled to the stool beside Katie and sat down, touched he thought of her dog first. "Thank you for seeing to Biscuit," she said as he washed his hands.

"He worked hard this morning," he said with a smile. "Chasing butterflies and rabbits." He dried his hands, then placed the towel on the counter before sitting down.

She took a breath and indicated the condiments on the side of his plate. "I wasn't sure what all you'd like on your sandwich."

"This is great. Thank you."

She shifted in her seat to observe him over Katie's head, and it struck her as odd that both father and daughter looked at each other with matching expectant, uncertain expressions.

But then Jake's face softened, and he tweaked Katie lightly on the nose. "Thank you, too."

"You we'come." Katie returned to coloring the picture Lexie gave her earlier.

She watched Jake add all the extra fixings to his sandwich and take a bite. "How's Dolly?"

Mouth full, he stopped chewing and looked at her.

She chuckled. "Sorry. Didn't mean to catch you with your mouth full."

He swallowed, then wiped his mouth with the paper towel she handed him. "Good, I think." He drank some tea. "Brett thinks the stress might send her into early labor."

"Oh no."

"She's pretty far along, and this is her second calf, so hopefully, won't be a big deal."

"What about the snake bite? Will it harm the baby?"

His eyes widened as though her interest caught him off-guard. "Uh, no. The calf should be fine."

"I'm so glad. Are bites common around here?"

"We have our share."

"Cody said they aren't usually fatal for cows."

"Not usually." Then he repeated what the cowhand said, adding details about how they treated a bite.

She enjoyed hearing him talk and asked more questions about Dolly, the other Longhorns, and the horses she'd seen in the pasture. He relaxed and answered each one, offering more information about the ranch. His voice made it apparent he cared deeply for his home, and her heart shifted once more.

He started to list things he still needed to do today, and she noticed his tea glass was almost empty. She rose and went to the fridge for the pitcher.

"You don't have to wait on me," he complained. "You're hurt, and I'm not helpless."

"No, you're not helpless. But you are a working man who has already put in a full day with no end in sight."

He opened his mouth, and she continued. "And I have been sitting on my fat and happy all day. It's the very least I can do." She raised one brow and grinned. "I'm whittling on that payback list."

Their gazes met, and suddenly, she couldn't get enough air.

His nostrils flared as heat flashed like lightning in those earthy depths, then disappeared so fast she questioned what she saw.

The very air around them pulsed with each beat of her thudding heart. Breathless and shaken, pleasure rippled through her body, the lone crutch the only thing keeping her upright.

Seconds ticked by before he hissed in a breath. "I'm, uh, I don't..." He pushed away and abruptly stood, colliding with her.

Knocked off-balance, she squealed and juggled the tea pitcher as the crutch hit the floor.

He grabbed her to him and sank back onto the swiveling stool so fast she didn't have time to react before the pitcher of ice-cold tea doused them both.

Chapter Sixteen

Jake's first thought was Katie, and he twisted around to check. Thankfully, none of the tea splashed on her, though a trail headed toward the picture she colored. He quickly used his paper napkin to divert the flow while keeping Lexie secured against him, her hip resting on his thigh. "You okay, kiddo?"

She nudged the paper towel dam away from her artwork. "Wexie got you wet."

He grinned. "Yeah, but it was an accident." He turned to Lexie, who rested between his legs, one hand still holding the half-empty pitcher in the air, the other resting on his chest.

Maybe it was the horrified look on her face. Or the sticky liquid dripping off the tip of her nose and down the front of her shirt. Or even Katie's concise observation. Whatever the trigger, the situation suddenly struck him as incredibly funny, and laughter tore through his gut and out his mouth in one great gasping wave.

Lexie joined in, laughing so hard she snorted. She froze a moment, and her wide-open, teary eyes met Jake's amused gaze before she fell against him in another spasm of uncontrolled mirth. Her forehead lay against his chest, one hand fisted in his shirt, the other still holding the offending pitcher aloft as her body shook.

"The...pitcher," she sputtered. "I'm going to drop it."

He held her against him with one hand and took the jug with the other. The soul-cleansing gurgles continued when he placed it on the bar.

Eventually, the hilarity stopped, and they took a deep breath but didn't move.

He savored the feel of her body against him, her head tucked under his chin. Just for a moment, he allowed himself to believe it was all real. This happiness, this desire, was real.

He cleared his throat. "Are you all right?"

Her wheezy giggles tickled his chest. "I laughed so hard—I have to—to...I don't," she inhaled, "think I'll make it," then dissolved in laughter.

"Is Wexie okay?"

He looked over his shoulder at Katie, whose upturned face wore a concerned frown. "She's fine. We both are." He gave her a quick grin. "Don't you think it's funny that she spilled tea on our heads?"

She giggled. "Wexie sounds wike a pig."

The comment made her snort again. "I hate when I do that."

"I think it's cute."

"Cute?" Lexie finger-poked his chest. "Sounding like a pig is cute?"

"Uh-huh." He shifted on the seat as desire flooded his veins. "On you it is."

Their eyes met and held until the gleeful smile on her face slowly faded. Her cheeks flushed a deeper red as her breath quickened, and those azure orbs darkened.

Lightheaded, he inhaled deeply, her scent creating a pleasant shiver that flowed through him like a fine whiskey.

She gulped but didn't protest when he shifted again, resting his hands on her waist.

The antique clock on the wall ticked away the seconds as they sat wrapped in a cocoon of slowly building desire.

He wanted, no, *needed* to kiss her again.

She took a sharp breath, lips parting when her gaze dropped to his mouth, then jerked up again.

And he knew she wanted it as much as he did.

Except they weren't alone.

He ran his thumb over her bottom lip and corralled his escalating emotions. "You need to change," he whispered, "I'll clean up this mess."

She searched his face, looking for what he couldn't guess, then tried to stand. But the awkward angle made her foot slip on the wet tile floor.

He grabbed her against him, and their bodies aligned chest to hips. She'd have to be numb from the waist down not to feel the effect she had on him pressing against her. He should probably be embarrassed, but he wasn't. And judging by the desire-clouded eyes meeting his, neither was she.

She inhaled sharply and rested her forehead against his chin. "This is crazy," she whispered as her grip on his upper arms tightened. "Crazy."

It took great effort on his part to get a grip on his skyrocketing emotions. "I know." Slowly, he pushed back and helped her stand, one hand on the bar for support, while he picked up the crutches. Silent, he handed them to her and ensured she stood on a dry spot.

"Thank you." She paused and looked at the suitcase by the door. "Um, I'll need my bag."

She indicated the bag by the door.

"Going somewhere?

She avoided his gaze. "Well, um, once Donna gets the boot on, I'll be able to get around better and thought I should go on to the cabin. You know, to get out of your hair."

Before he could say anything, she continued. "I can watch Katie there."

A myriad of thoughts rushed through his mind at once. He glanced at Katie and lowered his voice. "And if I don't want you to go?"

Her face flushed bright red, and she swallowed. "I really should go." The desire in her eyes contradicted her statement.

He stepped closer. "Why?"

"You know why," she murmured.

"What are you afraid of?"

She closed her eyes, then looked up. "You. Us." She shook her head. "It's...too fast."

He gently rubbed her cheek with his finger, and the spark in her eyes brightened. "Fast is good, isn't it?"

"In...situations like this," her words came in breathy gasps. "Slow is better."

"Are you sure?"

"No. Yes. Yes. Slow is better."

He watched the desire build, then slowly disappear from her eyes as she grappled with her emotions.

Knowing he wasn't the only one feeling this way helped. But hearing her say she wanted to leave hurt like a bitch.

Still, they had two weeks to work it out. "The cabin is less than a mile away."

She nodded.

"I don't have time this afternoon, so I'd rather take you in the morning." He stroked her cheek again because he had to touch her. "But if you can't wait, there's a gravel road behind the barn. When you get to the lake, take the road to the right. Your cabin will be the first one on the left. Key's under the doormat."

Dark brows shot upward, and she grinned. "Really? Under the doormat?"

He shrugged. "Few people know it."

"Wexie? Which one is brown?"

Katie's question broke the spell, and he turned around, found the crayon, and gave it to her.

He turned back to Lexie. "I'll take your bag back to your room so you can get cleaned up."

She slowly followed as he placed the bag on the bed and walked out.

Once back in the kitchen, Jake grabbed some rags, a sponge mop, and a bottle of spray cleaner from the laundry room. A few minutes later, the floor and counter were clean and dry. Then, he went to the sink, washed the sticky mess off his face and hands, and used a wet towel on his hair and neck. Tossing the cloth in the sink, he stared out the window, letting the tranquil scene calm the turmoil churning inside. After a moment, he returned to the bar and looked at the picture in front of Katie.

His first thought was to say something positive about her efforts. But how does one compliment a four-year-old's scribbled attempt at coloring a blue dog with a brown bow around his neck?

When she glanced up, the look on her face sent a stabbing pain right through his heart.

Suddenly, he saw a nine-year-old boy holding his first straight-A report card for his father's approval. He'd been so proud of his accomplishment and just knew this time, Jack Holloway would say how proud he was of him. Instead, his father glanced at it before passing the card to his mother without saying a word.

Raw emotions clogged his throat. *I won't be that man. I won't.*

He swallowed twice before speaking; still, his voice was husky and deep. "That's a very nice picture, Katie."

Slowly, her expression changed and became hopeful as she nervously extended it toward him. "...I made it for you."

The lump in his throat grew as he accepted her gift. "For me? Thank you. I love it."

"You wike bue?"

"It's my favorite color."

Her tentative smile widened. "Mine too."

From somewhere in his troubled mind came another memory from his childhood. He was visiting his best friend Sean's family, whose refrigerator door held all kinds of kid stuff. Drawings, photos, you name it. So, he went to the junk drawer, pulled out two magnets advertising the local bank, and stuck the picture on the front of the fridge. "What do you think?"

"I wike it."

"Me, too."

He squatted beside her chair. "I have to get back to work soon."

Silent, she nodded.

"So, you be good for Miss Lexie, okay?"

"I w'il."

"I know you will because you're a very good girl." Anxious to leave her with something more, he gave her nose another affectionate tweak. "And I'm very proud of you."

His heart swelled with gratitude and something else he couldn't name at the bright glow in her eyes. He said a silent *thank you* to Lexie for making this moment possible.

"Um, maybe tonight, I can read you Aunt Tina's book." He hadn't planned to say that. It popped out before he thought. Hopefully, Lexie hadn't read it yet. Or if she did, Katie wouldn't mind hearing it again.

"Okay." She fingered the worn box of crayons. "I wike to co-wour."

It never occurred to him to get her coloring books. Books, yes, but not coloring books. Lexie's thoughtfulness endeared her a little more. "I'm glad." He stood. "Want to color another page?"

She nodded, and together, they thumbed through the book on the counter and decided on a picture of two puppies and a kitten. He tore the page free and set the crayons within reach.

Just then, Lexie returned, wearing knee-length pants and a tee shirt, hair still in that off-kilter bun he found so attractive, horn-rimmed glasses perched on her nose. The woman oozed sex appeal, and he swallowed the saliva suddenly filling his mouth.

"Wexie!" said Katie. "Wook where Daddy put my pi-chure!"

"That's the perfect spot for it."

"His fabo-et co-wor is bue, just wike me." She held up another picture. "He gived me another one."

"That is so sweet of him."

Jake came around the bar and stopped, nodding toward the page Katie brandished. "Um, I hope you don't mind. She wanted another page to color."

"Of course not. I gave her the book."

"Thank you." He looked down at her bandaged ankle, now

sporting a tea stain. "Are you sure you're up to this?"

"I'm fine, Jake." She shifted on the crutches. "The swelling has gone down, and the pain isn't bad. Unless I bump it." She cleared her throat. "I've been thinking. Tomorrow is fine to move."

He refused to fist-pump the air.

"But I would like to take a look—if you don't mind me taking Katie along."

"The car seat's in the back of my truck. I'll set it on the porch. Do you know how to install it?"

Their invisible link held them in place like a tractor beam.

She cleared her throat again. "Yeah...I, um, could maybe cook supper tonight." She made a motion with her hand. "You know, to make up for dumping tea on your head."

It took massive willpower not to pull her to him and taste the lips that haunted him all morning. "You don't have to do that."

"I want to." She huffed out a breath. "I'm really sorry about the tea, Jake."

"Don't be. Besides, you got wet, too." Happiness warmed him like a ray of sunshine from within. "I haven't laughed so hard in years, so thank you."

"You're welcome."

"But don't put yourself out on my account."

"I want to help out in some way. And my mind's made up."

"Beautiful, but stubborn."

His comment caused her face to flush, but she seemed pleased.

She ducked her head, then gave him a sexy side-eyed glance. "Part of my charm."

He struggled for something else to say. "I'll, uh, probably be late getting home tonight. Maybe even after dark. I need to set out feed and check for new calves." He scratched the back of his neck where sticky tea from his collar lingered and itched. "Hogs got another section of fence, and we need to move some stock to the west pasture before rain hits later today."

"Rain?"

"Springtime in East Texas," he said with a grin.

"All by yourself?"

"Well, no. Cody helps. Derek sometimes, too. He's part-time." Suddenly aware of his rambling, he stopped and rubbed his chin. "Sorry. Didn't mean to bore you with my to-do list."

"You're not boring me." She met his gaze. "I rather enjoy hearing you talk about what you do."

Her sincere expression temporarily muddied his thoughts. "Yeah, well, wait until I tell you about baling hay and vaccinating cattle."

"I can't wait."

It felt so good to talk to someone who appeared interested and he didn't want the moment to end. "Derek will be with me, but Cody should be around the barn if you need anything and can't get me on my cell."

"I'll be fine."

"Oh, I'm expecting a feed delivery later today or tomorrow, but Cody should be around to handle it."

"Okay. Rain and feed delivery. If it's okay with you, I'll run out to the cabin before I put her down for a nap."

"That's fine." The longer he delayed, the longer it would be before he got home. He needed to leave. Now. "I better get going."

"Don't you want to clean up first?"

"I gave myself a lick and a promise at the sink—no point in doing more. Just get dirty again."

"Okay, well…don't work too hard."

"I'll see you tonight."

Ordinary people having a normal conversation.

A couple.

He shook away the tempting thought as something unattainable.

Or was it?

Things just felt right with her. The comfortable atmosphere of the kitchen, Katie at the bar coloring as they talked about simple things, and the possibility of a meal waiting—and someone there when he got home.

Home. Before Lexie, it was just where they lived. They were like pieces of a complex puzzle that fit together perfectly.

He glanced at Katie, who colored her new picture, back turned.

Unable to ignore the urge any longer, he stepped forward, placed one finger under her chin, tipped it up, and waited.

Eyes wide, lips slightly parted, she didn't back away.

Cautiously, he leaned forward and lightly brushed her lips with his.

She inhaled sharply. Balanced on the crutches under her arms, she gripped his waist.

He cupped her face, and she stretched to meet his kiss as he slowly covered her mouth. The gentle shiver racking her body fueled the flame inside, and the heady sensation threatened to rob him of coherent thought as shock waves of desire beset him.

Heart hammering in his ears, he deepened the kiss, unable to get close enough, deep enough to satisfy the hunger eating him alive.

The kiss went on forever, but not nearly long enough. Finally, reluctantly, he pulled back and leaned his forehead against hers as sanity slowly returned. Their heated breath swirled and mixed as they fought for control.

Before calm returned, the back door opened, and Donna walked in.

Chapter Seventeen

Jake's drugging kiss made Lexie long for so much more, even as Donna's sudden appearance flushed her face with embarrassment.

"Hey, I—oops."

"Wexie poured tea on Daddy, but it was a ass-i-dent." Katie giggled and continued. "And she wafes wike a pig."

Eyes wide, Donna stared at her niece. "Okaaay."

"And I helped make Daddy a sam'ich."

"That's great, sweetie." She placed a clunky black boot on the bar. "I see I missed all the fun." Donna's unreadable gaze fixed on Lexie. "Maybe I should have come by sooner."

Lexie noted the tips of Jake's ears turned bright red as he plucked his hat from the bar. "I have to get back to work." He strode for the back door, Biscuit on his heels. Jake raised a brow in a silent question.

"It's fine." She leaned the crutches against the bar and sat down. "I've obviously been relegated to second fiddle anyway."

"Only cause you think he's a city dog," said Jake as he opened the door, and Biscuit dashed out. "But he's country all the way." He paused. "See you at supper."

Once the door closed behind him, Lexie faced Donna. "Hey."

"I brought this boot for you to try."

Her crisp reply made Lexie do a double take. *Uh-oh. Is she upset about what she saw?*

"I'm sorry to cause you so much trouble," said Lexie, hoping to ease the sudden tension in the room. "And I do appreciate everything you've done."

"No problem."

Her short reply said otherwise.

Donna grabbed the boot and was all business as she explained its function and how to make adjustments. "Make sure you wear it all the time except in bed for at least a week," she said. "You should still use a crutch until you get accustomed to walking in it. Whether this is a grade one or two sprain, the support will help it heal faster." She pulled a white sock from her pocket. "You don't need to wrap it with the boot but wear a thick sock to prevent irritating your skin. I brought this from home. You can get one of yours later."

In a few minutes, the new boot was on and adjusted. "Now try and walk," instructed Donna. "But use the crutch."

After a few trips around the kitchen, Donna was satisfied. "Good. Call me if you have any questions."

She started for the back door but stopped when Lexie spoke. "Is everything all right?"

"If walking hurts, check the tightness like I showed you. If that doesn't work, call me."

"Donna?"

She wavered, then spoke to Katie. "Hey, sweetie, why don't you take your coloring to your room for a bit so Miss Lexie and I can talk."

"Okay."

She helped the child get down, then watched until she was out of sight. "I'm torn about what to do."

Even though she suspected the answer, Lexie asked, "About what?"

Silent, Donna moved to the fridge and gently touched the picture with one finger.

"Jake put it there," offered Lexie. "She colored it for him."

Donna groaned and raised her hands in the air. "See? That's what I mean." She took two steps toward the sink, turned around, and plopped down on a stool, her hands palm down on the top.

It was apparent Donna struggled with something significant, and Lexie sat quietly and waited for her to say whatever she needed to get off her chest.

"That child rarely speaks," she muttered, "and for damn sure never colored anyone a picture before. I didn't even know she had a coloring book."

"I gave her one," said Lexie.

Donna gave an exasperated huff. "Did you put her up to it?"

"Of course not. I gave her the book to keep her busy while I fixed his lunch. I didn't know she gave it to him until I came in a few minutes ago."

Her dark eyes narrowed. "You fixed his lunch, too?"

She shrugged. "It was just a sandwich. And the very least I could do after all he's done for me." When the silence became uncomfortable, Lexie tried again. "Donna, I—"

"What are your plans?"

"My plans?"

Dark, haunted eyes stared at Lexie, her expression a strange mixture of anger and sadness—with a tinge of hope. "My brother endured the worst hurt imaginable. He's guarded his heart ever since." She paused. "Which makes him vulnerable to someone like you."

Taken aback, Lexie whispered, "Someone like me?"

Donna rubbed her temples, clearly upset and searching for words.

"You come in here with your silly dog and coloring books, and suddenly, he's reminded of what it's like to have someone around besides Mom and me." She took a deep breath and let it out slowly. "But you're temporary." She leaned forward, hands tightly clasped together in her lap. "I can't believe how quickly Katie attached to you. It's obvious she already adores you. And Jake...." She paused. "I saw his face...." Her fierce gaze bore into Lexie. "He's been alone a long time." She slowly rolled her head side-to-side. "I admit, when I first saw the two of you together, I thought maybe it would be good for him if you hung around a while."

"And now?"

"I never expected this—reaction." She sat up straight. "But I do know this. You'll be gone in two weeks, and my brother, whom I adore, and his child, who is the most precious thing in the world to me, will be devastated."

"I—"

"I don't want him...them to hurt like that ever again."

"And you think I will?"

"Maybe not intentionally, but yes, I do." She stood, putting a chair between them. "I think it would be best for all concerned if you moved out to the cabin before he gets home tonight."

Lexie opened her mouth, but Donna continued, her voice firm and emotionless. "And limit all contact with both for the duration of your stay. Or better yet, get a room at the hotel in town."

The demand shocked Lexie into silence as her scrambled thoughts whirled. True, her stay was limited, but the idea of possibly never seeing them again made her stomach churn. How was it possible to become so attached in such a short period of time?

She'd been with Rodney for two years and never experienced the explosive white-hot shot of desire Jake elicited with a single glance. It was more intense than anything she'd ever experienced.

Donna's point was valid, too. If things didn't work out and she left, they would be hurt, and she couldn't bear that, either.

Feelings she'd denied from the beginning now begged for affirmation. Her attraction to Jake was instant and fierce and needed exploring because she sensed the mutual pull. Was it just physical? A rebound reaction on her part? Loneliness?

Or something else entirely?

And then there was Katie. The child tugged at her heart in ways she couldn't explain or ignore. She instinctively knew Katie needed her and suddenly realized she needed Katie, too.

Was she being selfish? Would her desire to explore the relationship possibilities between father and daughter end up hurting all concerned?

But a massive *what-if* made her reluctant to leave.

What if fate brought her here because they belonged together?

She took a deep breath and let it out slowly. She couldn't go. Not yet.

"You're not leaving, are you?" Resignation filled Donna's voice.

"I understand what you're saying, Donna. I do. And I promise to give it more thought."

"But?"

She took a calming breath. "I can't explain it. I've never felt this way before. It's like a part of me has been missing, and suddenly, it's within my reach." She paused. "Maybe you're right about one thing, though. I told him before you came in that I should go to the cabin. I think we both need the space to think."

She held up her hand when Donna started to speak. "But I won't leave without saying goodbye or telling him why." She took a breath. "And then there's Katie. The center is closed until next week, and I offered to watch her for him during the day."

"Mom hired someone to do that, but she can't start until Monday. I'll have Mom check to see if she can be available before then."

"That's not necessary. I can watch her at the cabin."

Undeterred, Donna continued. "Mom's bridge club is usually over around four, and she'll come to stay with Katie."

"There is no need to inconvenience your mother. She knows I'm here."

Donna rubbed both hands on her thighs and inhaled deeply. "Okay. Fine. Guess I'll go then." She stopped at the back door and turned around; her troubled gaze focused on Katie's drawing. "You appear to be everything they need, Lexie," her fragile voice shook with controlled emotion as she turned toward her. "But I'm terrified you won't be happy here either. And break his heart again."

Donna closed the door softly behind her, leaving the questions her comment generated unasked.

Lexie held Katie's hand as they walked through the cozy cabin.

The kitchen, dining, and living areas were open-concept. A short hallway off the kitchen led to the bedroom on one side and the bathroom on the other. A small laundry room covered the end of the hallway. A gas fireplace anchored the living space, and porches on the front and back ran the length of the cabin.

They stepped out onto the back porch, which faced the lake. Two wooden rocking chairs sat on one side of the door, and a glider rocker sat on the other with colorful throws draped over the arms. Cypress, pine, and oak trees dotted the water's edge, and a rustic pier stretched about ten feet out. Other trees covered the property, giving the space a private and secluded feel.

They sat in the glider, and she checked out the view. "Wow."

"Wow," mimicked Katie.

A quick inhale brought the smell of wet earth from a brief afternoon shower and things she could not identify yet found appealing. Birds chirped in a nearby oak tree, and a squirrel shimmied up another. A gentle breeze rustled the leaves. The delicate sound further eased the tension weighing her down as she sat back and sighed. "I've never seen anything so beautiful."

A light push with her toes put the chair in motion. The action and a gentle breeze leached away the restlessness cluttering her mind for months. Self-doubt and worry about the future vanished as her analytical mind sorted things out.

"I was right to come here," she said softly.

"Right," echoed Katie.

She smiled at the child. "If I remember correctly, Bobby said there's another cabin somewhere on the other side." She craned her neck to search the far side of the lake. "But I can't see it from here."

"I can't see it, e-vor, Wexie," said Katie, mimicking her action.

She smiled at her. "Did you know you're a very smart little girl?"

She yawned and nodded. "Daddy told me so."

"I think it's past time for your nap, young lady." She stood on the cumbersome boot and waited until her footing was stable before reaching for her hand. "Let's get you home."

By the time they reached the house, Katie was fast asleep.

She parked near the barn, hoping one of the hands was nearby since she could not get her in the house wearing the boot.

The rumble of an engine reminded her of the expected feed delivery, and she glanced up, surprised to see the red veterinary truck roll down the drive and stop in front of the barn. Worried it meant something happened to Dolly, she waited.

Sean Taylor hopped out, saw her in the car, and sauntered over.

She lowered her window. "Afternoon, Sean."

He glanced at Katie in the back. "Something wrong?"

"No. We were just down at the cabin, and she fell asleep on the way back." She looked toward the barn. "Could you check to see if Derek or Cody is in there? I need some help getting her inside."

"No need for that. I'll be glad to help."

He was a stranger, and she had no idea if Katie knew him, so she could not allow him to carry her inside.

"Unless you'd rather I didn't."

She chewed her lower lip. "To be honest, I don't know you, and since you're new in town, I'm guessing Katie doesn't either."

"Good point." He stepped back. "I'll go see if one of them is inside. I wanted to check on Dolly anyway."

Just then, Cody came outside. "Hey, Sean," he said quickly. "She's in labor. Don't see any issues, but since you're here, can you check her out?"

"That's why I dropped by." He patted the top of the car. "Lexie needs some help getting the kid inside."

Cody didn't appear comfortable in the task but quickly carried Katie inside and placed her on the bed.

"Thank you so much, Cody. Sean offered to do it, but I didn't know him and wasn't sure she did either."

"Don't reckon she does. He left 'fore she was born." He took a step back. "Let me know if you need anything."

As he left, she ensured Katie was covered and her bear tucked by her side, then returned to the kitchen. A few minutes later, with tonight's menu decided, she stood in the middle of the kitchen, wondering what to do now to keep her troubled mind occupied.

"I'll work. That's what I'll do." She retrieved her laptop from the bedroom, then sat in the comfy recliner. She finished her expense report, but the battery died halfway through the job invoices. She dug through her bags and groaned. She'd left the charger on her desk at home.

She opened the novel she brought and read until Katie woke from her nap.

She took her outside to the swing and discovered the child had never used it. The rope and wooden seat appeared weathered, so she tried it first to ensure it would hold, then sat Katie in it and helped her swing.

They returned to the house, and after a quick snack of milk and cookies, Katie asked to watch TV, so Lexie got her situated in the den.

Getting around on the walking boot was surprisingly easy. She made a quick pot of coffee and took a cup to the porch. She chose a rocker similar to the cabin's, offering a panoramic view of the barn, pastures, and the drive. Dark clouds hovered over the western horizon, which meant another shower was probable this afternoon. But, for now, it was enjoyable sitting there admiring the view.

The rocking action and fragrant breeze restored the sense of peace she enjoyed at the cabin earlier.

As usual these days, her thoughts immediately turned to Jake.

The sudden attraction was mystifying and intense, but was it love? Did she even know what love was? She considered herself in love with Rodney, but this thing with Jake was different and much more potent. What was it?

Whatever it was, it happened the instant Jake's coffee-colored eyes met hers on the side of the road in the pouring rain.

She stopped rocking when she recalled her mother's tale of meeting her father at a diner where she worked. On leave from the Army, he had stopped in for lunch. The moment their eyes met, they both knew. It was as though they'd known each other forever.

He sat in that booth all afternoon, and they chatted at every opportunity. When he took her home at the end of her shift, he calmly informed her parents he intended to marry her when he got out the following year. Forty years later, the romance remained as strong as ever.

She rocked slower as the seed of possibility sprouted, caus-ing a swarm of butterflies to invade her stomach. She pressed a hand against her racing heart. "I can't leave," she whispered. "I'm home."

She took a deep breath. *Okay, that's how I feel. What about him?* His kisses said he felt something, but what?

"I have two weeks to find out."

"Find out what?"

Sean's unexpected question made her jump.

"Sorry," he drawled. "Didn't mean to startle you."

Embarrassed to be caught so deep in thought she didn't hear him walk up, she huffed. "Well, you did."

"So, what do you have two weeks to find out?"

"How's Dolly? Is the calf all right?"

His dimpled grin said her evasive answer didn't put him off as he sat in the chair beside her without invitation. "Mother and daughter are both fine." He stretched his legs out. "Cody get the kid to bed?"

"Her name is Katie," she snipped. "Not kid."

He held his hands up. "Hey, I didn't know. Haven't been around in a while."

"So, you used to live around here then?"

"Yep. Born and raised here."

"Did you know Jake then?"

He rocked slowly back and forth in the chair. "Grew up together. Guess you could say we were best friends."

"Were?"

He stopped rocking and turned his head toward her. "Is that what you have two weeks to figure out?" The dimple was back—along with the unmistakable spark of interest in those cocoa-colored eyes. "How long I've known Jake?"

Before she could reply, he leaned over the chair toward her. "I'm disappointed you haven't noticed I'm wearing the smile you gave me."

She stared for a moment, then snickered. She couldn't help it.

He was a charmer. "That is, without a doubt, the dumbest pickup line I've ever heard."

"Maybe," he grinned. "But you smiled back."

When she didn't reply, he winked. "Which means I still have a chance."

Okaaaay. Time to derail this train wreck. "No. It doesn't." She picked up her cup. "I don't do casual."

He cocked his head and grinned as though he knew a secret. "I enjoy a challenge."

She moved to get up, and he grabbed the hand resting on the chair arm. "Just so you know, you're wasting your time on Jake."

His words glued her to the spot. "What do you mean?"

"Just what I said. There's only been one love in his life. That's never going to change." The sultry grin returned as he lightly caressed her arm. "Me, on the other hand..."

Her scalp prickled with unease as she jerked her arm free but stood too fast, wobbling on the unfamiliar boot.

Sean reacted quickly and grabbed her upper arms. "Steady there, blue eyes."

Angry at herself, she stiffened and regained her balance. "I'm good."

His hold remained, one thumb lightly caressing her arm. "You sure?"

Jaw tight, she stared without comment until he released her and stepped back, an I-won-this-round smirk on his too-handsome face.

"Hey, Sean," called Cody from the barn door. "Got a minute?"

Brazen eyes still on her, Sean spoke over his shoulder. "Be right there." His face turned somber. "Remember what I said." Then he winked and walked toward the barn, whistling a snappy tune.

Lexie stalked into the kitchen, fuming over her delayed ability to fend off his interest. She'd dealt with his type on countless job sites and board rooms without batting an eye. But she was so preoccupied with her sudden insight he caught her off guard. That would not happen again.

Still, his comment about Jake's one love wormed its way into her brain and wouldn't leave. It had to be his late wife. But if that were the case, why did he kiss her? And the desire she read in his eyes was real.

He didn't act like a man who engaged in casual relationships, but what did she really know about him? Other than the fact he affected her in ways no one ever had before and made it impossible for her to think straight around him.

Mind racing, searching for answers, she checked on Katie, then warmed her coffee in the microwave. As she gazed out the window over the sink, lightning flashed off to the right, followed by a rumble of thunder. She checked both directions and shook her head. "Bright sunshine and blue skies on one side of the pasture," she muttered, "rain clouds on the other." The microwave dinged, so she got her coffee and leaned against the counter.

The sharp peel of the house phone interrupted her musing. She hesitated, then picked up the cordless from the counter. "Holloway residence."

"Lexie, dear," said Aggie. "I hoped you'd answer since I didn't have your cell number."

Lexie opened her mouth to speak, but the older woman continued. "I just have a minute between games. Donna said you were fine with caring for Katie this afternoon?"

"Of course. She's watching TV right now."

"Good. I'm afraid our games are running a little long today, and I won't have time to come by and fix supper before I go home to cook for Jack."

"Don't worry, Miss Aggie. I'll take care of it."

"Are you sure, dear?"

"I'm sure. The boot Donna brought helps a lot."

"That's wonderful."

"Is there anything I should cook or not cook tonight?"

"Jake's not a fussy eater, but he does work up an appetite. I put some cubed steaks in the fridge yesterday to thaw, but feel free to fix whatever you like."

"Chicken fried steak is my specialty."

"Great. I'm so glad you're here. Oh, they're calling me. Gotta run."

Aggie's encouraging voice contrasted sharply with Donna's concern, and Lexie stared at the phone in her hand. It was almost like Aggie pushed her toward Jake, and Donna pulled her away.

Shaking her head, she focused on the questions foremost in her mind.

How do you tell a man you just met, a man with more baggage than Paris Hilton, you're falling for him?

And who is his only love?

Chapter Eighteen

J ake was dirty, dog-tired, and hungry when he and Derek herded the remaining stock into the new pasture. Thankfully, the rain had stopped earlier, but the air remained cool as dusk fell around him.

He'd never thought much about how days ended beyond getting the work done, but, for some reason, today, the beauty of it registered. Heaving a contented sigh, he shifted in the saddle to watch the sun slowly disappear below the horizon, painting the sky in brilliant shades of orange, purple, and blue. Despite the fatigue, he loved this way of life and couldn't imagine doing anything else. It was hard work and lonely at times, but it suited him just fine—until Lexie barged into his life.

She was easy to talk to and possessed a quirky sense of humor he found refreshing. She listened, asked questions, and seemed genuinely interested to the point he shared more than he had with anyone in a very long time.

And the way Katie responded to her was incredible.

How was it possible to feel this powerful connection so fast? Everything about her called to him like a siren's song. He shouldn't have kissed her again but couldn't resist her enchanting pull. Even now, the taste and feel of her lips lingered.

Part of his brain argued he read something into it that wasn't there. He'd been alone a long time, and she caught him in a weak moment. It was simply a physical reaction to a beautiful woman.

But the other part of his brain, the one he wanted to believe, insisted they were two halves of one whole.

Except, she wants to leave and spend her time at the cabin—away from him.

He didn't miss the conflict in her eyes when she said it, though. Hell, he was conflicted, too. Common sense said to take things slow, but slow was the last thing on his mind these days.

For both their sakes, letting her go, removing the temptation, was the sensible thing to do. But just the idea of being alone again made his heart hurt.

Let her go.

Make her stay.

I have Katie to think about.

I can't get involved with anyone.

All logical, sensible things to consider, but the desire to have her in his life persisted.

What am I going to do?

The answer evaded him as he watched Biscuit instinctively herd a calf back to its mother, then hunker down in the wet grass nearby.

Would Lexie take to ranch life the way her dog did? It was an absurd thought, but one that refused to die.

He got the impression earlier she wasn't happy working for her father. If so, what would she want to do instead? Can she do it from here? Would she even want to?

Disgusted with his wandering thoughts, he shook his head as Derek joined him.

"We're done, boss."

He whistled, and Biscuit trotted up beside him. On a whim, he patted his chest. "Here, boy." The dog immediately jumped, and Jake caught him mid-air, settling him on his lap. "You did good today."

"He's a born ranch dog, ain't he?" said Derek. "Never seen a dog take to herding the way he did."

"Yeah, he's special." *Just like his mom.*

"You gonna need me anymore this week?"

Derek was a part-time hand who typically worked when Jake needed an extra person. "No, I think we're good for now."

"Okay. I'm at the Benton place for the next week while Harper's on vacation. If you need something just let me know."

Jaked nodded and they finished the half-hour ride in silence.

"I got your horse, boss," said Derek as they approached the barn.

Cody met them at the entrance. "Dolly had a new heifer a couple of hours ago."

Jake dismounted and handed Derek the reins. "Is she all right? What about the calf?"

"Both are fine." Cody hesitated, and the expression on his face troubled Jake.

"What's wrong?"

"Sean stopped by just as they, Miss Lexie and Katie, got back from visiting the cabin."

"And?"

"Well, Katie was asleep, and Miss Lexie couldn't get her in the house what with her being on that boot thing and using a crutch."

Jake's patience, very weak lately, cracked. "Get to the point."

"He offered to carry Katie into the house."

Jake stiffened as Cody continued. "Miss Lexie said no. And, well, she asked me to do it."

"Okay. What else?"

"Well, I was walking to the front when I saw his truck was still here." He hesitated. "They was sitting in them rockers on the porch. She didn't look much like she wanted his company, so I called him back to the barn, and she went inside."

An unease he couldn't explain washed over him. Not because Cody helped Lexie but because Sean was here. Again. And it was obvious he was interested in Lexie.

Nope, dude. Not gonna happen.

Cody continued, seemingly unaware of Jake's sudden ire. "You should have seen Katie when Miss Lexie brought her out here. I've never seen a kid so excited. Miss Lexie, too."

On top of the other turmoil in his chest, Cody's wide grin irked Jake, and he tamped down the irritation. "She brought Katie to the barn?"

"Yeah. Didn't stay long. Said she had to cook your supper."

He didn't comment and entered the barn, stopping at Dolly's stall and smiling at the image of the calf nursing. "Good girl, Dolly," he said as the cow stretched toward him for a head scratch. "Good girl." He checked the calf and Dolly's injury, ensured she had ample water and feed, and then headed out of the stall, setting the latch behind him. When Biscuit ambled up, he stopped and stared. The poor dog was filthy and soaking wet. "Lexie will have a fit," he muttered. "Let's get you cleaned up."

Biscuit followed him to the washing area at the back and sat still as he hosed him down for a quick bath, then dried him with a towel. "Well, it ain't the best wash job in the world, but maybe she won't be too upset over it."

Troubling thoughts of Sean disappeared as he stepped onto the porch and toed off his boots. The image he saw through the window made his breath catch. Lexie stood at the sink, apparently washing dishes, when Katie came in wearing her favorite blue pj's, carrying a book, her hair piled on top of her head in a mini-me version of Lexie's.

She dried her hands, then leaned down, apparently listening to whatever the child said. Then she nodded and settled Katie at the bar, the book in her lap.

"Damn, Biscuit. I forgot I said I'd read that book tonight." He checked his watch, noted it was Katie's bedtime, and hurried inside, the dog on his heels.

"Daddy," Katie exclaimed. "Doh-wee had a baby."

"She did?"

"Uh-huh. I petted him, too."

He tried to hide his discomfort. "You did?"

"Uh-huh."

"I hope that was all right." Lexie's voice held a nervous quiver. "Sean told me—"

He jerked his gaze toward her, the mental picture of her and Sean together—on his porch, clouding his mind with a surge of unexpected jealousy. "Sean?"

Her cheeks turned bright pink, and she averted her eyes, making him think she hid something.

"Well, Katie and I went to the cabin after you left. It's beautiful, by the way. And she fell asleep on the way home."

The buzzing in his ears continued as she related Cody's earlier story—except for the part about them sitting together—on his porch.

Her eyes flitted around the room before connecting with his. "When Katie got up from her nap, I took her outside to swing. Then she wanted to watch this cartoon on TV, and I came outside to sit for a while. Sean came up and told me about the calf, stayed a few minutes, and left." She paused to breathe. "I'm sorry if I did something wrong."

His chaotic mind latched on to the mental image of her and Sean together, and he gave himself a mental shake. "No. It's fine." He glanced at Katie, who held the book close to her chest.

"...you read now?" Her tiny voice vibrated with uncertainty.

He hated to say no, but he really needed a shower first. Maybe it would wash away the disquieting images that kept popping up.

"Sweetie, I think Daddy should clean up first." Lexie leaned forward. "He kinda smells," she added in a stage whisper.

Katie grinned. "Yeah, Daddy 'tinks.'"

"Yes, I do." He stood across the island from her. "Give me a few minutes to shower, and then I'll come tuck you in and read. Okay?"

Her hair bobbed when she nodded.

"Biscuit worked hard today," he told Lexie. "He might be extra hungry."

"Okay," said Lexie as she lifted Katie to the floor and gave her the book. "Why don't you go hop in bed now? Daddy will be in soon."

Katie grinned at him, then hurried down the hall to her room.

Lexie turned her back to him and busied herself wiping the counter. "I'm sorry if I did something wrong. About the calf, I mean."

His first thought was that she had something other than the calf on her mind. The second was it shocked him to realize how quickly she picked up on his unease, even if she misinterpreted the reason. "I've never taken her to the barn before." He paused. "Animals can be unpredictable." Immediately, the image of Mary on the ground came to mind. It was difficult to shove it back into its darkened corner.

Lexie finally turned and faced him. "I was extra careful with her, Jake. But I should have asked you first. I'm sorry." A shadow of unease crossed her face as she waited for his response.

"No. It's all right, really." He rubbed that sticky spot on the back of his neck. "You had her on the swing?" The old rope swing had hung on the tree for as long as he could remember. It couldn't possibly be safe to use.

"I sat in it first to make sure it would hold her since I saw it was old."

Again, the strange feeling she knew what he was thinking. "I'm sure she enjoyed it." He sighed. "Frankly, I never even thought about it." He shook his head. "I usually work till dark."

She pushed away from the counter. "I'll feed Biscuit, then set your supper out while you shower."

"What's wrong, Lexie?"

She didn't immediately face him. "Nothing. Really. A lot on my mind tonight."

He wasn't buying that, but he let it slide for now because he had his own thoughts to contend with.

"Where're your glasses?" It was a stupid question to ask, but it popped into his head and out his mouth before he could stop it.

"Contacts."

"Your eyes are beautiful." He smiled at the light tint on her cheeks. "But that sexy librarian look is hard to beat."

The flush deepened, and she blinked. "Um, thank you." She hesitated. "I better see to Biscuit."

When she moved, he gently touched her arm. He hadn't meant to, shouldn't have, but he couldn't stop himself. It was torture to be this close and not touch her. Hold her.

She froze, her gaze ping-ponging from his hand to his face.

When their eyes connected, something sparked in the deepest part of him. The part he had kept deeply buried for years, one he thought never to live again. He didn't know what to call it, certainly not love, but it was different. Special.

And then he saw an answering spark in those electric blue eyes.

He sighed deeply, gathered her into his arms, and held her snugly against his stinky, wet body.

⬥

Something intense flared in Jake's eyes, and Lexie held her breath. Each time she saw him, the bond between them grew stronger. When he gently pulled her to him, it was a natural response to sink into his embrace and nestle her forehead under his chin.

All thoughts of Sean's comments vaporized as his hands explored the hollows of her back, and she snuggled closer. Despite his smelly, damp clothing, the heat of his body seeped through and warmed her from within. Content, she inhaled the masculine scent of rain, leather, and sweat. She abandoned trying to put a name to it. Knowing it existed was enough for now.

The kisses from earlier tantalized her memory all day, and she hoped for a repeat performance. But this was better, for he not only embraced her body, he also included her heart.

"I know I should have showered first." His uneven breath was warm and moist against her cheek. "But I...I needed this."

The rapid thump of his heart in her ear matched her own. "Me, too."

He pushed back slightly and cupped her chin with one hand, his thumb caressing her lower lip. "What have you done to me?" he whispered.

Then he teased her mouth in a series of slow, drugging near-kisses that sent hunger zinging through her bloodstream, and her hands fisted in his shirt.

He pulled back, then reclaimed her mouth in the passion-filled kiss of her dreams.

The slide of his tongue against hers sent the pit of her stomach in a wild swirl, and her senses reeled.

She had never, ever been so thoroughly kissed.

But it ended too soon, and he rested his forehead on hers, their rapid breathing the only sound in the room.

"Katie's waiting," he said hoarsely. "And I need to shower."

The big clock on the wall ticked away the seconds until Jake kissed the top of her head and stepped back. "I have to go now, or I never will."

Her knees wobbled, and she leaned against the counter as he walked away.

Sean's comment suddenly loomed to the forefront. How could he hold her, kiss her this way if his heart still belonged to his dead wife?

Chapter Nineteen

Jake lay propped against the headboard, the closed book resting in his lap. Katie fell asleep soon after he began reading. As he watched her now, he rubbed the heel of his palm over his heart where a sudden ache appeared. *I should have come home sooner.*

As he stared at the sleeping child, the riotous curls so much like Mary's, the past came rushing back.

To this day, he easily recalled the doctor's shocking words. "Your wife made it through surgery but remains in critical condition. We'll do our best, but we may not be able to save the child."

What? Was Mary pregnant?

Shock soon turned to delight, for he desperately wanted a child. But in the hours that followed, questions mounted. Why didn't she tell him? Did she know when she moved into the guest room? When she asked for a divorce?

Later that evening, the doctor estimated Mary was about twenty weeks along. Jake carefully hid his astonishment and mentally backtracked to the last time they made love, discovering a heartbreaking possibility.

The child may—or may not be his.

Questions without answers tortured him, but he kept her infidelity a secret. This was between them, and they would discuss it when she woke up.

Besides, blame was a two-way street, and he accepted his part.

But that didn't make her betrayal any less hurtful.

Days rolled into weeks as he divided his time between caring for the ranch and keeping a bedside vigil. At first, he just sat there, too hurt and stunned to speak. Slowly, he began talking about their life together, the good times, and the love they shared. He mentioned the child she carried, promising he would do the right thing despite the hurt eating away at his soul.

Doctors kept her sedated to alleviate some of the strain on her body. The first time they tried to stop it, a seizure resulted, halting the procedure. It was weeks before the next attempt. This time, they performed the process over several days and closely monitored her condition. After three days, she roused enough to briefly open her eyes before drifting off to sleep.

He never left her side, whispering words of love and vowed to do everything he could to make things right between them again. Finally, exhaustion claimed him, and he slept with his head on the bed near her hand.

Her soft moan woke him at dawn.

"Mary," he pleaded and rang for the nurse. "Sweetheart. Wake up."

Her face twitched as she struggled to open her eyes.

"That's my girl. Come on, baby, wake up."

He ignored the two nurses who rushed in. "Mary, please...wake up."

She turned toward his voice, eyes mere slits. "...Jake?"

Her ragged whisper was music to his ears.

"I'm here, baby. I'm here."

She lifted a hand toward him, and he grasped it, shocked by the coldness. "I'm here, baby."

Suddenly, alarms and rapid beeps exploded from the machines attached to her body.

"Mr. Holloway," a nurse snapped. "Please step back."

Terrified, he moved to the foot of the bed. "What's happening? Mary? Mary!"

She turned her head toward his voice and exhaled. "...J-Ja..."

More medical personnel pushed him aside as they charged in. He heard someone say they must take the baby now or risk losing them both.

Helpless, he watched them wheel her away, then numbly followed the aide to the waiting room. He called his parents and frantically paced around the small space until they arrived, Donna at their side.

His mother hurried toward him, her face pale, her voice strained. "How is she?"

He scrubbed his face with both hands. "I don't know. No one has said anything since they took her back."

Aggie and Donna stood on either side, hands gripping his forearms. "We're here for you, son," Aggie whispered.

"Always," Donna added, then lay her head on his upper arm.

His father stood to the side, face etched with concern, and cleared his throat. "Hang in there, son."

The doctor's sudden appearance, coupled with his grim expression, robbed Jake of speech. Adrenaline surged, and his heart raced as he waited for him to speak.

The doctor's jaw clenched and released once, and he sucked in a breath. "Your daughter weighs three pounds and ten ounces, which means our estimate on your wife's pregnancy was probably off a week or two, which is good. She'll still be in the NIC unit for some time, though."

"My wife?" Even as he asked, he knew.

"...I'm sorry."

The words hit Jake like a physical blow to his chest, and he staggered. "What happened?"

"Her blood pressure spiked, causing a massive stroke. There was nothing we could do."

His mother began to weep, and his father pulled her against him.

Silent tears streamed down Donna's cheeks as she clung to his arm.

Mary's unexpected death robbed him of answers and left him with a delicate child to raise alone. His promise to do the right thing mocked him now because he had no choice but to assume the role thrust upon him.

Thoughts raced through his mind all at once. Did Mary's lover know about the child or suspect he may be the father? And if so, what then? A paternity test would answer the question but tarnish Mary's memory and subject him to pity. He couldn't deal with either option. As time passed, he simply chose not to think about it. Self-preservation created a wall around his heart that lately began to weaken.

Katie mewed softly in her sleep, and the sound yanked him away from the dark abyss of uncertainty dogging his every breath.

He gazed at the angelic face, one hand fisted under her chin and something twisted inside. He'd spent the last four years focused on protecting his battered heart. He gave Katie everything—but himself. He looked but didn't see her. He provided for her but didn't show he cared.

No wonder she shied away from people. From him.

He ran a knuckle across her petal-soft cheek. So innocent. So trusting.

Sorrow mixed with shame brought a rush of heat to his face. When her mouth curled up in a tiny smile, guilt overwhelmed him. He was a shitty excuse for a man. And a father. But he could—and would do better than this.

Sean's unexpected return should be good news. They'd grown up together. When they were sophomores, he introduced him to Mary, who was new in town, and the three of them remained friends. He left town shortly after Mary's accident without a word to Jake.

He sat up straight in bed. Just how close were they?

⸻◈⸻

Lexie peeked around the doorframe as Jake gently touched Katie's cheek. The act was so tender, so loving that tears stung her eyes. Suddenly, feeling like an intruder, she backed away and hobbled to the kitchen.

But seeing the special father-daughter moment gave her more insight into the real Jake Holloway, and her chaotic emotions multiplied. Something about him called to her, but she needed distance for clarity. And there was still Sean's question to address.

Her shoulders drew up sharply, and she made a decision. "Dinner at the table," she muttered, then moved everything to the dining table instead of the breakfast bar, adding a place setting for herself across from his. On a whim, she added a bottle of wine she found in the pantry and two glasses.

She never liked eating alone. Even when she and Rodney were dating, she often found herself alone at mealtime while he worked late or networked. When they did share a meal, it was usually a work-related function. Even on those rare occasions when she cooked for them, talk centered on work and Rodney's desire to move up in the corporate world.

In hindsight, she saw what Bobby had from the first. Rodney was using her.

She shook her head to banish the past from affecting her future. Tonight was too important.

When Jake entered a few minutes later, her first thought was he made barefoot, wearing sweats and a tee shirt, look sexy.

Then she saw the scowl on his face and instantly knew something bothered him. He stopped at the bar, then noticed her in the dining room. The frown deepened, and suddenly, she questioned her actions.

She nervously placed the bowl of gravy on the table and faced him. "I hope you don't mind." She waved a hand casually at the table. "After such a long day, I thought this would be more comfortable than the bar."

He noted the two place settings and glanced her way.

One shoulder lifted slightly and fell. "I don't like eating alone."

He walked around the table and stopped in front of her. The soft smile on his face didn't quite reach his eyes, and the notion that something troubled him grew.

He has only one love.

She concentrated on him as he gently tilted her chin with one finger. "I don't understand."

"What?" she whispered, savoring the rush of desire his touch caused. "What don't you understand?"

"How you always seem to know just what I need." His hands dropped to her waist and gently pulled her forward. He hesitated, then brushed a tender kiss on her forehead. "Thank you," he whispered.

The heartfelt tenderness of his words sent a quiver through her body. "My pleasure."

He stepped aside, held her chair as she sat, and took his place across from her. "You went to a lot of trouble." He glanced up and smiled. "Thank you."

"You're welcome. Since Aggie had the meat thawing in the fridge, I assumed chicken fried steak would be okay."

"My favorite." He placed a steak on his plate and added potatoes and gravy. "Biscuits, too," he said as he slathered one with butter. "I'm impressed."

"Thank you." She fixed her plate, still wondering about what troubled him. Even though he sounded chipper, his eyes told a different story.

He has one love.

Was that it? His one love? His actions told a different story.

She couldn't let it go.

"Is everything all right, Jake?" she asked softly.

He stopped chewing, eyes fixed on her, then swallowed. "Why do you ask?"

She took a deep breath. "It's...you seem—never mind. It's none of my business."

He gazed at his plate without moving for so long Lexie regretted her habit of asking too many questions.

When he finally looked up, his whole demeanor changed. He sagged in his chair, shoulders drooped, and he looked dazed.

Her concern escalated. "Jake?"

"I can't do this anymore."

Chapter Twenty

Jake had no idea where that comment came from. He'd spoken without thought, and judging by the wounded look on Lexie's face, it was the wrong thing to say.

He shook his head. "I didn't mean that the way it sounded."

She folded her hands in her lap. "Okay. What did you mean?"

As he watched her now, the expression on her face altering with her thoughts, it suddenly occurred to him that having someone in whom to confide might help. Would she understand? Pity him? Think less of him?

Lexie leaned forward, eyes projecting compassion and understanding. "I'm a good listener, Jake. And I don't judge." She sat back and picked up her fork. "When—*if* you want to talk about whatever is troubling you, I'm here."

He knew honesty was a must for their budding relationship to succeed. But he'd kept his secret for a long time. Could he share it with anyone? Even Lexie? He hoped so. He wanted to. "It's a long story," he said softly, "and will take a while to explain." He gave her what he hoped was a reassuring smile. "Let's enjoy this delicious meal you've prepared, and we'll talk after."

"...Okay." She picked up her fork. "You had a long day today. Did you finish everything you needed to?"

And just like that, his whole body relaxed, and his burden became lighter. A few simple words from her changed the atmosphere to relaxed and friendly.

"I did." He picked up the wine. "I hope it's good," he said as he pulled the cork. "Donna left it last month when she stayed with Katie one weekend when I had to deliver some horses in central Texas."

"Do you have to do that often?"

"Not often, but it happens."

Glasses in hand, he hesitated, then lifted his toward her. "To better things to come."

"To better things."

For the first time in years, his life didn't feel so empty. He tucked the knowledge she'd be gone soon in a darkened corner of his mind. Tonight, he would enjoy feeling normal. He no longer questioned her ability to change things around her with words, a soft touch, or a smile. It was a gift he readily accepted.

Conversation came easy with her, and they chatted like old friends about everything. He marveled at how Biscuit instinctively herded cattle, progressing to how he raised and trained horses. Lexie was especially interested in the Longhorns and seemed delighted when he said he raised them because he loved the breed.

"Katie was so excited when she got to pet Dolly." Lexie's face lit with an inner joy that showed in her voice. "I think the horns made her a little afraid at first. But I held her when Dolly approached the gate, and she patted her head."

"Dolly's a sweetheart," said Jake with a smile. "She was the first Longhorn born on the ranch. I had to bottle-feed her when the mother rejected her, so she's accustomed to being around people."

"Rejected her?"

"Yeah, it happens from time to time. Sometimes, it's because she's a first-time mother and doesn't know what to do, as in Dolly's case."

Lexie nodded. "She was very friendly. And when the calf hobbled up to Dolly, I let Katie pet her, too."

Her light laugh filled the aching void in his world. He wasn't alone. He had someone to share a meal with, to share his thoughts—to care.

How many silent, solitary meals had he endured? The thought of losing this connection almost as soon as he found it made his heart twist in pain. He shook off the encroaching melancholy and focused on her voice.

"Of course, the calf didn't say put long and staggered away, but Katie got to pet her."

"Thank you for doing that." He pushed his empty plate aside. "I guess I was overly concerned about her getting hurt. It never occurred to me she might enjoy it."

"I think kids naturally love animals of any kind."

He picked up his wine and sat back in his chair. "I can't help but notice I've been doing all the talking." He nodded toward her. "I know you like to fish and work for your father, but not much else. So, who is Lexie Morgan, and why is she not married?"

———◈———

His question caught her off-guard, and she faltered. Where to start? But she hated to put a damper on their evening with tales of being dumped at the altar. And her decision to head for the cabin tomorrow would be the icing on the crap cake.

Jake's smile disappeared at her hesitation, and he sat forward in his chair. "I'm sorry if that's a sensitive topic. I just—"

"I was engaged." She sat up, flattened her hands on the table, and met his gaze. Hurt and embarrassment tinged her cheeks with heat. Her heart raced, and she lowered her head. "He..." Avoiding his gaze, she twirled the wine glass on the table. "I was the proverbial left-at-the-altar bride."

"I'm sorry. I know that hurt you."

It surprised her to discover the situation was more embarrassing than painful this time. "He sent my mother a text." She cleared her throat. "I had told him the night before I might be pregnant. I wasn't, but..." Her short laugh held no humor. "Seems Bobby was right about him. I wanted a family—he wanted a way up the corporate ladder."

He reached across the table and placed his big hand over her smaller one. "He didn't deserve you," he said softly. "Not if he could walk away so easily."

The warmth from his hand coursed through her. Tension evaporated, and past hurts vanished. And she knew that, no matter what, she could not return to her lonely, mundane existence. In her heart, she knew she belonged here—with Jake and Katie. But how to be sure? Everything happened so fast. And the thing Sean said couldn't be ignored. *He only had one love in his life.*

She shook away the troubling doubts. "Thank you for saying that." She shrugged. "Looking back—well, he did me a favor."

His sexy smile made her stomach flip as he released her hand and picked up the wine glass. "I'm guessing *The Swear Jar* got a workout."

She grinned. "Mom's idea." Her smile grew. "The one I have now is much smaller."

On more pleasant footing, she smiled at him. "Aside from *the event*, as Mom called that little debacle, I've lived a boring life. I work long hours and travel often, so there hasn't been time for anything else." She looked up. "What about you? Anyone special in your life?"

The minute the question left her mouth, she regretted it. "I'm sorry. That's none—"

"I haven't been with anyone in a long time." He took a breath, his piercing gaze fixed on her. "I'm hoping that will change."

"Me, too." Her crazy heart did another little roll, and she knew the time had come. Heart pounding, she tried to find the right words. "I'd like—"

Jake stood and picked up his plate. "How about we clear the table and continue this in the den."

Biscuit rose from his spot by Lexie and barked once as headlights from an approaching vehicle flashed against the wall.

Jake set the plate down. "Don't start without me." He looked down at shoeless feet. "I'm not putting on boots to answer the door. Be back in a flash."

Lexie snapped her fingers, and Biscuit lay down at her feet. "Good boy," she said and lightly rubbed his ears. "Oh, man," she said softly. "I hope I know what I'm doing."

She groaned when a familiar voice drifted in from the front door. "Son of a nutcracker. Why now?"

Chapter Twenty-One

The timing of the unexpected visit from her parents could not have been worse. His nearness and comfortable conversation distracted her to the point that she forgot to mention her mother's earlier text. Only the text said they'd be here tomorrow, not tonight.

She rounded the corner as her mother introduced herself.

"I do apologize for the unexpected visit, young man. I am Rose Morgan, and this is my husband, Henry. Of course, you know Bobby."

"I'm happy to meet you both." Jake stood aside, motioned them in, and closed the door behind them. "And no apologies are needed."

Her mother stepped inside, hands clasped in front, her father behind, one arm around her waist, their expressions open and friendly.

When her mother spotted her, she hurried forward and grabbed her in a fierce mother hug. "Alexa, sweetheart. Are you all right?"

She frowned at Bobby.

"Hey, I told them you were fine."

Rose Morgan stepped back, surveyed her head to toe, and inhaled deeply. "Are you? All right, I mean. What happened? What's that on your foot? Where else are you hurt?"

Henry Morgan moved to his wife's side, his features creased with concern. "Rosie," he said softly, "give her a chance to talk."

"I left you a voicemail, Mom." She sighed. "And an email."

"I got the messages, dear, and talked with Bobby." The pointed look she gave him made Bobby duck his head. "Your brother was very evasive with his answers."

"I said she was fine and staying with a friend," he muttered without looking up.

"She's using a crutch, and what's that thing on her foot?" Without waiting for a reply, Rose turned an appreciative smile on Jake. "I apologize again for barging in so late, but after talking with Bobby again, I had to see for myself. We are so thankful you were there for our girl."

"No problem, Mrs. Morgan. I'm glad I was there, too." He motioned toward the den. "Please, come in and sit down. It's more comfortable there, and Lexie needs to elevate her foot." He didn't wait for a reply as he took the crutch, put his arm around Lexie, and turned for the den.

She saw her mother's eyebrows jerk upward as Jake ushered her into his chair.

He grabbed a pillow off the couch and gently placed it under her foot.

"I'm not helpless, you know," she snipped. "And Donna said I didn't need to elevate it unless the swelling returns."

"No, you're not helpless, but you are prone to knit sweaters when no one is watching." He stood and smiled. "And you've been knitting all day."

"I didn't know you knitted, dear," said Rose as she lowered

herself to the couch. "When did you start?"

She rolled her eyes at Jake. "It's a joke, Mom. I don't knit." She scowled at Jake. "Thank you."

He dared to grin before facing her parents. "Excuse my bare feet. We had a late supper. Can I get you something to drink? Tea? Coffee? Something stronger?"

"No, thank you, Jake," said Rose. "We're fine. And we won't stay long."

He nodded and spoke to Lexie. "I'll do the dishes while you visit."

"I have to see this," teased Bobby, "so I'll go watch. Dad, let me know when y'all are ready to go."

As Bobby and Jake walked out, Lexie faced her mother. "How was New York? Did you enjoy the play you wanted to see?"

"New York was wonderful as always, and yes, I saw the play. Jake seems very attentive."

Her quick change in subject matter rattled Lexie. "Yes, well..." She couldn't think of anything else to say.

"And why did he call you Lexie?" Rose asked as she smoothed her skirt.

Nervous, Lexie rubbed both hands on her thighs. "Andy has called me that for years. I kinda like it."

"You've always been Alex," argued her father. "Why the sudden change?"

How could she explain something to them she didn't fully understand herself? The need to refocus her life and goals grew daily; the name was just the beginning. She hoped.

"Ever since...*the event*," she emphasized her mother's term for the failed wedding fiasco, "I've been, I don't know, in limbo.

Things needed to change—so I started with something simple. Like my name." Thinking about all the other changes she hoped to initiate made her heart jump. Would her father understand and support her wishes? Did she even know what she wished for? She shoved the doubts away and smiled at her mother. "And I like Lexie."

Rose glanced at her husband seated beside her on the couch, then back to her. "Bobby thinks quite a lot of him. Jake, I mean."

"Yes. They're close friends."

"You two appear very comfortable with each other," observed her father, "for so short an acquaintance."

Heat raced up her neck. Her father was very perceptive. "Yes, well...yes." What else could she say? It was the truth.

"His home is lovely," said Rose. "Does he live here alone?"

"No, he has a daughter, Katie. She's four." Happy with the change in topic, she continued. "Oh, Mom, she is so precious. I'd love for you to meet her. Maybe tomorrow since she's already asleep. You are staying the night, aren't you? You could meet her and see the ranch. And he has Longhorns."

"Really?" asked Henry. "Longhorn cattle?"

"Yes. About a dozen now since Dolly had a calf earlier today."

Rose and Henry exchanged one of their *special* glances that spoke volumes only to them. She was a teenager the first time she noticed these silent exchanges. It was uncanny how attuned they were and always seemed to know what the other was thinking.

"So," began her mother, "will you continue to stay here or move to the cabin as planned?"

Before she could answer, Katie walked in, dragging her stuffed bear by the arm, and shuffled to where Lexie sat. "Sweetheart? Are you all right?"

"I waked up."

The little bun she insisted on before bed now leaned to one side, curly strands framing her face. "I'm sorry if we woke you." She nodded toward her parents. "This is my father and mother, Mr. Henry and Miss Rose. Can you say hello?"

Katie stared for a moment, then, to Lexie's surprise, she smiled. "Heh-wo."

"Hello, dear," gushed Rose. "How pretty you are."

"Yes, she is," said Henry.

"Say 'thank you,' sweetie."

"Tank you." She turned to Lexie. "You tuck me in?"

"Katie," Jake's soft voice made the child jump when he came up behind her and placed one hand on her shoulder. "What are you doing up?" he asked softly.

She glanced his way. "I waked up."

"I can see that." He gently turned her back toward her room. "Let's get you back to bed. Miss Lexie has company right now."

"Can Wexie tuck me in?"

"I—"

"Go ahead, dear," said Rose softly. "Tuck the child in. We'll wait."

She peeked at Jake, who seemed undecided, and then he shrugged. "She'd rather you did anyway."

"Okay." As soon as she moved to lower the footrest, Jake held her leg and took the pillow before gently placing her foot on the floor. "Do you want the crutch?"

"No, it's not far, and I'm getting the hang of this boot." She clasped the hand he extended and tried not to react to the warmth of his other hand on her waist as she steadied herself, then reached out to the child. "Come along, Katie-girl," she said. "Let's get you back to bed." She paused, then looked down at her. "Can you say goodnight?"

Katie yawned, and her gaze drifted from Bobby to her parents before she gifted them with a tiny smile. "Nite."

"Goodnight, sweetheart," cooed Rose. "Pleasant dreams."

"Goodnight, Katie," said Henry. "It was very nice to meet you."

"Sleep tight, Lil Bit," said Bobby.

Lexie looked at Jake. His surprised expression made her wonder what she missed. "Coming?"

"Go ahead. I'll keep our guests company."

She took Katie's hand and started down the hall, accompanied by the warmth of Jake's gaze.

And the knowledge that he said *our* guests.

———◦———

Biscuit's soft whine drew Jake's attention from the sight of Lexie holding Katie's hand as they slowly made their way down the hall. The dog looked at the retreating figures and back to Jake. "Go on," he said softly.

Biscuit quickly caught up with the pair, and Katie stopped to hug him, then looked at Jake and smiled. His heart took that funny little stutter-step again, and he smiled back.

Once again, Lexie's influence on Katie was evident in the tentative smile she gave the Morgans when she bid them goodnight. She became a different child around her, and he liked the change.

Maybe too much.

The thought of Lexie leaving soon put an odd ache in his heart. *I'll deal with that when the time comes.*

"Man, she really took to Alex, uh, I mean Lexie," said Bobby from behind him. "I've never seen her so—happy."

Still smiling, Jake turned and faced the Morgans, who watched him closely. "Yeah. She likes her."

"She's a tiny little thing," said Rose. "How old is she?"

"Four," said Jake. "A little small for her age." He hesitated, then continued. "She was born early."

"Oh, dear," said Rose, as her face flushed. "I didn't mean that in a critical way at all. I just meant she's petite. And simply adorable." She took a breath. "Alexa was that way, too. Tiny, I mean."

"She grew out of that," snorted Bobby.

"There's nothing wrong with her size," snipped Jake.

"I didn't say there was."

Bobby's grin made Jake bite down hard to avoid responding to the taunt.

"Alex—I mean, Lexie tells me you have Longhorns," said Henry.

"A dozen as of this afternoon."

"A fascinating breed," said Henry.

Jake nodded as he sat in the other recliner. "I got my first pair eight years ago and was hooked."

"What do you do with them?" Henry leaned forward. "I mean, do you sell them, breed them?"

"I've sold a few over the years, but mainly, I like having them." He smiled at Henry. "What's a Texas ranch without Longhorns?"

"I've been all around the state," sighed Henry. "And I've never seen one up close."

"Dolly's in the barn with her calf if you have time to see her."

Henry looked at his wife, who smiled and patted his knee. "Go along, dear. I know how much you'd love to see her."

Jake stood and looked at Bobby. "Coming?"

"Y'all go ahead. I'll keep Mom company."

"I won't be long," said Henry.

Jake started for the kitchen, then stopped. "Are you sure I can't get you something to drink or maybe a snack, Mrs. Morgan?"

"Please. Call me Rose. And no, thank you, Jake. I'm fine."

Henry's excited questions continued as he stopped at the back door to slip on his boots and strode toward the barn. "I read somewhere there is more than one breed."

"Actually, there are five. I have the original Texas Longhorn variety," said Jake proudly. "It's the parent breed of the other four."

"Are they beef cattle?"

"You can eat them. And milk them, too, but I don't. I guess you could say I raise pets."

They entered the well-maintained structure, and Henry nodded approval. "Very nice barn, young man."

"Thank you. Dolly is down here on the right."

As they approached the stall, Dolly sauntered over for Jake to scratch her head.

"My goodness," murmured Henry. "Those horns are massive."

"Six and a half feet tip to tip. I have a bull who measures just over eight."

Henry cautiously stuck his hand through the slats to pet the cow. "She's very gentle. And, aside from the horns, not as big as I expected."

"They're peaceful and calm by nature and typically range from six to twelve hundred pounds. I bottle-fed Dolly, so she's especially comfortable around people." He stepped back so Henry could look closer at the calf as she approached.

"My daughter doesn't trust easily." Henry didn't glance around as he spoke. "Yet, she seems especially relaxed around you."

The out-of-the-blue comment surprised Jake, and he didn't immediately respond.

"And your little girl, who is adorable, seems quite taken with her."

Jake fumbled for words. "Yes, well...Lexie is special."

"Yes, she is." Henry paused. "I knew the moment I met my Rosie that she was the one for me." He paused, gave Dolly a final pat, and turned around. "Well, we best get back. It's been a long day."

He walked out of the barn, leaving a confused Jake to follow.

Chapter Twenty-Two

Lexie declined Bobby's offer to help as she sat back in the chair and slowly reclined. The throbbing in her ankle told her the swelling had returned, and it took a determined effort not to grimace, silently admitting she'd overdone it today.

"Is she asleep?" asked Rose.

"Yes. It didn't take long."

"And Biscuit is with her?"

"Mm-mm. They gravitated toward each other right away." She shifted in her chair. "I was covered in mud, and I guess she was scared. Anyway, Biscuit seemed to calm her down." She shrugged. "Now, he sleeps in her room."

"And Jake doesn't mind?"

"No, he likes Biscuit. Even takes him out on the ranch with him."

"Jake took your dog out?" Bobby's widened eyes conveyed his surprise.

She shrugged. "He seems to think Biscuit's a country dog at heart." She smiled. "I'm beginning to agree."

"What about you?" snickered Bobby. "Are you a country girl at heart?"

"What's that thing on your foot?" Rose's question, whether

intentional or accidental, saved her from a reply. "Are you sure you're all right?"

"I'm fine, Mom. I promise. It's just a sprain." She gently moved her injured foot. "It's called a walking boot. Jake's sister is a nurse practitioner and brought it by today." She sighed. "It makes getting around easier than the crutches."

"As long as you stay off it," added Bobby. "Which apparently, you have issues doing."

"I can't sit here all day twiddling my thumbs."

"So, you took up knitting, huh?"

She puffed out her cheeks and blew. "Don't start."

Silent, he held up both hands in an I-give-up gesture.

"Katie seems quite taken with you."

Rose's comment was unexpected, but Lexie quickly recovered. "She's such a sweetheart, Mom. It's hard not to love her."

"What about her father?" taunted Bobby.

Rose silenced her son with *the look*. "What your brother is trying to say, unsuccessfully, I might add, is one would think you'd known each other longer than just a few days."

Lexie avoided her mother's intense gaze. "We...get along."

Bobby's impertinent snort drew a scowl from her. "We..."

"You what, dear?" Rose leaned forward slightly.

"Get along."

"You already said that," goaded Bobby.

"Robert Earl." Rose's soft rebuke hushed him, and she turned to Lexie. "How long will you have to wear the boot? What about your other injuries?"

It took only a few minutes to update them on her progress. "So, you can see things aren't so bad, and I should return to normal within a week."

"I am glad to hear that, dear. Your father and I were so worried."

"I know, Mom. I'm sorry I troubled you and caused you to make the drive so soon after getting back from New York."

She waved away Lexie's concern. "We haven't seen Bobby and Tina in weeks, so we decided at the last minute to come this evening." She blinked a couple of times, then splayed one hand over her chest. "Jake being there was a Godsend." She paused, and a smile brightened her face. "I remember when—" She stopped speaking when Henry and Jake walked in.

"Rosie dear," said Henry, his step lively as he walked toward her on the couch. "It's getting late. I think it's time we left these folks alone." He extended a hand to assist her up.

Surely they aren't driving back tonight.

Before she voiced that thought, Jake spoke up.

"It's too late to drive back tonight. Why don't y'all spend the night? We have plenty of room, and I'm sure you'd like to visit longer."

Lexie's surprise doubled when he voiced her thoughts and said *we have room*. Were they a 'we'? Her heart skipped at the possibility. "He's right, Mom. It will be so late when you get back."

"Thank you, Jake," said Rose at last. "But we're staying with Bobby tonight." Her face brightened. "But, if you don't mind, maybe we can return tomorrow for a proper visit."

Jake grinned. "Absolutely," he insisted. "We'd love to have you."

"Good," said Lexie. "You and Dad can see how beautiful it is here and get a better look at the rest of Jake's Longhorns."

"I'd love to show you around the place," said Jake. "If it won't mess up your plans."

"We have no particular plans," said Henry. "Rosie wants to visit some antique stores in town, and we'll do that on the way out."

"By the way, Dad, I'm set to follow up on the Marshall project next week as planned," said Lexie. "I talked with Craig earlier to let him know."

"That can wait," Henry said firmly. "Or better yet, I'll have Andy do it. Take care of yourself first." He gave her shoulder a fatherly squeeze, then shook a finger in her face. "You're on vacation. No business at all. I mean it."

"We'll see," said Lexie as she started to rise.

He pressed down on her shoulder. "No, no, dear, don't get up. Jake can see us out." He bent down and placed a kiss on the top of her head. "Thank God you are all right." He glanced up at Jake. "And have someone around to look after you."

She opened her mouth to say she didn't need looking after, but her mother leaned down and whispered, "God works in mysterious ways." Then, she kissed her daughter's cheek and linked arms with her husband. "Goodnight, Jake. Thank you again for taking care of our girl."

"My pleasure, Rose."

Bobby led the way out, followed by her parents.

"I'll be right back," said Jake as he followed the trio to the door.

Their goodbyes drifted down the hall as her mind mulled over her mother's parting words: *God works in mysterious ways.*

———◈———

Jake waited until their car started down the lane before returning inside, mulling over their sudden appearance and departure.

He understood their desire to ensure their daughter's safety, but it was like they took one look around and decided all was right with the world.

Okay, so maybe he felt that way, but it didn't explain their reaction. Or Bobby's, who seemed to think the whole thing was funny.

Determined to put that aside tonight, he returned to the den and found Lexie sitting on the couch, her foot on the coffee table. He lifted one brow in a silent question.

"I was tired of the chair. Besides, it's yours."

"There are two chairs. And I conveyed it to you for the duration."

"Well, I'm giving it back."

"What if I don't want it back?" He took a step forward. "What if I wanted to sit on the couch?"

"Well," she murmured, her steady gaze locked on his. "Maybe we could...you know, share it."

His heart thudded as he closed the distance between them and gingerly sat beside her. Their gazes held a heartbeat before he slowly raised his left arm to rest on the back of the couch.

She let out a slow breath and relaxed against him.

Silent seconds ticked away.

He lowered his arm to support the back of her neck, and she moved closer to him.

He cleared his throat. "Your parents are great."

"Yeah, they are."

Out of his comfort zone, Jake didn't know how to resurrect the comfortable atmosphere of earlier. "Any trouble getting Katie down?"

"No, she fell asleep pretty quick."

He racked his brain for something to put off the conversation he knew needed to take place because it would certainly be a mood killer. "How's the foot?" he finally asked.

He caught a slight pause before she replied.

"A bit sore, but not too bad."

"You overdid it today, didn't you?"

Again, that pause before she answered. "Maybe a little. It's better since I'm off it." She paused. "But I think I'll wrap it tonight."

"Can I get you anything?"

She shook her head, and a strained silence followed.

"About what we discussed earlier." She drew a quick breath. "I should move to the cabin tomorrow after my folks leave."

The statement wasn't unexpected, but it did surprise him, given her response to his kisses. He removed his arm from the back of the couch. "I see."

She turned to face him, tears clouding her eyes. "Please. Hear me out." She clasped her hands tightly in her lap, and her voice shook when she spoke. "I'm doing this all wrong." She inhaled deeply, never taking her eyes off his. "From the first moment I saw you, I felt something—powerful. I can't name it, but it's there."

Silent, he waited for her to continue.

"Donna said—"

Body tense, he sat up straight. "Donna? She said you had to leave?"

"No, no...not exactly."

"What exactly did she say?" Anger at her interference made his voice hard as stone.

"I'm messing this up. I knew I would." She rubbed a finger

against each temple and blew out a puff of air. "This—this feeling is intense." She lowered her hands and clasped them together again. "And I think—I hope you feel something for me, too."

He sensed she waited for him to speak, but all his brain processed was *she's leaving me*.

"But I can't think straight around you."

"And running away will help—what? Decide how you feel about me?"

She looked down at her hands, then back to him. "Can you say with one hundred percent certainty, right here, right now, how you feel about me? About us?"

Her face clouded with worry when he didn't reply right away. How could he? He had more questions than answers. Maybe she was right, though. Maybe they needed distance. But damn it all, how could they find out if they were apart?

"My point exactly," she said softly.

Her comment pulled him back to the moment. "I know I care about you," he said at last, his heart thudding painfully against his chest. "I know when I'm around you, the world seems right again." He unclenched her hands and linked one with his. "And Katie adores you."

"And I adore her." She examined their linked hands. "When you look at me, I get lost." She shifted on the couch before meeting his gaze. "Is it a purely physical reaction? Maybe, but I can't be sure. And it's too important to take lightly."

"I see."

"Do you, Jake?" Her voice was barely audible when she continued. "You lost your wife. You've been alone since then." Her lips quivered, and her eyes glistened. "Maybe because you still love her." She took a shaky breath. "We both need to be certain about what we feel. And clear about what we want."

"I know I want you. Here. With me." His voice cracked with emotion. "I've never felt this way before. About anyone."

She chewed her lower lip and tilted her head as though considering his words.

"What about Katie?" He hated himself for playing the sympathy card, but he was desperate. "She'll miss you."

"I can watch her at the cabin."

"Your mind's made up then?"

Azure eyes shimmered as she faced him. "It has to be this way, Jake." She swallowed hard. "At least for now."

Resigned, he slowly stood, his body coiled so tight he could barely move. "Okay," he whispered. "I'll give you your space. Goodnight."

He thought he heard a muffled sob as he turned and walked away.

CHAPTER TWENTY-THREE

Lexie woke from a restless night of little sleep, Jake's tortured expression when he walked out foremost in her mind. Did she do the right thing? Her brain shouted "Yes," but her heart screamed "No."

Dejected, she rose early and hobbled to the kitchen, rolling her bag behind her, determined to follow the plan.

After hesitating, she started the coffee pot and quickly put a pan of biscuits in the oven. While they baked, she took her coffee cup to the porch and stood at the railing, staring at the eastern sky, still dark since dawn was over an hour away.

"The darkest hour is just before dawn," she murmured. "Is that an analogy for my life now?"

"You're up early."

Jake's unexpected voice from the other end of the porch startled her, and coffee sloshed on her hand. "Dammit."

"Sorry," he said as he moved forward. "Didn't mean to scare you."

She swiped her wet hand against her jeans. "Well, you did."

He stopped beside her and nodded at the cup. "Any more of that?"

"In the kitchen."

"Can I refill yours?"

"I'm good." She moved to the rocker she preferred and sat down.

When he returned, he silently passed her a quarter, no doubt for the *Swear Jar,* and took the chair beside her.

She tucked the money in her pocket. "Thank you."

The extended quiet was broken only by the creak of the rockers on the wooden floor.

"I'm sorry about last night," Jake said at last, tapping the rim of his cup with one finger. "I shouldn't have left like that."

"It's okay."

"No. It isn't." He leaned back and sighed. "If it's any comfort to you, I didn't sleep much."

"Neither did I."

Lexie finally broke the uneasy quiet. "I better check the biscuits."

Silent, he let her pass.

She placed the biscuits in the warmer, then picked up the bacon she'd left on the counter, conscious of his presence when he stopped behind her.

"I can't do this, Lexie," he whispered, his strong hands gently caressing her upper arms.

"D-do wh-what?"

His warm breath brushed her ear. "Be this close and not touch you," he whispered.

Unable to stop herself, she leaned back into his chest.

"Or kiss you."

She trembled as his lips trailed down her neck, then back up to her ear before he gently turned her to face him.

"Lexie," he whispered, then crushed her to him, his hungry mouth covering hers, his lips punishing yet thrilling as desire shot through her body.

His hands raked up and down her back, then anchored her hips against his, and a soft growl rumbled deep in his chest.

At last, he broke the kiss and leaned his forehead against hers, his breath coming in sharp, ragged gasps. Slowly, he gathered her into his arms, holding her snugly against him. "We never got to finish our talk last night," he murmured, then pulled back enough to see her face. "And I think we need to before going forward with—whatever this is."

She blinked him into focus. "Okay."

"But not now." He closed his eyes briefly. "Katie will be up soon, and your folks will be here after that. And I don't want to rush it."

Once again, Sean's words found their way into her brain. The fact he desired her was not in question. But would he ever love her? Would she be satisfied with only a part of him? She shook away the doubt and tried to smile. "I agree."

She watched his expression alter with his thoughts and prayed she wasn't making a mistake. "I'll take Katie to the cabin today after my folks leave. She can help me settle in."

When he didn't say anything, she continued. "We'll come back when it's time for her nap. That way, I can fix supper, and we can talk after she goes to bed."

His gaze narrowed. "Or," he said softly, "I can see if Mother will keep her tonight."

Jake parked the ATV behind the barn, and he and Henry stepped out.

"You have a beautiful place here, Jake," said Henry. "Thank you for the tour this morning, though I'm sure you had other things to do. A ranch of this size takes a lot of work."

"It does. But I enjoy it."

"And you're a single father. That's a lot of responsibility for one person."

Jake stopped and faced him. "My wife died when Katie was born."

"I'm sorry. I didn't know."

He shrugged. "I have two ranch hands who help out as needed. Any other questions?"

Henry paused and fixed dark eyes on Jake. "Alex, I mean, Lexie seems to be very content here. With you."

Jake didn't believe in beating around the bush and got to the point. "I hope she likes it enough to stay, sir."

"Do you, now?"

"Yes. I do."

"Have you discussed that with her?"

"Working on that part."

Henry looked to where two colts played chase in the field before them. "She's been hurt. She's vulnerable."

"She told me."

He jerked his gaze back to Jake. "She told you about—him?"

He nodded. "And *the event.*"

Henry's mouth opened and closed as he scratched his cheek. "That, too?"

Jake planted his feet in a wide stance, hands on his hips, then sucked in the scented air he thrived on. "I don't know how to explain this, Henry, but Lexie is—special to me. I know we just met, and the circumstances are—unusual, but—we just click." He shifted and shook his head. "I don't know where this will lead, but I aim to find out."

The cheerful sounds of birds singing and a gentle breeze settled around them as the two men studied each other.

Finally, Henry nodded slowly and walked toward the house. "I see."

Jake caught his arm as he passed. "That's all you have to say?"

Henry looked down at Jake's hand, then glanced up. "I'm the last person in the world to denounce immediate attraction." His chin lifted, and his gaze narrowed. "But, as a father yourself, you can understand I want what's best for my daughter. For her to be happy." His body relaxed, and he sighed softly. "Whether or not that happiness includes you and your little girl remains to be seen."

Jake didn't stop him again as he walked briskly toward the house.

Chapter Twenty-Four

Lexie's heart fluttered with happiness as she watched her mother and Katie at the bar, where the previously shy, reticent child happily worked on a big wooden jigsaw puzzle. Children gravitated toward Rose's affectionate nature, and Katie was no exception. Lexie experienced a momentary pang of sorrow over the lack of grandchildren for her to spoil.

Was that about to change?

"My goodness, Katie," gushed Rose. "You're really good at this."

Katie smiled and picked up another piece, then frowned.

"Hmmm...does it go here?" Rose pointed to the right spot. "See how the blue sky matches one side of the piece?"

Katie stared at the piece in her hand, then the spot Rose indicated, and snapped it into place. "Wook, Wexie, I making a puzzle."

"I can see that." She leaned over the bar and inspected the progress. "Only three more pieces, and you're done."

Katie's feet bounced against the bar as she quickly added the final sections. She looked at Rose and smiled. "Tank you. I wike puzzles."

Rose hugged Katie to her. "You are very welcome. I'll bring another the next time we visit."

Her comment surprised Lexie, for it implied Rose fully expected there to be a next time. Before she could respond, the back door opened, and Jake and Henry walked in, Biscuit following behind.

"Wook, Daddy." Katie pointed to the finished product. "Wexie's mommy gived me a puzzle. It's puppies, and I made it!"

Jake's surprised expression flitted between Rose and his daughter. "That was very nice of her." He stepped up to the bar to inspect her handiwork. "It's a great puzzle. Did you thank her?"

"Yes, sir."

"She's a precious child, Jake," said Rose. "I've enjoyed spending time with her."

"Thank you. She's a great kid."

Henry walked up beside Jake. "I believe that's the best puzzle I've ever seen."

Katie beamed as she looked at Henry, sneakered feet bouncing against the bar. "Tank you." Then she looked at Jake. "Wexie's mommy bing me a'nuver one when she comes back."

"Speaking of which," interjected Henry, "My Rosie and I should get going." He extended a hand to Jake. "Thanks again for the tour."

"But I wanted to show Rozy my room," pouted Katie.

Lexie glanced at Jake, whose face registered total surprise.

"Peeze, can I show her my room?"

"By all means," said Henry. "We must make time for that."

Without hesitation, Katie reached for Rose to help her down and took her hand. "Come on. I show you."

Lexie wasn't surprised at Katie's reaction to her mother, but one look at Jake's face said he was. When their eyes met, she smiled. "Mom has that effect on kids."

"My Rosie is something special," bragged Henry.

"Can I get you some coffee, Dad? Or maybe iced tea?"

"Tea would be great, sweetheart."

She looked at Jake, whose shocked gaze remained on the retreating figures. "How about you?"

He shook his head. "What? Oh, yeah, tea is fine." He moved to one of the barstools. "Any of that pound cake left?"

She served up the refreshments as the phone rang and glanced at Jake.

"You mind?"

She picked up the receiver. "Hello? Oh, hi...No, she's fine. Why do you ask... Oh, I see. Yes. I'll let him know. Okay. How's the water leak coming... Great. Thanks for calling." She hung up and looked at Jake. "That was Mrs. Tompkins from the daycare center. There's a virus going around, and three kids are sick. She wanted us to know in case Katie showed any signs of being ill. And the center should be open on Tuesday."

"A virus?"

"Yeah. Fever, upset stomach."

Jake sat up straight, one hand rubbing his thigh. "You said you thought she had a fever last night. Has she shown any signs today?"

"None at all. Which makes me think I imagined it. But I'll keep an eye on her anyway."

"Rosie called those things *daycare cooties*," offered Henry. "We enrolled Alexa in daycare when she was about Katie's age. The first two months, she was sick three times."

"Why?" asked Jake.

"Kids share germs. It's just part of growing up," said Henry. "I'm sure it's nothing to be worried about."

"Katie was premature." Jake's brow wrinkled, and uncertainty filled his voice. "She had a low resistance to infections for some time."

"Don't worry, Jake," said Lexie. "I'll keep a close eye on her. If she shows any signs of being ill, I'll call Donna right away."

He nodded, but Lexie saw his concern didn't ease.

She took the barstool beside her father and leaned over to speak to Jake. "Do you, by any chance, have a computer I could borrow? I can't find my laptop charger. I must have left it at home and wanted to look up some stuff online. Or I could use my phone, I guess."

"Feel free to use the computer in my office. Both it and the printer are older, but they work. There's no passcode since I'm the only one who uses it."

"Sure you don't mind?"

"Of course not."

"Remember what I said." Henry patted her arm. "Absolutely no work for two weeks. I've already contacted Andy about the Marshall project and told your secretary you are not to be disturbed." He picked up his iced tea. "You've earned the time off, Alexa. Enjoy it."

"I'll try, Dad, but you know I like to keep busy."

Jake speared a bite of cake. "There's a folder on the computer desktop labeled with Mary's name. She kept a bunch of games and stuff there. Maybe you can find some to occupy your time. Unless you don't want to go fishing after all."

She gave a theatrical sigh. "You drive a hard bargain, Mr. Holloway."

The next few minutes passed in friendly conversation as Henry and Jake discussed the pros and cons of different fishing gear.

"I still prefer a cane pole and a cork," said Jake.

"Me, too." Lexie grinned at her father. "Remember, Dad? That's what I caught that big grinnell on."

She looked at Jake when he laughed. He had a nice laugh—throaty and smooth and sent warm tingles through her body.

"I would have paid good money to see you toss him on the bank."

"She told you about that, too?" said Henry. He paused, then continued, a wistful sigh in his voice. "It's one of my favorite memories—I wish we could have had more of those times."

Lexie's heart swelled with love for her father, and she gently rubbed his arm. "We made the most of our family time, Dad. That's what I remember. That's what's important."

Henry glanced at Jake. "Yes. That's what is important."

The conversation ended when Katie bounced back into the room with Rose and Biscuit in tow.

"My Rozy wikes my room, Daddy."

"She does, huh?"

"Uh-huh. And guess what? She has a bear wike mine, and his name is Bobo."

"Thanks for showing me your beautiful room, Katie."

"You wek-kcome."

Henry moved beside his wife. "We should get going, sweetheart, if you want to do any shopping today."

Lexie stood between her parents and placed an arm around each. "Thanks for coming you guys. I'm sorry if I worried you unnecessarily."

"It's in the parent's job description," said Rose with a smile. "To worry about their children."

"I'm hardly a child, Mom."

Rose leaned toward Lexie and lightly stroked her cheek. "You will always be my baby, Alexa," she said, her voice soft and filled with love. "Always."

A sudden lump in her throat kept Lexie from speaking right away. "I love you, Mom." She kissed her mother's cheek, then turned to her father and kissed him as well. "I love you, Dad."

Their quiet "I love you, too" made her eyes sting.

Rose bent toward Katie, who watched them closely. "I had a good time today, Katie."

The child looked at Lexie, hesitated, then quickly kissed Rose's cheek. "Tank 'you for my puzzle."

Lexie knew her mother would positively affect Katie, but the kiss shocked her. She jerked her gaze to Jake, who looked like he'd seen a ghost.

"Come along, Rosie." Henry cupped her elbow. "Time to go." He smiled at Katie. "I hope we see you again real soon."

The child stood beside Jake and took his hand. "You bing my Rozy back, too?"

His laughter was light and bubbly. "I most certainly will."

Jake and her father shook hands. She hugged her parents again and walked them to the car while Jake and Katie followed.

Outside, the child happily sang "Bye-bye" when they left, then addressed Jake. "I wike my Rozy." She regarded them in turn, then clasped Lexie's hand as the car disappeared around the bend.

Jake stared at the surprisingly cheerful child and swallowed hard, his throat sliding up and down. Katie's bright smile never wavered as his gaze flicked from her to Lexie.

Tears stung her eyes as she glanced at the child between them, marveling at the sense of connection, of togetherness. Of family.

This is where I belong.

When she looked back to Jake, his ebony eyes glistened as he mouthed a silent "Thank you."

Chapter Twenty-Five

"Will you have to work late today, Jake?"

He heard Lexie's voice, but the actual words eluded him. He stood at the sink, unseeing eyes focused outward, his mind wrestling with the drastic change in Katie's demeanor.

The sight of her smiling and talking with Rose as she worked on the puzzle had stopped him in his tracks. Later, surprise turned to shock when she kissed Rose on the cheek as they prepared to leave. She'd never done anything like that before. Whatever possessed her to do so now?

Almost as soon as the thought surfaced, a possible reason followed. She tried to emulate Lexie by copying her hairstyle. It was reasonable to assume she'd copy behaviors, too, like Lexie hugging and kissing her folks when they got ready to leave.

He struggled to remember the last time he'd seen his father show affection toward his mother or anyone else for that matter. Nor could he remember the last time he'd kissed his mother's cheek or hugged his sister. He didn't doubt his family loved each other, but they'd never been demonstrative about it.

Lexie, on the other hand, was the exact opposite. Her family was openly affectionate with each other, and she freely lavished that affection on Katie. He thought nothing of it until Katie not only responded to it, she blossomed before his eyes.

"Jake?" A soft touch on his arm accompanied the question.

He looked to the side and saw Lexie's worried eyes on his face. "What's wrong?"

He turned and leaned on the counter, waiting for his troubled mind to settle.

Katie once again sat at the bar, studying them.

On impulse, he pulled Lexie in front of him and wrapped his arms around her waist.

"Katie's watching," she whispered.

"I know." He kissed her forehead. "I know."

She tilted her head to the side and met his troubled gaze.

"A child learns by what they hear, what they see—experience." Regret left a bitter taste in his mouth. "Until today, she never saw family members kiss or show affection for each other." He exhaled softly. "And that hurts my heart."

"Oh, Jake." She slid her arms around his waist and rested her head on his chest.

The weight around him lifted, and he knew *she* was the missing piece that made him whole and made them a family again. He didn't need time apart to know that. But if she did, he would give her all the time she needed.

When Katie smiled at him, his heart swelled in his chest. He would not let her grow up as he did. He had no idea how to fix the broken part of him, but he knew Lexie was the key.

He pushed back until he saw her face, tilted her chin, and lightly kissed her. "I won't be as late as yesterday." He moved away from her toward the bar. "I have a feed delivery coming sometime today, but Cody should be around to handle it."

He took a step away and snapped his fingers. "Almost forgot. Some lady, a nanny mother hired, should be by this afternoon to look the place over."

"Donna mentioned a new nanny. What's her name?"

He racked his brain and got nothing. "To be honest, I can't remember. I was upset they did it without my knowledge, and well, I guess I wasn't listening." He squinted at the floor. "Let's see...Beth, maybe. I know she's divorced; just moved here a couple of months ago." He looked up and caught Lexie's perturbed expression. "What?"

"Some lady? Someone who will care for your child, and that's all you have?"

Chagrined, heat washed over his face. "I'm sorry. But yeah, that's all I got." He raked his fingers through his hair. "I had a nanny for Katie before, but she moved away."

"I see."

He suddenly thought Lexie might feel slighted by the news and quickly explained. "Mother hired her without telling me and arranged for her to come by, probably this afternoon, so we could meet, and I could show her around. Just call me if she shows up."

"Fine. I'll call you if some strange lady shows up saying she's the new nanny."

Sarcasm was cute on her, and he grinned. "Thank you."

He stood beside Katie's chair, her innocent face turned to him, and swallowed twice to relieve the tightness in his throat. "I love you, kiddo," he said softly. Then he kissed the top of her head. "I'll see you both tonight."

While Katie watched a movie in the den, Lexie powered up the computer in Jake's small office. A quick scan of the icons on the home screen showed links to various farm and ranching sites, on-line marketing, email, and inventory links, along with multiple folders. She scanned the labels, found the one for 'Mary's games,' and moved it to the side before opening it. A quick check showed links to several online games and shopping sites.

After a moment's hesitation, she added a new folder labeled 'Lexie' to the desktop. Seeing it there made everything seem real, and she couldn't stop grinning. An hour flew by as she web-surfed learning opportunities for graphic artists, how to write children's books, and saved items to her folder.

The sound of an approaching vehicle drew her to the window. A truck bearing the name of the local feed store headed toward the barn. Even though Cody was supposed to be around, she decided to make sure. After closing down the computer, she headed for the back.

As she reached the kitchen door, a knock sounded. She was totally unprepared for the woman standing on the other side, a bottle of wine in one hand.

Wavy, platinum blonde hair framed a heavily made-up face. The top buttons of her too-tight blouse revealed a deep cleavage, while dark jeans encased long-shapely legs. The smile on her face faded as she frowned at Lexie. The hand holding the wine dropped to her side.

"Where's Jake?" Her voice lacked any semblance of politeness.

"Who wants to know?"

The woman raked Lexie head to toe in a contemptuous glare, then inhaled, expanding her ample bosom. Her eyes narrowed, and her shrill voice edged up a notch. "A friend. He's expecting me." One brow arched upward, and she smiled. "Along with his favorite bottle of wine."

Lexie's mouth refused to work as her brain tried to sort things through. Expecting her? Surely Aggie had not hired this—person as Katie's nanny? Jake did say she'd be here this afternoon. But this didn't feel right.

So, maybe there was another reason altogether for her to be here—a reason she didn't want to consider.

Jake said he hadn't been with anyone in some time. Did he lie? The fact she couldn't picture him with someone like her didn't mean it wasn't true.

Once, she and Rodney saw one of her site supervisors out with another woman and she became upset. Rodney saw nothing wrong, adding, "A man has needs."

Was this woman taking care of Jake's needs? She didn't know him well enough to answer.

In fact, she didn't know him at all.

"It's his favorite."

The woman's sultry voice jolted Lexie back to the present.

"I promised to bring it for later."

"I see," was the best Lexie could manage.

The woman looked around the yard. "Where is he? He insisted I make his delivery the last one of the day." She looked up and smiled. "So we wouldn't be rushed."

Lexie took a calming breath. "Then he should be here anytime.

If you'll excuse me, I need to check on Katie."

"Oh, how is that precious child? She loves it when I tuck her in."

No way in hell would Jake let her anywhere near Katie. Or would he? Maybe she had tucked Katie in before. And she and Jake enjoyed that damn wine. Together.

Just the thought made her stomach roll.

"Aren't you going to let me in?" She arched her neck as though daring Lexie to say no.

She wanted to refuse but didn't know if she should.

"Jake wouldn't want me to stand out here."

Against her better judgment, she stepped aside and pointed to the bar. "You can wait there."

The woman paraded past her and headed for the den. "I'll wait in here."

Lexie hurriedly followed, catching up to her as she entered the den and stopped. She moved around her and spoke to Katie. "Sweetie, why don't you come into the kitchen with me."

Katie eyed the woman as she took Lexie's hand.

"Hey, kid," she said. "Long time no see."

Katie ignored her as she and Lexie walked back to the kitchen.

"Daddy don't wike her."

"He doesn't?"

She shook her head. "He make her weave."

"Okay. I'm going to talk to her for a minute. You stay here, okay?"

"Okay."

She returned to the den and found the woman sprawled on the couch, thumbing through a ranch magazine. "I'm sorry, I didn't get your name."

The woman looked up and snarled. "I didn't get yours, either. What are you doing here?"

"I'm staying here for a while." She saw no need to elaborate further.

The woman pushed up from the couch and strolled toward Lexie. "Whatever ideas you got about my man you best forget 'em."

Shocked didn't begin to describe how her remark struck Lexie. "Your man?"

"That's right." She straightened her shoulders and fingered a platinum curl beside her cheek. "My man."

Nope. No way. "I'll call Hawkins Feed and have them verify why you are here."

The woman grabbed her arm when she turned to go. "No need for that," she cooed. "I'm Janet. Janet Orms." She fingered the top button on her blouse, head cocked to one side. "Jake and me are...old friends."

The fake smile put Lexie's teeth on edge. "Well, Miss Orms, I'll call Jake and let him know you're here."

Before she could say anything, the front doorbell rang.

Now what? "Excuse me." She left Janet standing in the den and hobbled to the front door. She would need to wrap and elevate her foot for sure tonight.

She opened the door and froze. "Elizabeth?"

Chapter Twenty-Six

Jake caught himself whistling as he parked the ATV in its spot. The afternoon had passed quickly and uneventfully, and he couldn't wait to get home. No call from Lexie meant the new nanny never showed, which was fine by him. He had more than enough to stress him out right now.

He entered the barn, found Cody lifting feed sacks from the back of the truck, and moved to help.

"Did I hear you whistling, boss?" teased Cody.

Jake grinned. "Maybe."

Cody hefted the sack over his shoulder. "Wonder which one caused it?"

Jake stopped in the act of lifting a bag. "Which one?"

"Yeah." Cody adjusted the sack on his shoulder. "Janet, Miss Lexie, or the other woman who just showed up."

"What?"

"Janet went inside about fifteen minutes ago." He adjusted the sack on his shoulder. "Don't know who the other one is."

"Shit."

Jake turned and hurried toward the house, his mind racing with things Janet might say or do to upset Lexie. The other woman could only be the new nanny, which presented a whole new pile of shit for him to shovel.

He entered the kitchen and saw Lexie, Katie, and the unknown woman sitting at the bar.

"Where is she?" he barked.

Lexie's face revealed nothing. "The den."

He turned and stalked in that direction.

Janet sat on the couch, legs tucked under her, thumbing through a magazine. When she saw him, she stretched out, one elbow on the arm of the sofa, the other draped over her hips in a blatantly seductive pose. "Well, hello there."

"What the hell are you doing here?"

"Waiting for you, of course." She leaned forward, her breasts nearly spilling out of her blouse as she reached for the wine. "I even brought wine."

He marched to the couch and reached for her hand.

Surprised, she sat up and clasped it, an eager smile on her lips. "I knew you'd be glad to see me."

"Not the word I'd use." He pulled her toward the kitchen.

"Where are we going?"

"You're leaving."

She slowed and pulled on her hand. "I just got here."

When he entered the kitchen, Janet in tow, he stopped mid-stride.

Three pairs of wide eyes stared at them.

Lexie reacted quickly and hopped down from the stool. "Katie, let's go see if *Paw Patrol* is on TV."

Once they were gone, he continued toward the French doors leading to the porch and walked outside, hauling a whining Janet along until she pulled to a stop.

"Why are you acting this way? I told you I'd deliver your order at the end of the day and bring some wine."

Jake sucked air through clenched teeth. How the hell could he get through to her? With a dismal shake of his head, he knew the direct approach was his last resort. "I thought you understood the last time."

"Jake, honey—"

"I've tried to spare your feelings, Janet, but you won't listen." Hands planted on his hips, he tilted his head back, closed his eyes for a quick mental ten-count, exhaled, and faced her. "Going out with you was a mistake. A big one. But I felt sorry for you, and—"

"Wait. What?" she screeched and poked a finger in his chest. "*You.* Felt sorry—for *me*? That's why you went out with me?" Her voice rose with each word, and her face flushed with indignant fury. "Why, you conceited, self-centered bastard," she shouted. "How dare you say you felt sorry for me!"

The slap was unexpected. But if that's what it took to eliminate her unwelcome attention, he'd gladly endure another.

Janet angrily jabbed a finger at him. "I'll have you know plenty of better-looking men are just waiting for the chance to go out with me." She shoved hair away from her face. "You think that mousy little thing is woman enough for you?" She turned and stalked down the steps. "Well, don't come sniffing around me when you find out she ain't."

At the bottom, she looked at the bottle in her hand, then threw it on the ground, sending glass shards and wine everywhere. Back straight, she stomped toward the truck and got behind the wheel as Cody closed the tailgate.

Gravel and rocks sprayed the barn as she accelerated down the drive.

Fury rolled off Jake in waves. He couldn't go inside until he cooled off, so he headed toward the barn in long, angry strides.

"Sorry, boss. I didn't know it was her until I saw her on the porch," offered Cody. "I couldn't stop her from going in."

He shook his head, too upset to speak.

"She's a piece of work, for sure," he added. "Thought old man Hawkins put a stop to her harassing male customers." He removed his hat and ran stubby fingers through his hair. "She even tried to hook me once." He looked at Jake. "Whatcha gonna do?"

Jake grabbed a shovel. "Find a stall to muck." He marched down the barn and went to work.

❈

Once Lexie had Katie and Biscuit in front of the television, she rejoined Elizabeth in the kitchen in time to see the woman slap Jake and storm off the porch.

Lexie brought a hand to her mouth. "Shut the front door." Unsure of what prompted the action, it was apparent the woman was furious.

She sped away and Jake charged to the barn. "Crap on a cracker. He ain't happy, either."

Despite never having seen this side of his personality, she wasn't scared so much as concerned as to the reason behind what happened.

But she didn't have time to worry about it right now. Elizabeth Adams sat in her—his kitchen. Her ex-husband, a contractor with her dad's company, recently left her for Lexie's former assistant and moved to Austin.

"I'm so sorry, Elizabeth. Not a very encouraging welcome."

"She certainly wasn't happy with him." She sipped lukewarm coffee. "Who is she?"

"I wish I knew." Lexie hesitated, then changed the subject. "How have you been?"

She ducked her head, then fixed tired grey eyes on her. "Starting over at my age sucks. But you do what you must, right?"

"Jake told me someone was coming by, but I didn't realize it was you. What are you doing here?"

She slowly shook her head. "I had to get away. Too many memories. Too many people who know what he did, too many pitying looks."

"Been there, done that."

"I'm sorry. I didn't mean to bring up painful memories for you."

"No apology needed, Elizabeth, I—"

"If you don't mind, I go by Beth now. Changes, you know."

She smiled. "I do, indeed. I'm Lexie."

"Lexie. I like it. How did you end up here?"

"Long story short, a jinxed vacation and wild hogs."

She nodded toward the crutches. "How bad?"

"Just a sprain. Be fine in a week or two." She paused. "What about you?"

She took a deep breath. "As you know, the divorce was...difficult. I eventually had to sell the daycare center. My sister, Cindy, is married to a local real estate guy and convinced me to move here until I got my life back together."

"How did you end up with this job?"

She smiled. "Small town networking. Cindy knows Mrs. Holloway and discovered her son needed a nanny. I had experience with kids, so a few calls, an interview, and here I am." She glanced toward the barn. "Am I going to regret accepting the position?"

"Well, I have no explanation for what we just witnessed, but I can tell you Jake is an honest and kind man and Katie an absolute doll."

After several minutes of conversation about expectations, which Lexie winged since she had no idea, she showed her around the house before ending up back in the kitchen. "So, any questions?"

Beth eyed her closely. "I must admit the only question that comes to mind is your relationship with Mr. Holloway."

Lexie huffed out a long breath. "It's...complicated."

"But you're a couple?"

Were they? She hoped so. "Yes. We are."

"Good. For the record, I'm not looking for another man in my life except as an employer." She glanced toward the barn. "Does he often work this late?"

"It varies depending on what's going on." She secretly thought another reason was no one to come home to and had mixed feelings about Beth being here—particularly since Katie had warmed to her right away.

Lexie's interaction with Beth was limited to company events. And while she didn't know her very well, she was always open and friendly and ran a successful business.

And she was undoubtedly attractive with ash-blonde hair clustered in short curls around a heart-shaped face and a pasted-on smile. Her body was curvy and toned, but raw hurt glittered in the depths of hard, grey eyes.

"Okay," said Beth. "As I understand from Mrs. Holloway, I will pick Katie up at daycare starting Monday at three-thirty, bring her home, and stay until Mr. Holloway returns. I'll cook dinner each weeknight and get Katie ready for bed. Unless he's home by then."

"Then that's the plan. Jake intended to go over all this with you, but well, you know." She shook her head to get back on track. "Almost forgot. The center is closed through Monday. Water leak. They expect it to reopen on Tuesday."

"Ahh. So, what time do I need to be here Monday?"

It was awkward talking schedules with her like she was the lady of the house or something, but someone had to. Beth deserved answers. "Will eight work for you?"

"Yes. I'll be here." She took a pad from her purse and scribbled a number on it. "This is my cell phone. If something changes, just let me know." She took a step back and stopped. "I did tell Mrs. Holloway I prefer no weekends, but I know things can happen, so if y'all need me before then, just call."

"I—we will. Thanks. And I'm glad you'll be the one watching Katie." She swallowed hard. "She's an exceptional child."

"Don't worry. I'll take good care of her for you."

They walked to the door, and Lexie watched her leave, emotions across the board. At least she knew Beth and thought she'd be good for Katie. But at the same time, she didn't want anyone but her to fill that role.

Subdued, she shuffled back into the den and watched Katie playing with Biscuit. She considered saying something more to her about Beth but decided Jake should handle that part. "I'll be in the kitchen if you need something."

Katie tossed a red foam ball and laughed as Biscuit chased it. "Okay."

She stood in front of the sink and watched the dusky sky change colors. *Do I really need to leave? What's the answer?*

Shaking her head, she looked around. Roast and bread were in the oven, peas and potatoes on the stove, so she had nothing else to occupy her time. In her earlier explorations, she'd found a small liquor stash in the pantry and decided a margarita was in order. Maybe a double. It was that kind of day.

When Jake finally came in, she'd just sat down with her drink. "So, how was your day?"

He stared for a heartbeat, then gave her a sexy, lopsided grin that turned her insides to mush. "Got another one of those?"

"Uh-huh." She got up. "Single or double?"

"Double."

A few minutes later, glass in hand, he looked around. "Where's Katie?"

"Playing fetch with Biscuit in the den."

"Let's take this to the porch."

"I'll let Katie know where we are."

"Okay."

When she joined him, he sat sprawled in a chair, long legs stretched out and crossed at the ankles. He took a drink and silently patted the rocker beside him.

She sat and waited.

"This is good."

She sent the rocker in motion with her foot. "We call it a MawRita." Ice clinked as she swirled the glass. "Mom's best friend's recipe. Her grandkids call her Maw, and she has this special recipe. Hence, a MawRita."

"Hmmm."

An owl hooted in the distance, followed by the deep moo of cows in the field. The evening breeze carried the scent of damp earth and the croak of tree frogs as they rocked in companionable silence.

"How much did y'all see? Or hear?" Jake asked softly.

She sipped her drink. "Enough to know she was angry at you about something."

He snorted, then turned his head to face her. "I went out with her once, maybe three months ago. I realized it was a mistake almost from the start and ended the evening early." He eyed his drink. "She wasn't happy and apparently doesn't take no for an answer." He downed a healthy portion. "Maybe she will now."

"Women can be fickle."

"Are you? Fickle, I mean."

She rested her head on the back of the chair and smiled at him. "Nope. No hidden agendas. What you see is what you get."

"Good enough for me." He leaned over, put his hand around her neck, and pulled her toward him to capture her lips in a searing kiss.

Heat curled up and down her spine. She couldn't get enough air in her lungs. How could something as simple as a kiss do such chaotic things to her body? Her mind quickly discarded the word simple—there was nothing simple about it.

Never before had she experienced anything remotely similar. And it terrified her. How could something so strong be real? And last?

Her parents' love was an almost tangible thing. You saw it in every touch, every look. More than anything, she wanted that intangible something, and every beat of her heart said she'd found it.

Here. With Jake.

"Is it too early to send Katie to bed?"

His voice, hoarse and filled with need, sent a pleasant shiver through her as desire percolated between them.

"...yeah." She pulled back to see his face. "And you haven't had dinner yet."

"I'm more interested in dessert."

She huffed out a strained laugh. "That's the MawRita talking."

He twisted and set their glasses on the floor, then pulled her from the chair, shifting her to his lap. "No. It's you," he whispered. "Just you." He lightly brushed another kiss across her lips, then cradled her against him as their breathing steadied.

A delicious warmth coursed through her, a feeling both sensual and comforting. She nestled closer, savoring the sense of rightness in his arms until a sudden thought broke the spell. "Please tell me Cody isn't still in the barn." She muttered. "If he is, he's getting an eyeful."

She groaned, and he pulled her closer. "I'm sure he's gone by now." He leaned his head back and sighed. "I'm guessing the new nanny got an eyeful, too?"

"'fraid so."

"What do you think about her?"

"I actually know her. And like her."

"You do?"

"Her name is Elizabeth Adams, but she goes by Beth now. Her ex worked for Dad's company." She gave him the condensed version of a marriage gone wrong and how she ended up on his doorstep.

"What did she say about all the drama?"

"Not much. She asked if it was a common occurrence. I told her you were an honest, decent man despite what the scene suggested."

"Thank you."

"I spoke the truth. Then we chatted about expectations – which I just winged since I had no idea, and I showed her around and introduced Katie, which went well. Since the daycare is closed, she will be here Monday morning at eight, but left her number if you need to change anything."

Just then, the door opened, and Katie stuck her head out. "I hungee, Wexie. So is Bistit."

Reluctantly, she pulled away and stood. "Okay. Let's get y'all fed."

He held her hand a moment longer. "Dessert," he whispered, lightly brushing his lips across her hand.

Chapter Twenty-Seven

Jake enjoyed supper at the dining table again, but Katie seemed unsure since she'd never eaten there. He made a mental note to find a booster seat for her since the chair was a little low and required a pillow to sit on. She watched him and Lexie, then mimicked their actions before finally settling down to eat, chattering like a magpie.

This new animated, talkative child amazed and pleased him to the point he encouraged more interaction instead of telling her to stop and eat. He would gladly spend the evening finishing a meal that generally took twenty minutes to see her this way. And Lexie's presence made everything better.

After supper, the three of them worked on the wooden puzzle again, then Katie sat in his lap—another first, and he re-read Tina's book.

While Lexie got her ready for bed, he did the dishes.

A typical family evening.

God, how he wanted there to be more of those.

But she needed to know everything first. Tonight's incident was nothing compared to the potential drama he anticipated, and she may not want any part of it.

A bundle of nerves, he fidgeted on the couch and waited for

her to join him. His expectations for the outcome of this evening ran from high to low as she sat down, and he drew her to his side. "Tonight was perfect," he said. "And I can't get over the change in Katie." He tipped her chin up. "Because of you." He kissed her, a light brushing of the lips that didn't begin to satisfy the need inside as his heart pounded against his chest wall.

Now or never.

"I can't explain it," he began quietly. "Sure as hell don't understand it, but it's like I've known you—waited for you all my life."

She rubbed her hand across his thigh. "I feel the same way."

He caressed her upper arm with one hand. "I hate deception," he said at last. "Secrets."

"Honesty is important." She placed a hand over his heart. "For any relationship to work."

She couldn't possibly know the importance of honesty to him. His throat ached with the need to get the words out. To have another person share the torment he'd suffered alone for four years. "There's something you need to know. About me. And Katie."

She pulled back to see his face, her hand making slow circles over his racing heart. "Whatever it is, Jake, tell me. I'll understand."

He looked at the ceiling, then closed his eyes, resting his head on the back of the couch. It took several attempts to get sufficient air past the band of anxiety constricting his chest. "We met in high school. Our sophomore year." He took a ragged breath. "I was crazy about her."

Lexie moved her hand in soothing circles as though she sensed his pain and wanted to ease it. "How long were you married?"

"Ten years."

Each pass of her hand over his heart eased the tension a little more.

"I thought we wanted the same things." He stopped to gather scattered thoughts. "I grew up here and bought the ranch from my folks after we married. Dad was getting older, had some health issues, and wanted to retire." He shrugged. "Ranching is hard, demanding work. Throw in bad weather, the economy—it adds up." He inhaled and let it out slowly. "I had no idea she was so unhappy. In the end, I mean. I should have known."

A long silence ensued before Lexie spoke. "What broke your heart, Jake?"

The soft-spoken question left him speechless, and tears stung his eyes. After so many years carrying this burden alone, the thought of sharing it with anyone—with her, squeezed his throat so tight he could hardly breathe. And saying the words out loud would bring all the betrayal and pain back to the surface.

But he'd passed the point of no return.

She stopped rubbing his chest and laced their fingers together before kissing the top of his hand. "Take your time," she whispered. "Take your time."

He sucked in a breath, swallowed his pride, and told her.

All of it.

⁓◈⁓

Lexie couldn't imagine holding so much hurt inside this long. To share it with her now spoke volumes about his feelings.

"No one knows," he said softly, his voice drained of emotion. "About the divorce or her lover."

Silent, she slipped her arms around his waist and laid her head on his chest. He responded by holding her uncomfortably tight, but she didn't pull away. He needed her, and she wanted to be there for him.

She had questions, of course, but they could wait. This moment was about Jake letting go of the past to embrace the future.

But could he let go of his only love? The one who broke his heart?

Unwilling to dwell on those discouraging thoughts, she stuffed them into a darkened corner of her mind—*one thing at a time.*

Several minutes lapsed before he spoke again, his voice hoarse and strained as his embrace relaxed. "They said Mary was about twenty weeks along at the time of the accident. I did the math, so I may worry about a problem that doesn't exist. But what if it does? And did she know when she moved into the guest room? When she asked for a divorce?"

Silent, Lexie blinked away the tears stinging her eyes at the devastating hurt his voice carried.

And he suffered alone. Her embrace tightened. He wasn't alone anymore.

"I was in shock, I guess, and didn't think beyond one day at a time. Katie spent three months in the NIC unit. When she finally came home, she was—so fragile and required constant monitoring." He rested a moment and continued. "I don't know what I would have done without Mother and Donna. They took turns staying here that first year until I hired a nanny."

Like a deflated balloon, he sank against the back of the couch, and his voice dropped to an anguished whisper. "Mary's deceit…killed something inside me, and I buried it with her." He sucked in a ragged breath. "Until you came along and made me want to be whole again." His voice cracked with controlled emotion. "You made me realize how unfair I've been to Katie. She deserves so much more. When I watched her sleeping tonight, I knew the time had come."

"For what?"

Air hissed through pursed lips, and he shook his head. "I don't know." He scrubbed one hand over his face. "One part of me says do nothing because it doesn't matter. Another says what if he shows up one day and decides he wants to have a part in her life."

"It's been four years, Jake. Surely he would have spoken up before now."

"I've thought about that. There could be any number of reasons why he hasn't. Maybe he wasn't sure. Maybe she didn't tell him." He rolled his head side to side on the back of the couch. "Maybe she didn't know."

Her rapid-fire brain began constructing possibilities. "Under normal circumstances, I think she had to at least suspect something at that point."

His brow furrowed, air filled his cheeks, then released as he arranged his thoughts. "Which can only mean she questioned who was the father and didn't say anything."

That seemed the most logical conclusion to Lexie, but she didn't comment.

"I see Mary in her eyes, her hair," he murmured. "But I don't see me."

The sorrow in his voice nearly broke the tenuous hold on her emotions, and she struggled for encouraging words. "DNA can be tricky, Jake. It's not uncommon for a child to resemble only one or neither parent. Bobby looks nothing like my folks but is the spitting image of my paternal grandfather at his age." Before he could refute her comment, she continued. "Is there anyone she would have confided in? A close friend who might know something?"

He shook his head. "She grew up here but didn't have many close friends. Like Katie, she was shy and didn't do well among strangers. Spent a lot of time online and rarely left the ranch except to shop in town. We'd go out to dinner, sometimes with friends, sometimes alone, but, in hindsight, I don't think she enjoyed that much, either." Disgusted with himself, he shook his head. "Another thing I didn't notice."

Lexie's heart hurt for him. He'd taken on full responsibility for everything. Mary's unhappiness, the accident. She tiptoed through the emotional minefield and chose her words carefully. "It's only natural for you to feel a certain amount of—liability, Jake, but she was a grown woman, old enough to be accountable for her own happiness. She could have done something, said something to you." Even as she spoke, another idea popped into her head. "You said she rarely left the ranch, so if she *were* seeing someone, could it have been online?"

"I suppose. She used the computer a lot, but all I ever saw on there were games." He tilted his head to the side, and his eyes narrowed as he processed the information. "If it was someone she met online, how did they get together?" He shook his head. "No. I can't see her doing something so out of character. And she would never meet a stranger in town. Everyone knows everyone here." He rubbed his thigh with one fisted hand. "So, it has to be someone who came here."

"Possibly." She paused, her mind categorizing options. "You said y'all broke up when you joined the Army. Did she date anyone in particular while you were gone?"

"No. She dated some, but it was more like friend dates. And she told me about them in her letters." He paused. "We got married three months after I got out."

"What about her parents? Or other family members?"

"She was an only child. Her mother died when she was a senior. Her father remarried a couple of years later and moved to California. Didn't even come to Mary's funeral." He looked down at her. "What are you thinking?"

"I'm not sure. Let's table this part for the time being." She patted his chest. "What are you going to do right now?"

He leaned his head back against the couch again. "I know I should have done something before now. But I—couldn't face the possible outcome. Now, I risk someone showing up one day to take my child away." His warm breath brushed over the top of her head when he exhaled. "I've done a shitty job of showing it, but in every way that matters, Katie is my daughter. She's Mary's child and my daughter." He swallowed hard. "That's the first time I've said it out loud. What the hell kind of father does that make me?"

She shifted until they faced each other and cupped his face. "She knows you love her, Jake."

He shook his head. "Does she? Half the time, I don't even know what I'm doing."

"But you try anyway," she said softly. "That's what matters."

"I hope so," he whispered, pulling her against him. "I hope so."

The fierce desire of earlier gave way to an overwhelming sense of contentment. The hard pounding of Jake's heart against her ear slowed to calm, even beats, and his ragged breathing steadied as tension left his body.

She needed answers, too, because the thought of losing him and Katie was unbearable. She pushed back until their gazes met, one hand on his chest. "Whatever happens, Jake, I'll be here for you." She inhaled and wagged a finger back and forth between them. "There's something here. Connecting us. I don't know what exactly, but we owe it to ourselves to find out." She licked suddenly dry lips. "What do you think?"

"I wanna know, too."

The kiss was surprisingly gentle, his lips featherlight but powerful.

He pulled back and inhaled deeply. "I've never brought a woman here and haven't been with anyone in a long time. Haven't wanted to. Until now." He cleared his throat. "I enjoy being with you, talking to you. What I feel is—beyond friendship, and I want to know you better." He brushed a thumb over her lower lip. "Would you have dinner with me tomorrow night?"

The question surprised her, and she blinked. "Dinner? Like on a date?"

"Yeah. Like on a date." He gave a one-shoulder shrug. "What do you think?"

"I'd like that." She looked down at her booted foot. "As long as dancing isn't involved."

His light chuckle warmed her heart.

"No dancing. There's a decent steakhouse not far from town. Nothing fancy, but the food is good."

She grinned and fingered the buttons on his shirt. "Mmm...It just so happens I have access to this cozy little cabin. Very secluded."

"You don't say."

"Uh-huh." She lightly brushed her lips against his. "Maybe we could have dessert there...and get to know each other on a more—in-depth level."

She watched his eyes darken with desire, and that sexy smile came quickly.

"I'll get Mom to let Katie spend the night."

"Are you sure you want to stay at the cabin all by yourself?"

Jake's lazy smile made Lexie's mouth water. "I won't be alone tonight, will I?"

The look he gave her was filled with promise. "No. You won't." Jake rose from the breakfast bar and placed his empty plate in the sink. "I have two horses to deliver to Texarkana this morning but should be back by early afternoon."

"Okay."

"I'll put your stuff in the car for you before I help Cody load the horses."

"Are you weaving, Wexie?"

Katie stood at the entrance to the kitchen, wearing her favorite blue pj's and her bear clutched in one hand.

She and Jake exchanged looks. "Just to the cabin, sweetie."

"But I want you here wif me."

"I won't be far away, and you can still come and stay with me while Daddy works."

"I don't want you to go."

The sadness in Katie's doe eyes tore at Lexie's heart.

"Katie," said Jake softly as he squatted beside her. "The cabin's nearby, and you'll still see her every day."

"We'll go exploring when we get there today," added Lexie. "We didn't get to do much last time. We might even see a deer or a bunny rabbit."

"And guess what?" added Jake. "Mimi is coming by this afternoon. She wants you to spend the night with her and Pops."

"I want to stay wif Wexie and Bistit."

"I know, but you haven't had a sleepover with them in a long time, and they really miss you." Her head dipped, and he continued. "Mimi will bring you back in the morning."

Lexie hated to see the child so downcast. "It's just for one night, sweetie. I know you'll have a great time with Mimi. And when you get back tomorrow, we'll go exploring again."

Katie nodded but didn't speak.

"I have to get busy," said Jake as he stood. "Your stuff ready to go?"

"By the door in my room." Lexie smiled as she watched him move. He had a great body. That thought sparked another one and had her cheeks burning.

He caught her stare, winked as though he read her thoughts, and headed down the hall toward her room.

When he returned with her things, she and Katie walked to the porch behind him while Biscuit raced down the steps.

"No, big guy," said Jake. "You stay home today."

Like a petulant child, the dog whined and sat down.

Jake grinned and put her things in the trunk. He walked back to where she and Katie stood watching. He tweaked Katie's nose and faced Lexie. "I'll call when I'm headed home."

"Okay. Safe travels."

They watched him disappear behind the barn, presumably to help Cody with the horses, and Lexie took Katie's hand. "How would you like pancakes for breakfast?" The child didn't move. "Katie?"

"Are you going to weve us?"

The barely audible question brought back Donna's concerns and made her heart ache for the child. Despite the mutual attraction, there was still a chance things might not work out with Jake. The thought of hurting this child was almost too much to bear, but making a promise she couldn't keep was worse. The cumbersome boot made squatting to her level difficult, so she leaned down and tilted Katie's chin. "I'm just going to the cabin, sweetie. And we'll see each other every day."

Katie looked toward the road beside the barn leading to the cabin, then back to Lexie. "I see you tomorrow?"

"Of course."

She hesitated, then gave Lexie a half-smile. "I wike pancakes."

"Then let's make you some pancakes."

Her subdued demeanor continued through breakfast but quickly improved when they reached the cabin and spotted a bunny hopping toward the lake.

"Oh, let's hurry and get this stuff in the house. Then we'll explore and see what else we can see."

"Yes!"

After unloading the car, she grabbed her sketch bag, and they walked outside.

Katie's amazed reaction to seeing a squirrel and later a deer said she didn't get outside much, which gave Lexie the perfect idea for her first children's book. When she pulled out her sketchpad and began drawing, Katie was fascinated and looked for things to point out, like a robin chirping in the tree and ducks landing on the pond.

The morning passed way too fast, and once they returned to the ranch and Katie was down for her nap, she braced herself and called her father.

"Hey, Dad. I hope I didn't catch you at a bad time."

"It's never a bad time to talk with my favorite daughter."

"I'm your only daughter." She smiled at the long-running joke. "And you're biased."

"A father's prerogative."

She took a sip of water to soothe her suddenly dry mouth. "I, um, I wanted to discuss something with you, Dad. It probably should be an in-person conversation, but..."

"What is it, sweetheart? What's wrong?"

"Nothing's wrong, Dad. It's just..."

"Just what?"

"I'm...um, the thing is, I'm thinking about a career change."

Silence on the other end of the line made her heart race. "It's not that I don't love working for you, Dad, it's, well, I..."

"Alexa, your mother and I have known you were unhappy for some time."

His leather chair creaked when he shifted in the seat. "Even before Rodney, we knew. I even wondered if you were trying to force something you didn't feel."

He continued before she could reply. "I saw no joy in your eyes, heard no laughter in your voice. It seemed you were merely going through the motions."

Her father's perception shouldn't have surprised her, but it did.

Obviously, she didn't do as good a job hiding her true self as she thought.

"When we saw you this week…"

She heard him inhale.

"Everything about you was different. The happiness we prayed for was in every glance between you and Jake. And the connection with his daughter was obvious and heart-warming."

His astute observation spurred her to speak. "I can't explain it, Dad. I've never felt this way before," she babbled. "I don't understand it—this, this thing between us. But I have to stay and find out where it leads."

He inhaled deeply. "I understand, Alexa. I do—because it was that way when I met your mother." He paused. "Take all the time you need to make sure this is what you want. Your happiness is all your mother and I care about."

She heard a pencil tapping on the desk as he switched gears.

"You mentioned a career change."

Now that the time had come, she hesitated. Would he understand? Support her as he did Bobby when he wanted something different.

"Whatever it is, Alex, you can always talk to me about it."

I hope so, Dad. She sat up straight. "You're going to think I've lost my mind, Dad. But I want to write and illustrate children's books." Once she started, the words flowed with enthusiasm. "I've wanted to do so for a long time. And today, I got my first idea and began sketching. I don't know what's involved in this new endeavor, but I'll learn. I've already done some research online."

Pride infused his voice. "I know you will succeed in whatever career path you choose sweetheart." He waited for a beat. "God has a way of putting us where He wants us to be, though we don't always see it at the time." He paused. "I'm so proud of you, Alexa. I don't tell you that near enough. I just want you to be happy. With your profession. With your life. It's all I've ever wanted." He cleared his throat and continued. "Your mother and I will always support whatever makes you happy."

She had to swallow twice before she could reply. "I love you, Dad," she murmured. "Thank you for understanding and always being there for me. For all of us. You're the best." Tears of joy rolled down her cheeks as the discussion moved to what needed to happen next.

By the time the call ended, she was on cloud nine and ready to focus on her date with Jake.

And dessert.

———◦◉◦———

While Cody loaded the two horses for him, Jake moved to the far corral and placed a call to Beth Adams, who answered on the second ring. "Miss Adams? This is Jake Holloway."

"Good morning, Mr. Holloway."

He cleared his throat. "I, um, I wanted to apologize for not greeting you properly yesterday, and for...the thing is..."

"Apology accepted, Mr. Holloway, and thank you for the gesture."

"Please call me Jake."

There was a moment's hesitation before she replied. "If you don't mind, Mr. Holloway, I'd prefer we kept things on an employer/employee level."

"Oh, yes, of course." *Dumbass. You should have known that.* "Well, um, I wanted to assure you the—spectacle you observed yesterday was a one-time thing and won't happen again. Ever. And I hope it didn't cause you to decline the position."

"I admit, I was a little uncertain at first. But after talking with Lexie and my sister, I see no cause for concern now."

He released the pent-up air in his lungs. "Good. I'm glad." He picked at a splinter on the rail he leaned against. "I hate to ask, but could you drop by again later this afternoon? My mother is picking Katie up for a sleepover around three. We can meet properly, review things again, and I'll answer any other questions you might have." It suddenly occurred to him she may get the wrong idea about his request. The last thing he needed or wanted was another Janet to deal with. "Lexie will be here, too. We have plans for the evening," he hurriedly added.

There was a slight hesitation before she replied. "Okay. Would you prefer I arrive before or after Katie leaves?"

"Before, if you don't mind. I'd like her to get accustomed to you."

"Will two-thirty work?"

"Yes. Thank you. And my apologies again for yesterday."

"No problem. I'll see you this afternoon."

Jake ended the call and sighed. "That went better than I expected." He then quickly called Lexie to alert her to his appointment with Beth. Task handled, he leaned against the top rail and stared out across the pasture, his mind drifting to tonight's date with Lexie.

"Sure you don't want me to make the run, Boss?"

Cody's question wasn't unusual since he sometimes made these trips. "No, I'm good. I have something else to do while I'm out." He didn't bother to mention *something else* involved stopping at a drugstore where no one knew him.

Cody nodded, and they strolled toward the trailer. "Saw Miss Lexie leaving. Said she was gonna be staying at the cabin."

"Yeah."

"She and Katie sure hit it off."

When Jake merely grunted, Cody continued. "She does brighten up the place."

"Yes, she does. Call the clinic and have one of the vets check on Dolly. If they give the all clear, put her in the small pasture where we can watch her for a few days."

"Will do."

Once on the road, Jake cranked up the radio, his thoughts consumed by his date with Lexie.

Chapter Twenty-Nine

"Higher, Wexie!"

Katie's excited squeal made Lexie smile, and she gave the rope swing another push, being careful not to go too high. "Hang on tight."

"I will."

The rumble of a truck coming down the driveway drew Lexie's attention. Aggie and Beth were expected at any time, so seeing the veterinary truck stop in front of the barn surprised and concerned her. Afraid something happened to Dolly, she stopped the swing as Sean exited the vehicle.

When he saw them, he turned in their direction, stopping a few feet away. Mouth agape, his attention totally focused on Katie.

Something in his expression caused unease to crawl up her spine, and she took the child's hand. "Is Dolly all right, Sean?"

If he heard her question, he didn't respond.

His eyes widened in surprise, then he blinked and stepped closer. "My God," he whispered. "So much like Mary." His shocked gaze remained fixed on Katie, and his voice shook with emotion. "I had no idea."

Unease grew, and she eased Katie behind her. "Is Dolly all

right?"

He continued to stare until Lexie spoke again. "Sean? Is Dolly all right?"

"Huh?" He shook his head, and an artificial smile instantly appeared. "Oh. Yeah. Jake asked me to check and see if she can be moved to the small pasture."

He squatted on the ground, extended a hand toward Katie, then rested it on his knee. "So much like her." He took a shaky breath. "You deserve better, too."

Gooseflesh peppered her arms at his whispered comment, and Lexie moved into his line of sight. "You need to check on Dolly now, Sean." She made no effort to temper the iciness in her voice.

He slowly stood and faced her, the amiable man she had met before gone. His whole body radiated tension as his nostrils flared and a vein in his temple throbbed. "I failed her once." His jaw clamped, then released. "Not again." He took one last look at Katie and stomped off toward the barn.

Shaken by the encounter, she took the child's hand. "Come along, Katie. Mimi will be here soon, and so will Miss Beth. We need to get ready."

Katie shuffled to the house with her head bowed. Inside, she looked up to Lexie. "I want to stay wif you."

"It's just for one night." She squeezed her hand. "You'll be back tomorrow."

"And you be here?"

"I'll be here." Sean's behavior concerned her, but she forced a smile. "Let's get your backpack ready before they get here."

A short time later, Lexie carried the loaded bag to the kitchen and placed it on the bar. "How about some milk and cookies?"

Katie grinned and nodded. "I wike cookies."

"So do I."

As she placed Katie's snack in front of her, she saw Beth's car coming down the driveway with Aggie not far behind.

"Ah, they're here. Stay here and eat while I get the door."

"Okay."

She hobbled to the front and greeted the new guest, noting Aggie parked to enter through the kitchen. "Hey, Beth." She stepped aside for her to enter. "Please come in."

Handbag gripped in front of her, she nervously stepped inside. "Mr. Holloway asked me to come back so we could meet."

"Yes, he told me." She motioned down the foyer. "Katie's having a snack. Aggie just arrived, too, and I expect Jake at any time."

They entered the kitchen as Aggie came through the back door.

"Mimi, wook," gushed Katie. "I eat all my snack."

Eyes wide, she stared at her grandchild. "I see." Aggie glanced at the other women. "Glad to see you getting around so well, Lexie. And Beth, it's so nice to see you again."

"Likewise, Mrs. Holloway."

"Jake wasn't able to meet Beth yesterday," offered Lexie. "So, he asked her to drop by this afternoon."

Aggie nodded and faced her granddaughter. "Are you ready to go?"

Katie nodded and looked at Beth. "I having a seepover at Mimi's house."

"My, how exciting."

"Uh-huh. Me and Wexie packed my bag."

"Well, I am certain you'll have a great time."

"Wexie?"

"Yes, sweetie?"

"Did you put my puzzle in my bag?"

"I don't think so. But I packed your books."

"I wanted my puzzle, too."

She glanced at Beth. "Why don't you and Miss Beth get it while I visit with Mimi?"

"Okay." Katie turned in the chair toward Beth, who helped her down. "I be wite back, Mimi."

Lexie smiled as Katie led the way down the corridor and turned back to Aggie, who watched misty-eyed. "Aggie? Are you all right? Is something wrong?"

The older woman shook her head. "No, dear. Nothing's wrong. It's just that I've never seen Katie so open before." She rested a beat. "I can't believe the change in her—because of you."

"She's an adorable child, and I care deeply for her."

Aggie watched her closely. "Sometimes, I feel like you're too good to be true. Other times, I know it's meant to be." She inhaled deeply. "I've waited and prayed so long to see my son happy again."

She debated how much to reveal; so much was at stake. In the end, honesty won out. "Katie may be uneasy tonight."

"Why? What happened?"

"She overheard Jake and I talking about my moving to the cabin. She's concerned I'm leaving."

Aggie fixed too-seeing dark eyes on her. "Are you?"

"No." She waved her hands. "There are things Jake and I need to discuss and deal with, but no. I'm not leaving anytime soon." She maintained careful eye contact, hoping his mother would understand how serious her intentions were. "I want to be here, Aggie. With Jake and Katie." She clasped her hands together to keep from wringing them. "My life has been in limbo for so long. It wasn't until I met them that I realized what was missing. I know this is hard to believe, but I love them both. Have from the moment we met." She swallowed hard. "I've already told my father I'm quitting the company. I want to make my life here. With them."

Aggie hesitated, then released pent-up air from her lungs. "That's good." She walked to where Lexie stood and gave her an awkward embrace as though it was an unfamiliar gesture. "That's good. I hope you and Jake have a nice night out tonight. You deserve it."

"Mimi," said Katie as she and Beth returned. "My Rozy gived me a puzzle. I show you and Pops how to make it."

"I can't wait," said Aggie. "We love puzzles. Pops is waiting so we best get going."

"You pomise to bing me back tomorrow?"

Aggie glanced at Lexie. "I promise I will have you back here tomorrow afternoon. And guess what?"

"What?"

"We're having pizza for supper."

"I wike pizza."

"Me, too."

Katie faced Lexie. "You be here tomorrow?"

"As soon as I know you are home, I'll be here."

She added the puzzle to the backpack and handed it to Aggie. "I included her favorite pj's, her bear, and two favorite books." Taking a breath, she looked down at Katie. "I know you'll have a great time with Mimi and Pops." She smoothed down the child's wayward curls, then kissed her forehead. "I'll see you tomorrow."

When Jake arrived a few minutes later, Beth and Lexie enjoyed the beautiful spring day on the porch.

He took his hat off as he approached. "Ms. Adams," he began. "Thank you for coming back."

She stood and extended her hand. "My pleasure, Mr. Holloway."

"I need to speak to you, Jake. Now."

Sean's sharp voice interrupted whatever Jake planned to say.

He glanced back, then faced the ladies. "Excuse me. Must be something with Dolly. I'll be right back."

They watched in shocked surprise as Sean met Jake halfway there and promptly laid him on the ground with a punch to the face.

Chapter Thirty

Stunned by the unexpected blow it took Jake several seconds to react.

Biscuit's response, however, was instant, and he lunged off the porch toward Sean, his growl deep and menacing.

Jake rolled over, grabbed his collar, and held on tight. "No, boy! Stay." He struggled to stand and control the angry dog. Once upright, he glared at Sean. "What the hell was that for?" he shouted.

"She deserved better." Face scarlet, body rigid, Sean exhaled loudly. "I should have done something."

"What are you talking about?"

"Like you don't know." Sean ran both hands through his hair. "I failed her—just like you. And she deserved better."

Jake stared for a moment as comprehension dawned. "Who? Mary?"

"Who else?"

Wheels turning in his head, he quickly categorized the facts. She and Sean were friends before he met her. Afterward, the three of them remained close for years—until shortly before the accident when Sean informed them he'd taken a new job in San Antonio.

Jake caught him and Mary in a heated conversation in the kitchen a few days later. When he questioned her, she passed it off as a disagreement about the move. He thought nothing of it then, but suddenly, it grew in significance. Had their relationship gone beyond friendship? Was he the reason she wanted a divorce?

"Was it you?" Emotions tangled, he ground out the words through clenched teeth.

Sean remained silent; his face so tight it stretched into a snarl.

Jake took a step toward him, and Biscuit growled. "Was it?"

Sweat coated his brow, and skin bunched around his grief-stricken eyes as Sean opened his mouth and clamped it shut. He whirled toward his truck, Jake and the dog three steps behind him.

"Answer me, dammit!"

Sean opened the door and got in. "Dolly's alive." He started the engine. "Unlike Katie's mother." Tires kicked up gravel as Sean sped off.

Nausea churned in his stomach. No. It couldn't be Sean. A friend wouldn't do that. But it had to be. Otherwise, he would have denied it.

Wouldn't he?

He yanked his hat off the ground and beat it against his thigh.

Biscuit whined beside him.

Long-buried questions returned. Who was Katie's father? Was it him? Maybe. Maybe not. Was it Sean? Someone else?

He searched his memory for shared traits that would give him what he needed and found none. Katie bore a striking resemblance to Mary, period.

"Boss? You okay?"

Cody's question jerked him back to the present, and he jammed his hat on his head. "Just damn peachy."

The cowhand's brows edged upward. "He said Dolly's fine now, so do you want me to move her or what?"

He shook his head, trying to get his whirling thoughts in order. "Give it another day. We'll move her to the small pasture tomorrow where we can keep an eye on her."

Cody glanced at the dog standing at Jake's feet, then toward the two women watching intently from the porch. "Lot of excitin' stuff 'round here lately." He spit a stream of tobacco juice off to the side, then chuckled and turned for the barn. "Don't think I'd wanna be in your boots, though."

Jake heaved a sigh. He didn't even want to be in his boots right now. He bent down and patted the dog's head. "Good boy, Biscuit. Good boy."

Cheeks burning with a twisted mixture of anger, confusion, and embarrassment, he strode toward the women, stopping when he reached the top step.

He took off his hat and glanced between them, his cheeks so hot he expected them to flame up any minute. "I don't even know what to say."

"Jake?" Lexie's voice held only concern as she placed one hand on his arm and squeezed. "Are you okay?"

He took a deep breath and looked at Beth. "I must apologize once more for subjecting you to another unseemly display. All I can say is this is not normal—not who I am." It took massive willpower to maintain eye contact. He'd never been so embarrassed in his life.

Well, except for yesterday.

Her face revealed nothing. "At least you didn't set the dog on him."

Lexie rubbed his arm. "Come inside and let me clean your lip."

No one spoke as they entered the kitchen. Jake and Beth sat at the bar while Biscuit lounged at his feet.

Jake cleared his throat. "There's a first aid kit in the pantry. Just inside the door on the right."

While Lexie looked for the kit, he faced Beth, heat once again racing up his neck to the tops of his ears. "I have no explanation for what just happened." He shook his head. "And I'll totally understand if you want to leave and never look back. But this isn't—things are…"

"Complicated?" Her soft voice held no malice.

"Yeah. Complicated is a good word for it."

He easily read the hurt buried in the ebony eyes watching him before they shuttered.

"If there's one thing I've learned these last few months, Mr. Holloway, it's that we're not always in control of our lives. Sometimes, we're the victim of someone else's agenda." She gently rolled her shoulders. "I suspect that's what you're dealing with here."

"Thank you for saying that, Ms. Adams."

Lexie returned and stood beside him, placing her hand on his shoulder. At her gentle touch, the tension tying him in knots slowly eased.

"Let's tend to this cut."

✦

Lexie watched until Beth's car disappeared around the bend in the drive, then returned to the kitchen, where Jake still sat at the bar folding and unfolding a paper napkin.

She sat down and gently rubbed his back. "Are you okay?"

He pinched off a corner of the napkin. "I don't know." He tore off a second piece. "I honestly don't know."

"Do you want to talk about it? It's okay if you don't. But I'm here for you."

He sat up straight and cut anguished eyes toward her. "It might be him."

Her heart thudded hard against her chest, their recent conversation about his late wife filling in the details. *Oh no. Sean is—was his friend.* "What makes you say that?"

He shrugged. "Just trying to connect the dots." He inhaled deeply, then exhaled. "He said something about her deserving better and how he should have done something." He shook his head. "They were best friends before I met her, so I can understand his being upset about the accident. But I don't know. Something doesn't add up."

She straightened her shoulders, hesitant to say anything but knowing she should. "Okay. This is probably nothing, but Sean said something that, well, bothered me, I guess is the word."

He whirled around. "What did he say?"

"Well, he seemed shaken when he first saw Katie earlier and surprised by how much she looked like Mary."

"And?"

She noted the tightness in his jaw and debated how much to tell him but wouldn't lie. "He said he wouldn't fail her again."

"Is that all?" The words were a harsh whisper.

She looked down at her hand on the bar.

"What else, Lexie?"

A knot formed in the pit of her stomach, and she licked suddenly dry lips. "The day Dolly was hurt, he stopped by again that afternoon. I was on the porch, and he came over."

When she hesitated, he placed one hand on her knee. "Go on."

She straightened her spine. "I thought he might be hitting on me, so I said I wasn't interested. Then he told me if I had any interest in you to forget it." She failed to keep the tremble from her voice. "Because you had only one love of your life, and there'd never be another."

Chapter Thirty-One

Jake's head spun, and time slowed to a crawl as he processed her words, trying unsuccessfully to see how they related to what Sean said. He slowly wadded up the napkin pieces with one hand and placed them on the bar. "I can only assume he meant Mary." He took her shaking hands in his and pulled them to his chest. "She was indeed my first love, Lexie." He brought her hands to his lips and softly kissed the knuckles. "But you're my last."

He felt the rush of warm air against his face when she released a breath.

"Oh, Jake," she whispered. "You're my last, too."

He stood and pulled her against him in a rough embrace. Events of the last two days jumbled his thoughts and threatened to ruin his perfect evening plans. He held her tighter. "I don't want to talk or think about anything else tonight—except us."

"Sounds good to me."

"I have a few chores and some paperwork to finish. Think you can be ready by five for an early dinner?"

She ducked her head, then looked at him with desire-filled eyes that nearly stopped his heart.

"After the last couple of days, I think a nice, quiet evening at home is in order." She slipped her hands around his waist. "Thanks to Tina, I have a well-stocked pantry and fridge at the cabin." She stretched up on one foot and lightly kissed his lips. "What do you say?"

"Are you sure? You've been cooking all week, and I wanted tonight to be extra special."

"I'm sure." She kissed him again. "We can get to know each other without interruption. All. Night. Long."

Jake smiled, the troubling events disappearing like fog in July. "I'm good with that."

She patted his chest and stepped back. "Then I'll head home and get ready. See you at five." When Biscuit rose to follow, she motioned him back. "Stay with Jake for now. I have work to do." She turned for the door, then looked over her shoulder. "Don't be late."

Anticipation had his nerves snapping. "I can't wait."

He watched her limp out the door, then swung around and headed for the office, too hyped to be still, the urge to hurry through his tasks growing. "This will be the longest two hours of my life."

Biscuit gave a light woof that sounded like agreement, and Jake laughed as he headed for his office.

Chores completed in record time, he hurried inside to prepare for his date. He showered and dressed quickly, checked his watch, changed shirts—again, and stared at the frazzled man in the mirror. "What the hell, Holloway?" he mumbled to himself. "It's not like you haven't done this before." He sighed and closed his eyes, rubbing sweaty palms against his thighs. "It's not like your whole life depends on the outcome."

Except it did. His future—his happiness, hung in the balance.

There was no question in his mind Lexie was it for him. She cared for him, too, but things between them happened so fast, and there were still issues to be handled. Plus, they'd had few opportunities just to be themselves. He prayed tonight would prove what he knew in his heart. They belonged together.

He took a last look at his reflection and grumbled to Biscuit. "I should have gotten a haircut." Annoyed with himself, he dug around the cabinet for cologne, twisted it open, and sniffed. "Does this stuff go bad?"

Biscuit snorted and shook his head.

"Yeah, smells okay to me, too."

Ablutions completed, he grabbed his keys from the dresser, stuffed the package he'd purchased earlier in his back pocket, and strode out to greet his future.

———⊗———

Lexie couldn't remember ever being this nervous before. She hadn't anticipated needing anything other than shorts or jeans for this trip but had included a baby blue sun dress at the last minute.

She exhaled slowly and checked her reflection, suddenly wondering if she should go with the sexy librarian look Jake mentioned liking. "Too late now," she muttered.

The cap sleeves, deep vee-wrapped bodice, and lightly flared skirt skimmed her body, accentuating a slim waist and full bosom. She'd left her hair loose, hanging in gentle waves over her shoulders, and hoped Jake would approve her efforts.

The clunky boot certainly took away from the look, and she debated removing it but heard Jake's truck out front. Her pulse jumped, and her breath hitched as air whooshed from her lungs. "Showtime."

When he knocked, she opened the door and stared. "Wow, Holloway," she said through suddenly dry lips. "You clean up real good."

Slowly, seductively, his gaze slid down her body and back up again. "So do you."

The intensity of his gaze, the huskiness of his voice, took her breath away. "C-come in."

She noted his hand trembled when he extended a bouquet of wildflowers toward her.

"Saw these and thought you might like them."

"I love Indian Paintbrush. Thank you."

He rubbed one hand against his thigh. "I should have gotten some real flowers from town."

"These are perfect. Why don't you pour us a glass of wine, and I'll put them in water."

Task completed, she hobbled toward him on the couch. Her heart hammered, and her skin prickled with pleasure at the potency of his gaze.

He stood as she approached and waited for her to sit before joining her, a glass in each hand. She took one and sat back on the couch. "Thank you."

Side by side, they silently sipped their drinks.

Jake cleared his throat. "Biscuit took off after a rabbit."

"He won't go far."

"He's a good dog."

"Yes, he is." She quickly glanced at him, then smoothed down the front of her skirt with one hand.

"I like your hair down like that."

"Thank you." She tucked a curl behind her ear. "Um, the grill is ready to light, but the steaks need to marinate a bit longer."

He gulped his wine. "Okay."

Her mind exploded with self-doubt. They acted like complete strangers, not two people fiercely attracted to each other. Maybe she misread things. Or perhaps she was rushing him. She straightened her spine. When presented with an issue, you face it. You don't leave it hanging. Resolve in place, she turned to face him.

"This is crazy."

"This is crazy."

Their simultaneous comments broke the tension, and they smiled at each other.

"I've never been so nervous in my life," said Jake. "Or tongue-tied."

"Me neither."

"How about we start this evening again?" He moved forward and brushed a kiss across her lips. "I've been looking forward to this all day."

"Me, too." She nestled against his side, the warmth of his body sending a different kind of heat through her.

He put his glass on the end table and added hers beside it, then tipped her chin with his finger. "This is more what I had in mind."

His kiss was slow and thorough, sending spirals of ecstasy through her.

He pulled back and looked deeply into her eyes. "You are a unique woman, Lexie," he whispered. "Beautiful on the outside, but, more importantly, on the inside, too."

She caressed his cheek. "It's safe to say we both had pieces missing from our lives and space in our hearts we never expected to fill." She took a shaky breath. "I knew when I woke up that first night to find you beside the bed, holding my hand, that the missing piece of me was you." Tears threatened when she touched his cheek. "I know it's crazy to feel this way so soon, but it is what it is. You complete me."

His voice grew hoarse, and he swallowed hard. "You're everything I didn't know I needed. Life without you is meaningless."

"I didn't know what love was until I met you. And I can't imagine my life without you."

Her lips instinctively found their way to his, and she kissed him, lingering, savoring every moment—a kiss for her weary soul to melt into.

Suddenly, he took control, and the hunger of his lips shattered her calm. This was what she wanted. This man. This moment.

Panting hard, he pulled back. "You got anything cooking that needs attention?"

"No."

"Any objections to a late supper?"

"No."

"Good." He swept her into his arms, headed for the bedroom, walked inside, and kicked the door closed with his foot. He sat her gently on the edge of the bed and stood. "Okay if I take off the boot?"

"Yeah. Was about to when I heard you drive up."

"Let me know if I hurt you."

Moments later, the boot was gone. As suspected, the foot was slightly swollen and throbbed with intermittent pain.

Jake took one look at it and frowned. "It's swollen again. Does it hurt? Do we need to wrap it?"

Her initial inclination was to say no and get on with the program, but common sense prevailed. The wrap would—hopefully, help. She huffed. "Yeah. Wrap is on the dresser. Talk about a mood killer."

He leaned down and kissed the tip of her nose. "I don't know about you, sweetheart," he purred. "But nothing short of a bomb going off in this room will affect my mood."

His grin was so damned sexy; her whole body shivered in anticipation.

He helped her sit so her feet were on the mattress, then he sat down and gently placed the injured one in his lap. Long fingers caressed her bare leg as he wrapped, adding to the sensual upsurge as nerve endings tingled and stirred. She braced her arms behind her on the bed and took a jerky breath. *Holy crap on a cracker. Who knew wrapping a sore foot could be so stimulating?*

Finished, he continued to lightly skim his fingers over her bare skin a moment before moving to the other side of the bed and stretching out beside her.

"How do you feel?"

"Fabulous."

He smirked. "I mean, is your foot okay."

"Oh. Yes. A little sore, but no biggy."

Eyes locked on hers, he ran one finger down the edge of her bodice, then followed the same path with his tongue, his breath hot against her skin.

She arched up, gasping for air as his hand gently caressed her breast, its tip marble hard and aching.

He showered kisses around her mouth, her neck, and between

her breasts as he worked the little cap sleeve down her shoulders.

She pulled at the buttons on his shirt, then tugged it from his pants. "I want to touch you," she murmured.

He sat up and jerked off his shirt, tossing it onto a nearby chair.

"Oh my," hummed Lexie as she ogled his impressive chest, covered with dark hair sprinkled with grey.

He lay beside her again, his upper body supported by one elbow on the bed. "Where were we?" Light and painfully teasing, his hand skated across the hardened peaks of her breast, past her waist, then skimmed her hip. "You are so beautiful," he whispered, moving his mouth over hers in a kiss that sent shock waves crushing through her body.

Lexie couldn't get enough air in her lungs. She raked her fingers over his broad shoulders, down his back, marveling at the flexing muscles underneath. She gripped his waist and sucked in a ragged breath as his lips left a trail of warm moist kisses from her chin, down her neck, to the hollow at the base of her throat, and lower still to the space between her breasts.

While his lips ignited the blood in her veins, one hand slid under her skirt, over her thigh, and then skimmed over her quivering stomach.

"Jake..."

He raised up, one hand sliding behind her back.

"Zipper's on the side." She barely raised her arm before he had the zipper down, and the dress pooled around her waist. He massaged the soft fullness of her breast, then bent down and teased the pebble-hard peak with his teeth through her bra.

He discovered the front clasp of her lacy bra and pushed it aside, quickly tantalizing one taunt bud with his tongue before pulling it deeply in his mouth. His hand explored the soft lines of her stomach, inching down to her waist before it disappeared beneath the waistband of her panties. Heat rippled under her skin as the flush of desire consumed her. His arousal pressed against her hip, and she instinctively arched toward the hand cupping her.

Then his mouth followed the trail of his hand down the length of her body, stopping when he reached the dress crumpled at her waist. Rising, he straddled her legs, and the dress soon joined his shirt on the chair.

He sat on the side of the bed and removed his boots. His jeans and boxers came off in one quick move before he rejoined her on the bed.

The touch of his rough skin against hers—the smell of his freshly showered body played havoc with her senses as her passion sprang to life. He worshipped her body with his mouth and his hands, the gentle massage sending currents of desire screaming through her. She writhed under the fingers skimming down her body and past her waist as his lips made their way down her neck.

Her fingers fisted in his hair, holding him in place as his mouth covered an aching tip while his hand shaped and molded the other breast.

She couldn't be still. The fire inside raged out of control as he took one stiff peak, then the other in his mouth.

Arching up, she flailed her arms on the bedsheet, then raked her nails up and down his back. "Jake..."

He continued to suckle each tip in turn as his hand slid lower until his fingers slid under the thin material covering her core. She bucked up and cried out when his fingers rolled over the sensitive flesh.

She angled her hand to explore his length in tight, even strokes. He groaned against her breast, and she increased the pressure.

He stopped and grabbed her hand. "Keep that up, sweetheart, and this will be over before it starts."

She squeezed lightly. "Are you saying you have no stamina?"

He grunted, then, in one swift move, her panties disappeared, and he jerked his jeans off the floor. He grabbed a foil pack from the pocket and sheathed himself.

Poised over her, he paused. "My Lexie," he whispered and lowered himself until his chest hair brushed the tips of her breasts.

The sensation was amazing, and she gasped, pushing her chest up.

"Like that?" He moved against her again.

"Yes," she gasped. "Yes."

And then he crushed his mouth against hers and joined them in a primal act of possession.

Pleasure beyond anything she'd ever experienced engulfed her. Nothing else existed. Just them. Like this. Together.

His expert touch took her higher and higher, her nails digging into his back, her legs clamped around his waist, and she gasped in sweet agony.

Bodies in perfect harmony, the tempo ebbed and flowed. Slow and easy became fast and furious as passions flared to explosive levels. Labored breathing and the sound of flesh against flesh filled the tiny room as they inched closer to the brink. The pressure grew.

His thrusts came harder, faster. Their bodies begged for release until they crested the pinnacle together in a staggering explosion of pleasure.

Chapter Thirty-Two

Lexie woke to the soothing sound of Jake's steady breathing and his warm body spooned against hers, one arm across her middle.

He stirred behind her. Strong hands circled her body and pulled her closer. "Mmm," he murmured, his warm breath tickling her ear. "Morning."

She pressed against him and smiled. "Good morning."

"It certainly is." He nuzzled her neck, sending a shiver of delight through her, then ran a calloused hand down her side, across her stomach. "What do you think about my stamina now?"

"Not bad."

He rolled her over to face him. "Not bad?"

She smiled and rubbed his chest. "Okay. It was fricking awesome."

He lay back and pulled her on top of him. "That's more like it."

His smile faltered, and she suffered a moment's concern. "What's wrong?"

He rubbed her upper arms. "How..."

Her heart stumbled. *Please don't let him be sorry.* "How what?"

"This is probably something we should have discussed last night instead of..."

She rested her palms on his chest. "Making love all night? Do you regret it?"

"Not for a minute. You?"

"Not at all."

"Good. As I was saying, how will this work?" He rubbed his hands over her exposed derriere. "I mean, you're leaving soon."

Immediately, her concerns vanished. "I've known for some time I no longer wanted to be an engineer for Dad's company. I just didn't know what I *did* want."

"And now?"

She ran her hand over the course chest hair, loving the feel of him. "I want to be here. With you. And Katie."

"I want that, too." He paused, and concern filtered back into his face. "But are you sure you'll be happy here?"

She heard the fear in his voice and struggled to find the right words to banish it and convince him she was home now. "As long as I have you and Katie, I'll be happy anywhere."

He inhaled deeply. "What about your career? And we're fifteen miles from the nearest town. And a small one to boot. No close neighbors. None of the things you're accustomed to."

She gently caressed his cheek. "I've spent my whole adult life doing what someone else thought was best for me. By the time I realized something was missing, I was over thirty, single, with no prospects." She chewed her lower lip. "Which is probably why I turned a deaf ear when Bobby insisted Rodney just wanted a leg up. His desertion, while hurtful and embarrassing, was a blessing in disguise—because it brought me here." She swallowed and met his probing gaze. "Yes, I had a career, and it's been a good one, but it's not what I want to do with my life."

"What *do* you want?"

After spending time with Katie, the idea solidified. "I want to explore writing and illustrating children's books. I think I have a knack for it and enjoy art."

"What else?"

She met his steady gaze. "I want to be here with you. And Katie."

He swallowed hard. "What about your father?"

"I've already talked with him."

"You have?"

She nodded. "He will support whatever makes me happy." She paused. "I might have to travel back and forth to Dallas until he finds someone, though. But a lot of what I do can be done from here. That is—if you want me."

His face beamed with happiness. "I want you any way I can have you."

Her body hummed with pleasure. "Ummm...sounds interesting." She drew circles around his nipple with her nail. "What time is Aggie bringing Katie home?"

"Not till after lunch."

"Wanna check your stamina this morning?"

When Lexie entered the kitchen sometime later, Jake stood at the sink, a coffee cup in his hand, Biscuit near the front door. He'd been outside most of the night and still appeared miffed at them.

A quick pat on the head sufficed for an apology. "Sorry, boy, you ran off after a rabbit. But Jake shared his steak with you later."

Biscuit didn't even open his eyes.

She straightened and found Jake's gaze fixed on the beautiful view of the lake. Her breath caught at the expression on his face. Happiness. Contentment.

As though sensing her presence, he turned, placed his cup on the counter, and extended a hand toward her.

She limped toward him, the stupid walking boot making a graceful approach impossible, and took his hand.

He eased her in front of him and wrapped one arm around her waist as they stared out the window. "I'll even share my coffee with you."

She took the cup in both hands and inhaled the hearty brew before taking a cautious sip. "You do make great coffee."

"I'm a man of many talents."

She grinned. "Amen to that."

She took another sip and handed it back, her mind drifting back to last night.

The second time they made love was breathtakingly slow and sweet as they took the time to explore each other's bodies with infinite care. His raw sensuousness carried her to greater heights until, once again, they soared past the peak of passion and pleasure together, then basked in the afterglow until hunger insisted they eat.

He grilled the steaks while she put together the sides. They ate at the tiny table, his bouquet of wildflowers in the center. After-wards, they snuggled on the couch for two hours talking about everything, then made love again in front of the fireplace.

It was the most romantic night of her life and everything she hoped it would be. And this morning, well, it was special, too.

She leaned back against his broad chest, knowing this moment would live in her heart forever, for it solidified this was where she belonged.

Neither spoke as the sun topped the trees in the distance. Varied shades of blue layered with gold-tinted clouds changed to bright orange as giant rays fanned out behind the foliage, reaching toward the sky. As the forest slowly materialized, trees in the distance turned from dark shadows to distinct shapes.

Lexie's breath caught as the tip of the sun peeked over the tree-tops. "I've never seen anything so beautiful," she whispered. "I can't remember the last time I watched a sunrise."

"My favorite time of day," murmured Jake.

She sighed. "Mine, too—now. Thanks for sharing this with me."

Silent, he kissed the top of her head and tightened his arms around her waist.

When the sun finally crested the trees in the distance, she tilted her gaze to him. "New day, new possibilities."

"New possibilities," he whispered as he lightly brushed his lips against hers, then slowly stepped back. "I've got stuff to do before Mother brings Katie home, and I'm already behind." He tapped her nose with his index finger. "Someone kept me in bed too long."

"You complaining, Mr. Holloway? Because I can ensure it doesn't happen again."

He tenderly pulled her against him. "Don't you dare."

She wrapped her arms around his waist, loving the warmth, the feel of him. "I can have breakfast ready in half an hour or less. You can't work all day on an empty stomach."

"I need to get going. I'll grab something later."

"Okay. I promised Katie I'd be there when she got home, so I'll be there around one or so."

"You sure you don't mind? Babysitting, I mean." He slid his hands up and down her upper arms. "You're supposed to be on vacation."

"...I don't see it as babysitting." She hesitated. "It's more like...practice."

He pulled her against him in a tender embrace. "I like that idea." Then he kissed her cheek and started for the door, stopping when he approached the dog. "You coming with me?"

The disgruntled mutt dared to snort and lay his head back down.

Jake laughed and grabbed his hat off the rack. "I can't believe you're still pissed at me. I even shared my steak with you."

Lexie chuckled behind him. "He'll get over it."

She touched his hand when he reached for the doorknob, and he stopped. "Don't work too hard." She reached up and kissed his cheek. "I'll see you later."

✦

Jake's stomach growled so loud Cody looked up from mending a harness. "Did I hear a foghorn, boss?"

"Skipped breakfast." Heat tinged his cheeks, and he turned away from his observant helper. "Let's break for an early lunch. Mother should bring Katie home soon, and I'll need to get her situated until Lexie gets here."

"She down at the cabin?"

"Yeah. For now."

Cody nodded without comment and sauntered off, whistling a nameless tune as Jake stomped to the house and entered the kitchen. He stood at the bar and looked around, surprised at how empty the place felt without Lexie. *But she will be here soon, and everything will be perfect.*

He went through the motions of building a sandwich and devoured it as loneliness surrounded him. The thought of things going back to the way they were scared the hell out of him, and his meal threatened to reappear. The sharp ding of an incoming text made him jump. Until he saw it was from her.

> Hey, just checking to make sure you got something to eat.

He smiled as he read the text, his somber mood instantly forgotten.

> Finishing a sandwich. Thanks for checking on me.

> I'm sorry, but I'll be home later than expected. Dad set up a conference call for one o'clock with a prospect. LOL..he suspected I wasn't happy for a while and had some feelers out.

The smiley face emoji and two hearts at the end further elevated his mood.

Okay. I'll see you when you get home.

Please tell Katie why I'm late. I don't want her upset because I'm not there when she gets home.

I will.

He grinned like a jackass eating briars and added: *I love you.*

I love you, too. Be home soon.

He rose, washed his dishes, dried his hand on a towel, and leaned against the sink, eyes focused out the window. Something about this place called to his soul. Maybe too much. Or maybe his life was empty before, and the ranch filled that void. But today, he saw things differently. Today, he was whole again.

"Stop mooning, Holloway," he scolded himself. "You've got work to finish before she gets home."

When his mother arrived at one-thirty, he worked with a new horse in the main corral. He stopped and climbed the fence as she got Katie out of the back. "Hey, kiddo," he said with an easy smile. "Did you have fun with Mimi and Pops?"

She shoved hair out of her face with one hand and clutched her bear in the other. "Uh-huh. We made the puzzle My Rozy gived me, and know what else?"

"What?"

"We had pizza, and Pops gived me another puzzle, and we

watched a show about a mermaid."

"Another puzzle and a movie? Wow, it sounds like you had a great time."

He glanced at his mother, her expression one of puzzlement. "What's wrong?"

"Nothing. It's just..." She flicked a tear off her cheek. "You both are so different," she whispered. "Katie is so happy. And you. Something has changed about you, too."

He smiled and slipped an arm around her waist, and kissed her cheek. "I'm happy, Mother." He nodded down at Katie. "We both are."

"I can see that."

"Where's Wexie, Daddy?" asked Katie. "Her pomised to be here."

"She's at the cabin now but will be here soon. She had to talk to her father."

"Is everything all right, son?" Aggie's soft voice was full of concern.

"Everything's fine. Her dad arranged this call—" The ring of his cell phone cut him off. He glanced at caller ID. "It's Lexie. Hey, everything okay? Oh, no problem. Yeah, I'll let her know. Okay. Love you, too."

Aggie's eyebrows nearly touched her hairline as she gaped at him.

"Yes. You heard right. I'm in love, Mother. For the last time in my life." He squatted down in front of Katie. "Sorry, kiddo, but Lexie's gonna get here a little later."

"Why?"

He knew she wouldn't grasp the concept of a conference call

and settled for calling it a meeting. "The meeting with her dad started late. She'll be here as soon as it's over."

"Where is she?"

"At the cabin, so she isn't far."

"Her said her be here."

"And she will, sweetheart, just a little later is all." He stood and looked at his mother's shocked expression. "I love her, Mother, and she loves me." He looked at his daughter, who watched the exchange. "And she loves Katie, too. Very much and can't wait to get back here to us."

"Wexie wuv's me, too?"

He ruffled the soft curls on her head. "Yes, she does. Very much."

"And I wuv Wexie," Katie gushed. "Is Bistit wif Wexie, too?"

"Yes, and they'll both be here soon."

"Do you need me to stay until she gets here?" asked Aggie. "I don't mind."

"No, I have paperwork and some small things to handle outside, but I'll be close. And Lexie shouldn't be much longer."

"Okay. If you're sure."

"I am."

Aggie made no move to leave. "Son, are you sure about this?"

He knew she referred to his feelings for Lexie. "I've never been more certain. We both knew it from the start."

Her lips trembled when she smiled. "Then I'm happy for you, son."

He watched her drive away, then looked down at Katie. "It's just you and me, kiddo. What shall we do?"

She ducked her head, then looked toward the old swing but

didn't speak.

"Would you like to swing a bit before we go inside?"

Her face brightened, and she smiled. "Yes!"

It humbled him to realize he'd spent so many years wallowing in his own pain and grief he failed to see how he neglected his child. He saw to her basic needs, of course, but neglected the most essential one of all. The one he, himself, just realized was missing from his life.

The need to *know* you are loved.

Her impish laugh as he put the swing in motion put a lump in his throat, and tears stung his eyes. He vowed then and there to be the kind of father she deserved.

— ❖ —

Lexie was beside herself with worry. One conference call became three as her father sorted through prospects, then two glitches in the West Texas project meant an extended call with Craig Bennet, which left her fuming, and then her assistant had questions for her. By the time she headed back to the house, it was after three o'clock.

When she pulled up in front of the barn, she saw Jake in the small pasture behind the house with Dolly and her new calf. She honked and waved, then headed inside.

"Katie? I'm home."

Noise from the den drew her attention. The TV was on, her bear on the floor, but Katie wasn't there. She checked her bedroom and found it empty as well.

"Katie? Where are you?"

Frantic now, she searched the house to no avail.

Biscuit, attuned to her every mood, whined and followed behind.

"Maybe Jake took her with him to the corral."

She hobbled outside and found Jake coming around the house.

"Hey, there you are."

"Is Katie with you?"

"What? No. She's inside watching cartoons."

"No, she isn't. I've looked all over. She's not in the house."

Jake hurried inside, and she followed.

"I've looked everywhere. She's not here."

Jake ran outside, and she followed him to the barn, where he yelled for Cody.

"What's up, boss?"

"Have you seen Katie?"

"Not lately."

"She was watching TV. I told her to stay put till I came back." He paced in circles. "We had to chase Dolly down and get her back in the pen." Anguish shredded his voice. "It's all my fault. Oh God. She has to be around here somewhere."

His tortured voice tore at Lexie's heart. "Kids are easily distracted and wander off, Jake," said Lexie. "We'll find her."

"Cody," barked Jake, "look around the barn. I'll check around the house."

His helper started for the barn, then stopped and turned. "Boss?"

"What?"

He scratched his chin. "This may not mean anything, but Sean was here a while ago."

"Here? When?"

"I saw his truck leaving while we wrestled with Dolly. Thought nothing of it at the time. Figured he seen us moving her and left."

Lexie and Jake stared at each other; the unspoken question settled between them.

Did he take Katie?

Chapter Thirty-Three

"It went straight to voicemail." Jake plunked his phone down on the bar, his rage barely contained. "I swear, if Sean took her, I'll kill him with my bare hands."

Lexie gripped his forearm. "Your folks and Donna are on the way. So is Bobby. We'll find her."

"It's all my fault," he groaned again, clutching her bear against his chest. "I wasn't gone long, but I shouldn't have left her alone."

"She can't have gone far, Jake," said Lexie. "We'll find her." She moved to the counter and started a pot of coffee.

Jake couldn't think straight. He placed the bear on the bar and went to the back door. "I'm going to look around the yard again." He rounded the front and saw Sean's truck coming down the drive. He rushed forward before the vehicle fully stopped and jerked open the door. "Where is she?" he shouted, pulling the surprised man from the seat. "Did you take her?"

"Take who?" roared Sean. "I don't know what you're talking about."

Jake pinned him against the truck, one arm against Sean's throat, the other hand fisted in his shirt. "Where's my daughter?"

Sean pushed against Jake's chest, but he didn't move.

"I don't know."

"I swear if you're lying, I'll kill you."

"I don't have your kid," shouted Sean. "I haven't seen her since yesterday."

Jake's soul began to shatter. If Sean didn't have her, who did?

"I don't have her. I swear to you."

Deflated, Jake stepped back. "Then why were you here earlier?"

Sean glanced at Lexie, who now stood by Jake's side. "I wanted to explain about the letter."

"What letter?"

"The one I left this morning."

Jake stared at him. "I haven't seen any letter."

Sean raked long fingers through his hair. "I slid it under the door. A chickenshit way to do it, I know. I thought you'd find it by now."

"I've been searching for my daughter."

His body was rigid, and sweat dotted his brow as Sean faced him, his voice filled with regret. "She made me promise."

"Mary."

"Yeah," snorted Sean. "Mary. Your wife."

"Were you lovers?" Jake snarled.

Sean jerked his head back and squared his shoulders. "No." His jaw clenched and released. "But I loved her. I would have done anything for her." He slowly shook his head. "Even deliver that damned letter." His body slumped, and he leaned against the truck. "I actually tried to talk her out of leaving you, though you didn't deserve her."

"That night in the kitchen. When y'all argued."

He nodded. "She gave me the letter the next day. Asked me to wait until the divorce was final. After the accident...I didn't see the point."

"But you kept it?"

"Yeah."

"Why?"

He shrugged. "I made a promise." He shook his head slowly. "And no, I don't know what's in it. And after all this time, it may not mean anything, but it was important to her then."

Bobby's motorcycle roared down the drive, followed by Jake's parents. "We'll continue this later. I need to find my daughter."

"Can I help?"

When Jake didn't immediately reply, Sean added, "She's Mary's daughter. Please. Let me help."

Jake nodded and moved to greet the newcomers.

Just then, Biscuit whined and circled Jake's feet.

"I know, boy," he gave the dog a light pat. "We'll find her."

An hour later, the searchers re-convened near the barn, their downcast faces telling Jake what he didn't want to hear. They didn't find her.

Thunder rolled in the distance as another spring storm threatened, and his panic grew. Where the hell was she? She must be terrified.

"She couldn't have gone far," said Jake. "She didn't have enough time."

"Are there any lakes or ponds, or maybe a well close by where she might wander and..." Sean didn't complete the thought.

"No," said Jake, his despair growing by the second. "She always stayed in the yard." He stared into the distance, trying to figure out where to search next when another roll of thunder sounded. He looked at the concerned faces of his family and swallowed hard. "We'll fan out and start again."

Lexie grabbed his hand and squeezed. "We'll find her, Jake. We will."

"But will it be too late?"

Biscuit continued to circle them, his whine growing louder.

"Biscuit," said Lexie, her voice rising in excitement.

"What do you mean?"

"The bear. Show Biscuit her bear."

It took a moment for her plan to register. "Of course." He ran into the kitchen, grabbed the bear off the bar, and showed it to the dog. "Find Katie, Biscuit. Find Katie."

No one spoke as he sniffed the bear, then circled the yard, his nose to the ground. He ran in and out of the barn, around the swing, then hesitated near the corral. He looked at Jake as thunder rolled closer and whined.

"It's okay, boy. You can do this. Find Katie."

He circled half the corral, backtracked to the side of the barn, then headed down the road.

"I'll follow him in the ATV," shouted Jake as he ran to the shed. "Someone drive the truck."

"I'm coming with you," Lexie said, grabbing his hand.

Hope flooded Jake's chest as they followed the dog, only to fade when he appeared to lose the scent several times, crisscrossing the road before going forward again.

When the first raindrops fell, Lexie smothered a cry with her fist. "Oh God, no! The rain will wash away the scent."

"No, it won't," said Jake. "It won't."

Then he prayed he was right.

Half a mile from the cabin, Biscuit worked his way along the edge of the road on the left, circled back to the right, and sat down.

"Oh no," said Lexie. "He lost it."

Jake and Lexie exited the cart and squatted down by the dog.

Sean's truck stopped behind the cart, and everyone piled out.

"Good boy, Biscuit," said Jake. "Good boy." As more raindrops peppered down, he petted the dog in long, soothing strokes. "Good boy, Biscuit."

Lexie pushed the bear closer to his nose. "Katie needs you, Biscuit. We need you. You can do this. I know you can. Find Katie. Please find Katie."

He whined and licked Lexie's face, then went back to work, only this time, he ventured into the woods on the side of the road.

"She must have gone off here," said Jake. "I think he's confused by all the different scents, so fan out." He helped Lexie stand. "Katie," he shouted. "Katie! Where are you?"

The thick brush and Lexie's boot made walking difficult for her. "Go on," she said at last. "I'm holding you back. I'll follow."

He didn't bother to argue. His daughter was out there somewhere. He had to find her.

<hr>

Lexie tripped over a fallen log and barely kept from crying out. The damn boot was a nuisance, but at least it kept the throbbing pain down.

Sean suddenly appeared and helped her stand.

"Thank you," she said stiffly, unable to determine exactly how she felt about him.

She'd lost sight of Jake and Biscuit but heard him shouting Katie's name. "This way." She didn't wait to see if he followed.

"Katie! Where are you?"

"I'm not the enemy, you know."

"I guess that remains to be seen, doesn't it?" She could hear the others calling out as they trudged through the forest but only saw Bobby.

A rabbit scampered out from under a nearby brush pile and startled Lexie. "Fruitcake!"

Sean snickered.

She ignored him and continued forward. "Katie!

Biscuit's excited bark had everyone rushing toward the sound. She had no choice but to accept Sean's help navigating the under-growth as the rain increased in volume.

"Katie! Katie!"

Jake's frantic shout and Biscuit's bark sent her heart rate through the roof. Did they find her? Was she alive?

They crashed through the brush to a small clearing and saw Biscuit frantically barking at the edge of a steep embankment.

"Don't move, baby! Daddy's coming!" He turned around and shouted at Sean. "Do you have ropes or straps in your truck?"

"Yes." He checked the drop-off. "I'll be right back." He looked down again. "That's a thirty-foot drop. Is she all right?"

"I don't know. She's not moving."

Jake couldn't wait for Sean to return. The heavy rain caused the creek at the bottom of the gully to rise. A few more minutes and the water would reach her. But the bank was too slippery and steep to navigate without a rope. "I have to get down there," he said at last. "The water is getting closer."

"Maybe one of these long vines will hold you," said Bobby as he pulled on it. "It's up in this tree pretty far."

"Daddy."

His heart nearly stopped at the painfully soft cry. She was alive! "Don't move, Katie! Daddy's coming." He jerked the vine from Bobby's hand. "I'm coming! Don't move!"

"Be careful!" cried Lexie as she helped tug the lifeline into place. "I love you both."

Their eyes met, and he saw the tears mixed with rain. "I love you."

He stepped over the edge, hit the slick red clay, and immediately went to his knees, barely keeping his hold on the vine. Blinded by the heavy rain, worked his way down. *Please, God. Please let her be all right. Let my little girl be all right.*

He made it halfway before the vine snapped, and he plummeted to the bottom, grunting in pain when his left wrist twisted, taking the brunt of the fall.

He heard Lexie's cry above the thunder and water rushing in the creek. "I'm okay," he shouted. "I can reach her."

"Daddy," she whimpered.

He rushed to her side, afraid of what he would find, and used his body to shield her from the rain. "Don't move, baby. Let Daddy see where you're hurt."

"I fall down."

"I know." He gently. "I know. " He ran his hands over her arms and legs, noting numerous scratches and tears on her clothes. A cut on her forehead still oozed blood, but he couldn't see anything serious. "Can you wiggle your feet for me?"

He breathed a sigh of relief when she showed no pain. "What about your arms?"

She slowly lifted each one.

"Good girl." He smoothed back her hair. "You're gonna be fine."

"Sean's back with the ATV, and an ambulance is on its way," shouted Bobby. "How bad is it?"

"I don't know. Can't see anything broken, but she needs a doctor."

"I think we should wait for the ambulance and a backboard," shouted Bobby. "Can you hang on?"

He looked at the water two feet away. "If they hurry."

He heard the distant wail of the siren and gently kissed her forehead. "You're gonna be okay. Daddy's here."

Her trembling smile melted his heart.

"I wuv you, Daddy."

"I love you, too, Katie. Don't ever forget that."

Chapter Thirty-Four

"**I**s she asleep?"

Aggie's hushed voice conveyed the general mood of those gathered.

"Yes," said Lexie. "Jake is still with her. So is Biscuit."

"He saved her life today," said Bobby. "We would never have found her otherwise."

"How on earth did she get so far?" Aggie wrung her hands together while her husband absently patted her shoulder.

Bobby, Tina, Donna, and Sean watched silently near the fireplace.

"From what we gathered, she decided to walk to the cabin and got sidetracked by a bunny. She chased it and fell in the ditch."

"Why was she going to the cabin?" snapped Donna.

"She was looking for me." Lexie faced Jake's sister. "She won't ever have to look for me again because I'll be here. Where I belong."

Donna's worried expression barely relaxed. "Are you sure?"

"Positive."

Bobby grinned and walked toward Lexie. "Remember a couple of weeks ago when I said there was this guy I wanted you to meet?"

"Don't start, Bobby. I told you I'm not interested."

He grinned and tweaked her nose. "Yes. You are."

She stared at her brother, then shook her head. "No. Really?"

"Why do you think I arranged for you to stay in his cabin?"

"Jake is the guy you wanted me to meet?"

"You can thank me later." He turned to his wife. "Let's go home and let these folks get some well-deserved rest."

"Thank God she wasn't too badly hurt," said Donna as she came to stand beside her mother.

"Yes," said Lexie. "A few cuts and scrapes but nothing serious."

Jake entered, put his arm around Lexie's waist, and scanned the people in the room. "We can't thank you all enough for what you did today."

"We're family," said Bobby. "That's what we do." He leaned over and kissed Lexie's cheek. "Night, kiddo. I love you."

"I love you too."

Aggie moved forward and embraced Jake. "Son, are you all right?"

He hugged her tightly. "I am now."

She stepped back. "Is there anything I can do for you?"

He looked at Lexie. "No. I have all I need right now."

Soon, only Sean remained, the envelope clasped in his hand. He stepped forward and held out the letter. "It was still on the floor by the door." He ducked his head, then met Jake's steady gaze. "I blamed you for what happened even though I knew better." He swallowed hard. "She was so unhappy." He hesitated. "I tried to convince her to talk to you, explain what she was feeling, but..." He took one last look at the letter. "It's overdue, but I kept my promise." He met Jake's gaze. "And I was wrong about you. Katie does deserve a father like you."

He nodded to Lexie, turned, and walked out.

———◆———

Jake stared at the unopened letter in his hand. Did he truly want to know what it held? Would his questions be answered, or would more be generated? Did it even matter anymore?

Lexie's gentle touch on his arm broke the spell.

"I remember it like yesterday," he said softly. "All the hurt, the anger, the betrayal." He lightly shook the envelope. "This won't change any of that."

"No. It won't," she murmured. "But maybe it will help you understand why she did it."

"What if it says I'm not Katie's father?"

She clutched his arm. "*You* are her father, Jake. In every way that matters, you are her father."

His hands shook, and his heart raced. He blew out a long breath and opened the envelope.

ONE MONTH LATER...

J ake sighed and sipped his drink, waiting for his wife to join him on the porch. He smiled at the thought—*his wife.* She pulled off a perfect wedding in less than a month. Of course, both families helped, but it was still a huge accomplishment. Especially since what was initially going to be a small affair at the ranch turned into a community event in short order.

He closed his eyes and relived the moment three days ago when he became whole again.

As Katie slowly walked down the aisle, her smile radiant, her hair and dress a mini-me version of Lexie, tears threatened to fall as four years of anger, pain, and doubt dropped away like the petals Katie spread before her. In its place was a love so deep it would never end. Love for his soon-to-be wife and his daughter. Because regardless of what was in the letter he had yet to read, Katie was his daughter. Nothing would ever change that.

The moment Lexie walked toward him on the arm of her father, he couldn't name a single person in the church. He only had eyes for her.

The ceremony was short and sweet, the reception long and joyful. They spent the weekend here at the cabin and would return to the ranch tomorrow.

He smiled as he recalled Katie's disappointment at not going with them to the "moon of honey". However, discovering she would spend time with her new grandparents soon had her smiling again.

The door opened and Lexie walked out, wearing the jersey she wore that first day. God, he loved that shirt. And her in it. Or out of it.

"Everything okay?" he asked.

"Yes. She just wanted to say goodnight. After she told me about going to the zoo today." She curled up in the glider beside him and sipped from the glass he handed her. "I'm afraid my folks will spoil her rotten."

"She deserves some spoiling."

Lexie took a breath and looked out over the lake.

"I can tell you have something on your mind. What is it?"

She turned to face him. "She asked Mom what getting married meant."

His brows shot up in surprise.

"Not that part." She sighed. "Katie said it meant that since you are the daddy, then I am the mommy. We hadn't talked about that part, and I didn't know what to say. But she was so excited, I just said that was right. I hope you don't mind."

"Why on earth would I mind? I'm thrilled—if you're okay with it, that is."

"Of course I am." Her eyes grew misty as she placed a hand on his arm. "It's a dream come true for me—to be your wife. And a mother."

"You're a great mother, too. You were the missing piece of our lives." He leaned over and kissed her. "We're so very lucky to have you."

"And you're the best thing that ever happened to me."

He pulled her close to his side as happiness wrapped around them.

She touched the letter resting on his knee.

"No. Not yet."

"Why not?"

He shrugged. "I don't know. Scared maybe. I keep thinking about those old sayings, being careful what you wish for and the truth setting you free. But will it?" He rubbed a finger over his neatly written name on the front of the envelope. "In the end, it won't change how I feel."

She placed a hand on his knee. "No, it won't." She paused. "But hopefully, it will give you answers."

"Or more questions." He handed her his glass, pulled out the single sheet from the envelope, and began to read.

Dear Jake,

I know this is the coward's way out, but even so, this is hard to write. I honestly can't say what happened to change things between us because we were so happy once. It wasn't any one thing or a single moment in time. I just woke up one day and realized I wasn't happy anymore.

This will sound crazy I know, but I still love you, Jake. I'm just not **in** *love with you.*

As much as you may care for me, this ranch means more to you than I ever will. Which makes me think maybe you're not in love with me, either; that we have just been going through the motions.

But I want more than that, more than you can give me.

I've known for some time that I wanted a divorce but lacked the courage to say so because I know it will hurt you. And despite everything, that knowledge pains me, too. But I can't wait any longer.

I never really explained why I avoided the issue of having a child. Well, it's because I couldn't bear the thought of bringing one into your world. A world where we would always be in second place. I won't do that to our child.

That's right, Jake. Our child. I was as surprised as you undoubtedly will be to discover I was pregnant. I found out this week it's a girl, and I realized I couldn't wait any longer. And despite what I will tell you tomorrow, there is not and never has been anyone else in my life. But if you knew the truth, you would never let me go. I will not deny you access to her, but I will not raise her here. I'm sorry for the pain my words will cause you. And knowing I left carrying your child will hurt even more than the divorce. I'm sorry for that, too.

I hope Sean keeps his promise and gives this to you so maybe you'll understand. He's angry with me; accused me of being selfish and cruel and said I'm making a huge mistake. Maybe I am, but we, your daughter and I deserve more. We deserve to know we are loved.

I hope and pray that one day you will find someone who will take the place of this land in your heart. Maybe then you can forgive me.

Love,

Mary

Jake swallowed hard and passed the letter to Lexie, took his glass, and downed the contents. "Read it." Even to him, his voice sounded harsh. "I'm sorry. Please. Read it."

He sat in silence as Lexie read, then placed it on the seat beside her. "Are you okay?"

"Yes and no," he murmured at last. "I'm relieved to know what I already decided in my heart is the truth—Katie is my daughter."

He took a shaky breath. "But at the same time, I'm so ashamed and so sorry for what I didn't see. Didn't do. I never meant to hurt her. Or Katie." He swallowed hard. "I was so deep in my own grief, that's all I saw."

"You can't change the past, Jake," she said softly. "You can only learn from it and move forward."

He brought her hand to his lips and kissed it. "You're right. And I've learned a lot lately, not the least of which is to never give up on love. It will find you when you least expect it."

"Like in a muddy ditch in the middle of a thunderstorm?"

He smiled and took a shaky breath. "I swear to you, Lexie, you and Katie will never doubt how much I love you. And every day for the rest of my life, I will thank God for my second chance at love."

"We both will." She gave him a teary-eyed smile. "You know what they say. Love is better the second time around."

The End

PREVIEW OF
"THE DETAIL"

"I'll only be gone a couple of days, Mom. I'll drop by when I get back. I know. I'll think about it."

Detective Jessie Foster heard the click when her mother ended the call without a goodbye. Again. She paused, then slapped the receiver in its cradle. Two seconds later, she flung a pencil across the room where it ricocheted off a corner of the cushioned cubical wall before it landed on the other desk.

Her mom could turn a good day into a bad one in a heartbeat.

"Whoa, there, Texas. What's got your panties in a wad this time?"

The question from Seth Hamilton, her partner and co-habitant of this padded cell, reminded her she wasn't alone. "Can it, Hammer. I'm not in the mood." She sighed and tugged the red scrunchy from her ponytail, tossed it on the desk, then leaned back and raked slender fingers through dark, shoulder-length curls. A tension headache crept up the back of her neck. *Perfect. Just damn perfect.* "And stop calling me Texas. And Tex."

"I would, but I hear bitch isn't politically correct these days."

Despite her anger, she snorted. "You're such an ass."

"Says you." He sauntered over and rested his hip on the corner of her desk. "She still after you to take that job with the feds?"

Before she could reply, he continued. "And in Dallas, no less. You hate the traffic."

"A desk job is a place to start." Even as the lie slid off her tongue, her inner voice chided, 'Coward,' and she caught herself before she blurted out the hard truth. *It's killing me to work side-by-side with you every day and not tell you how I feel.*

"You like working in the field, Tex. A desk job isn't for you, and you know it. So, what gives?"

She didn't address his comment. She also knew he wouldn't let it go. "I'm a damn good cop whether I'm behind a desk or out in the field."

She ignored the teasing snicker from Seth. He delighted in getting her riled. Today, she refused to take the bait.

"I have my last interview with them next week." She stood and scanned her work area. Small, crowded, and noisy, it was nonetheless a decent space. The police force in Walker, a quiet town southeast of Dallas, was a small, tight-knit group. Granted, most called her names behind her back, mainly because she refused to take any crap from them, but if push came to shove, they'd be there for her. Did she really want to start over somewhere else?

Or was she simply running away?

"They don't deserve you," said Seth. "And we'd miss you here."

She grunted. "Yeah. Right."

He had the audacity to laugh. The throaty, masculine sound made her stomach quiver. *Aw, hell. I've worked side-by-side with him for over a fricking year, and now my stomach flutters when he laughs. Or winks.*

Or breathes.

Just shoot me.

If she were honest with herself - which she always tried to be – he was nice-looking, handsome even. Five years older than her at thirty-eight, he carried his age well. Cognac-colored eyes framed by long, dark lashes she silently envied, and heavy brows were the first thing she noticed about him.

The second was his mouth—those lips. Women paid a fortune to fake what God gave him free gratis. Even a slight overbite and crooked nose didn't detract from his rugged good looks. From the top of his military cut, salt and pepper head to the souls of his cowboy boots, he was six feet three inches of blatant masculinity coupled with a compelling sex appeal hard to ignore, but she managed.

Well, most of the time.

Lately, not so much.

One whiff of his cologne, coupled with a provocative man-smell, was enough to send rational thought straight to the gutter.

It took determination to get her wayward mind back on track. "You're just playing nice cause you think you'll get lucky."

"Yeah, right. I relish the idea of sex with a buzz saw."

She flinched and buried the hurt his comment elicited; defensive walls shored and braced. She knew him so well and knew he liked to tease, but still, it gave her pause. Had the job finally robbed her of all femininity? Desirability?

Is that how he saw her?

Suck it up, buttercup. It is what it is. "Time to rock and roll," she snapped and gave herself a mental shake. Focus on their detail—pick up Jack Walls in Denver and bring him back to Walker to stand trial. Suspected of killing two of his former girlfriends, Jess couldn't prove the first one, and by the time they got the evidence needed to arrest him for the second, he vanished without a trace. Until now.

"With any luck," continued Jess, "we can get there before midnight tonight and be back late tomorrow night."

The grueling fourteen-hour drive was just another part of the job. Hours alone with her partner presented issues she did not want to dwell on.

Seth smirked. "What's your hurry, Tex? Hot date?"

"The sooner this is over with, the better."

He stood, grabbed his jacket off the rack, and draped it over one arm. "Personally, I can't wait to spend the next three days trapped in a car with Miss Congeniality and a deranged sociopath."

She lifted the paperwork and her purse off the desk, grabbed her go-bag, and headed for the hallway. "Wonder why you got stuck with me for a partner."

"Obviously, somewhere along the way, I spit in someone's Cheerios."

Jess shook her head. An anomaly, Seth always spoke his mind. She liked that about him, though he sometimes goaded her to no end. For whatever reason, they clicked from the start, probably because they were more alike than different. Neither liked all the hoops they jumped through daily to get the bad guys, and both sported a wicked sense of humor not everyone could handle. Plus, they each tended to call a spade a spade without apology.

Unable to curb the impulse, she cast him a quick sideways glance. Immediately, butterflies the size of a roadrunner took flight in her stomach.

Probably some kind of hormonal-biological-clock thing. I am thir-

ty-three now. It will pass. Probably like a kidney stone, but it will pass.

Disgusted with her wandering mind, she strode toward the elevator, Seth following a few steps behind. She barely managed to smother the temptation to strut a bit. *What the hell is wrong with me?* She gave the elevator dial a harder-than-necessary push. *I don't care what he thinks of my ass in these slacks.*

The doors opened, and she walked in, pressing the garage button as she turned.

Seth met her gaze, sensuous mouth curved up in a Cheshire-cat smile. "I appreciate the show."

"Shut up."

He winked.

It was going to be a long three days.

———————⊗———————

Seth knew he skated a fine line with Jess. The department's stand on sexual harassment left no room for doubt. One word from her, and his ass was in a sling.

But he was just vain enough to believe she enjoyed their suggestive banter. And she gave as good as she got, too. He liked a woman who spoke her mind and didn't get all ticked off when a man did the same.

His transfer to Walker coincided with her last partner's move to Austin. He didn't miss the snickers drifting among his fellow officers after the announcement of their partnership. Later, he discovered most didn't like working with her, calling her testy, hardheaded, and bitchy. But he never saw that side of her personality. Instead, he saw a first-rate detective, intensely dedicated to the job, with a warped sense of humor to match his own.

She was also a beautiful, fascinating woman who worked hard to hide that fact from the rest of the world. And it was the woman behind the badge who captivated his thoughts these days.

Granted, he sometimes took things a bit too far, like the buzz-saw comment. The brief flash of pain he saw in her eyes tore at his conscience. Filters he found so easy to employ around others failed him completely around Jess. From day one, she took whatever he dished out and gave it back in spades. So much so, he inched further and further across that invisible line just to see how she would respond.

Lately, though, something was different. *She* was different. An occasional look in her eye that quickly disappeared made him wonder. What if she saw him as more than her irritating partner with a propensity for spouting out useless trivia?

What if she saw *him*?

Finally.

That *what-if* kept him awake most of last night, and he vowed to use this trip to explore the prospect in depth.

After she got over being mad, of course.

Man, she was something when riled—like now. Her cheeks were a flattering shade of red, and that sexy, sassy mouth formed a tight line across her face. Her anger never lasted, so he'd just wait her out.

And try not to think about other things that could put such an enticing flush on her cheeks.

The door slid open, and she started to exit ahead of him, then stopped and scowled.

He grinned and strolled out. "How about I take the first turn at the wheel. Your driving makes me nervous."

"Since when?"

"Since you go into a cussing rampage in traffic, and we'll hit the start of rush hour through Dallas."

"Whatever. Drive." She pitched him the keys and walked to the passenger side, throwing her bag into the back seat before buckling in.

He placed his go-bag beside hers and climbed behind the wheel of the older model SUV.

Jess dug through the paperwork and pulled out a map. "The GPS is on the fritz again, and cell service may be iffy."

He glared at the map in her hand. "I don't need a map."

"Need I remind you of the last time we had this conversation?"

"That was then. This is now. I don't need the map."

"I swear, Hammer, you will sincerely regret it if you get us lost and drag this trip out any more than necessary."

"Duly noted."

He put the car in gear and headed out of the garage toward the interstate through Dallas. Traffic would be horrible, the drive exhausting, but he looked forward to the hours of proximity with his feisty partner, who of late pressed every male button he possessed.

It was time he located a few of her female ones.

The Detail available now in
print, e-book, and audiobook.

RECIPES

If you've enjoyed my last few books, you know that I include recipes at the end. Sometimes they are ones the characters prepared in the story or ones I simply like. Here is the MawRita recipe Lexie enjoyed and prepared for Jake.

———◆———

The MawRita

- 1 part Cuervo Gold (or any good tequila) tequila

- 1 part Grand Marnier

- Splash of orange juice

- Pinch of coarse sea salt – optional but adds to the flavor

- 2 parts Margarita Mixer (I use Cuervo skinny variety – less tart)

Place all ingredients in a tall glass, add ice, and enjoy!

Chicken Fried Steak

This dish is a staple in any southern household. This recipe came from a dear lady in our Sunday school class, who is one of the most renowned cooks in our town. Round steak can sometimes be a little tough, so I tenderize it first, then soak it in buttermilk for about an hour. You can also use those tenderized cubed steaks you buy at the market.

- 2 lbs round beef teak

- Salt and pepper to taste

- 1 cup or so of all-purpose flour

- Vegetable oil for frying

Using a sharp knife, trim any excess fat from meat. Cut into portions, 4-6 oz each. In a small bowl, combine the flour, salt, and pepper. Fill a 10" iron skillet with oil about ½" up the sides. Place skillet over medium heat. As the oil heats, sprinkle a tiny pinch of flour on top to test. If it sizzles immediately, it is ready for frying. Coat the meat in the flour mixture and gently place it in the skillet. Be careful as the oil may pop and spatter. Cook until golden brown on the bottom. Flip it over and continue cooking until golden brown and cooked through. Adjust the heat as needed to avoid burning. Drain steaks on a plate lined with paper towels to remove excess grease. Serve with creamed potatoes, gravy, and biscuits. – Miss Ouida

ACKNOWLEDGEMENTS

When I published my first book in the summer of 2016, I had no idea how long my writing career would last. I only knew I wanted to write, and I hoped that people would enjoy what I wrote. Fast forward seven years. I have published seven award-winning books and cookbook, with more in the to-be-written file! I am blessed beyond measure.

But I did not get here on my own. First of all, I thank God for gifting me with a talent for words, and a wonderful husband who understands and supports me in every way possible.

I cannot express the depth of my gratitude to Patty Wiseman, mentor-extraordinaire, my favorite nitpickers, Phyllis Still, Beth Howlett, and Ruth Buck, as well as members of my writers' groups. I would not be able to do what I do without them. Your support means everything to me.

About the Author

Dana Wayne is a sixth-generation Texan, an admitted die-hard romantic, and a lover of good food, good wine, and good company. She routinely speaks to book clubs, writers' groups, and other organizations and is a frequent guest on numerous writing blogs. A strong advocate for new authors, she started a podcast in 2020 called A Writer's Life, where she shares her experiences on the road from writer wanna-be to award-winning romance author. Her romantic stories are filled with strong women, second chances, and happily ever after. Among her many accolades are the prestigious international Best Indie Book Award, Readers Digest Bronze Medal, three RONE Award Nominations, two Finalists in Page Turner Awards, and is listed in the *Top 50 Indie Authors You Need to Read*.

"I am all about the romance and strive for realistic characters. My work is character-driven with a lot of emotion. While they are steamy, I believe romance is about emotion, not sex, and the journey is more important than the destination."

She is a long-time member of The Writers League of Texas, East Texas Writers Association, Northeast Texas Writers Organization, and East Texas Writers Guild

ALSO BY DANA WAYNE

Secrets of The Heart

Mail Order Groom

Whispers on the Wind

Chasing Hope

Unveiling Beulah

The Detail